LIGHT
IN ROSADERO

LIGHT
IN ROSADERO

Jay Kristensen Jr.

Written in unceded Tohono O'odham and Coast Salish
territories.

Part I

…people who shut their eyes to reality simply invite their own destruction, and anyone who insists on remaining in a state of innocence long after that innocence is dead turns himself into a monster.

—James Baldwin, *Notes of a Native Son*, 1954

The Americans have an excessive awareness of an identity that they don't have.

—Donald Judd, "Notes," 1983

The country is most barbarously large and final.

—Billy Lee Brammer, *The Gay Place*, 1961

· One ·

Blue Rain Canyon

THREE HUNDRED MILES from where she would disappear, Mariazul Lluvia Cenote Bautista walked alone in the shadows of Lordsburg, New Mexico. Silhouetted in the predawn light, she shivered against a row of abandoned businesses; cold, boarded-up structures of adobe and rusted steel that had stood empty for decades. She was young, dark brown, her black hair tied into two braids. Her clothing was a uniform of pink—pink sweatpants, pink hooded sweatshirt, pink headband—and her sneakers were white. A heavy black backpack hung off her chest and abdomen like a baby, strapped tightly against her body. Her stature was petite, and every now and then, she looked over her shoulder down the desolate frontage road behind her. On the interstate, eighteen-wheelers roared into the magenta west and sunrise east. Ten hours from Los Angeles and ten hours from San Antonio, Lordsburg subsisted off the profits of its hundreds of motel rooms and trio of truck stops, the town's prosperity fixed to the traffic speeding forever along its margins.

Ninety miles to the south lay Mexico.

Driving onto the vacant street, I didn't see Mariazul until I passed by her side. At first glance, she seemed like a teenager on her way to high school, an illusion that vanished the moment she looked at me. In her eyes, I could see stress and terror. She slowed down as my vehicle drifted by, studying the black finish of my hybrid, memorizing my Oregon license plates, vigilant to every detail.

A woman so alone.

Yet a woman almost unstoppable.

Almost.

I came to a halt and rolled down the front passenger window. Before we could speak, I took a moment to check my appearance in the rearview mirror. Grayness underscored my eyes. The brown roots on my scalp contradicted the blondeness of my ponytail. My pale skin burned against my all-black ensemble: black knee-high boots, black tights, black corduroy skirt, an oversized black t-shirt flowing across my lap like a flag, its golden hem shimmering. I hadn't changed or showered in two days. A tattoo of an Alaska cedar sapling graced the surface of my left hand, a corresponding female pinecone nestled inside my palm. As I studied myself, my tattoos seemed like the only permanent aspect of my appearance. Everything else was fleeting.

On the dashboard, the temperature registered nineteen degrees Fahrenheit. All night, violent winds had pummeled my motel room, battering the door, rattling the hinges. From underneath my cigarette-burned blankets, I could almost feel the air devouring the community. Before my departure, I had smoked a cigarette on the second-floor balcony, incredulous at the autumn chill. Somewhere, a guard-dog was howling at the screech of a freight train, protecting its owner's rugged casita.

Checking out of my room and returning to my car, I had indulged in the luxury of heat, a luxury that could amount to survival if shared.

The woman on the sidewalk halted by the window, her breath crystallizing in the air.

Need a ride? I asked.

She stared, saying nothing. I opened the door, patting on the seat and gesturing in the direction she was traveling.

Truck stop? I asked.

She looked down the street again. Chills were visible across her skin. Her teeth were chattering. Finally, she came to a verdict.

Yes, she said. Truck stop. Yes. Thank you.

She stepped into my car, closing the door behind her, and rolling up the window. Her eyes widened at the self-warming seat.

Thank you, she said again.

I nodded. She buckled her seatbelt. For the two-minute ride to the nearest truck stop, she kept one hand on the door handle, the other on the backpack. As we pulled up to a fuel pump, she stared at the Border Patrol van in front of the Tex-Mex restaurant attached to the convenience store. The van's green stripe glinted like a blade against its white surface.

Mariazul turned to me.

Texas, she said. ¿A dónde vas? Please.

For several seconds, I drummed my fingertips on the steering wheel, unsure what to say. Finally, I reached behind my seat to pull out an atlas of the continental United States. Mariazul took the atlas from me, opening to a section dividing the Lone Star State into five regions: Trans-Pecos, the Panhandle, Central Texas, East Texas, and South Texas. She turned to the Trans-Pecos region, placing the tip of her index finger where westernmost Texas met New Mexico.

El Paso, I said.

She nodded.

Sí, sí. Texas. El Paso. You drive to El Paso?

I stared. For a moment, fear flashed across her eyes. Taking out my smartphone, I pulled up a translation app and typed out a message in English. I read aloud the results in Spanish.

Me voy a Rosadero. Pero, yo puedo parar en El Paso. ¿Cuál es la dirección?

She stared.

Rosadero? You drive to Rosadero, Texas?

I nodded. She unzipped the front pocket of her backpack, extracting a business card and passing it to me. On the front side of the card was a picture of an orange brick motel sitting on a hill of yellow desert grass. On the back of the card, white letters on a black background listed a name and address, along with a phone number. I studied the card in disbelief.

> The Celenia Inn
> 1600 US-90
> Rosadero, Texas 79843
> (432) XXX-5930

I passed back the card, then typed out another message.

Sí. Es la verdad. No hay problema.

Mariazul's expression brightened. She unzipped the backpack, reaching into its depths and pulling out a brown wallet, torn and held together by duct tape.

I can pay, she said. Dollars. How much?

No gracias, I said. No money, no money. No es necesario.

Deciding to accept my words, she took out a small golden crucifix necklace hidden beneath her hoodie, closed her eyes, and whispered a prayer to her Creator. I turned away, trying to provide privacy. When she was done crossing herself, she returned her attention to me. I remembered we still had not introduced ourselves. I tried to draw on the rudimentary Spanish retained from high school.

Mi nombre es Anna, I said. ¿Cómo se llama?

Mariazul, she said.

Mucho gusto, I said.

Yes, okay, she said.

Later, I would find her full name written on a white label stitched inside her backpack. Someday, I would learn that her mother named her after nature, a name she carried with her to far-distant places that looked nothing and felt nothing like home.

Do you want breakfast? I asked.

She nodded.

Huevos rancheros. Thank you.

She took out the frayed wallet again, passing me several crumpled dollar bills. I left her alone in the hybrid, crossing the cold parking lot quickly and stepping into the store. Inside, three Border Patrol agents were congregating around the coffee machine, filling their thermoses, and laughing. They were all men, heavyset but strong, all Latino, with trim gelled hair. At the counter, I placed an order for huevos rancheros, then left to use the restroom. A poster outside the women's room detailed warning signs of human trafficking in several languages, with a 1-800 number to call to report suspicious activity. Upon my return to the food counter, the three agents were gone. Waiting to pick up Mariazul's breakfast, I looked out the window, checking for her outline in my car. She was still there.

I couldn't believe it. Any of it.

Receiving the huevos rancheros in a cardboard takeout container, I approached the cash register to pay. Copies of the Hidalgo County newspaper sat in a stack by the scanner. The frontpage headline was about a notorious Japanese internment camp in the area during the 1940s. I read the first few sentences before realizing the cashier in front of me—a large young woman dressed in the truck stop's red and yellow uniform— had nodded off, though she continued to stand upright. Her breathing was heavy, as though she were in a trance. She stood there until her manager shook her shoulder.

ELONGATED MIRAGES MELTED across the eastern sky, a range of phantom mountains vanishing into dawn. Two hours after leaving the truck stop, Southern New Mexico broke into Texas, erupting into the strip malls and interchanges of El Paso. As we drove through the city, Mariazul stared at Ciudad Juárez rising on the other side of the international fence. She looked up at the cinderblock houses, her hand on the window as though trying to touch the craggy neighborhoods. Most of the hillside shacks were tagged with graffiti and coated in dust. Razor-wire encircled the yards, piled tires and sheet metal forming makeshift defense barriers. On the other side of downtown El Paso, Juárez opened into a huge industrial valley, an iron bar of smog hovering over the export manufacturing plants that sprawled in every direction. For a moment, Mariazul turned to me as though she had something she wanted to say.

She said nothing.

THE SIERRA BLANCA Border Patrol Checkpoint funneled interstate traffic into an outdoor shelter between the hills of Hudspeth County, contracting the countryside of yucca and dry soil into the restrictive architecture of security. Mariazul—who had been asleep—looked out at the idling line of semi-trucks and passenger vehicles. She was expressionless.

My hybrid stopped in front of a small army of surveillance cameras and orange cones. An agent standing in front of a security booth gestured for me to come forward. As I complied, a flash indicated that my license plates had been photographed.

The border agent smiled at us with practiced warmth. His uniform tag identified him as Agent Gallegos.

Morning, ladies. Where are you traveling today?

Rosadero, I said.

The agent nodded at Mariazul. She glanced at me before answering.

Yes sir, she said. Rosadero.

Are you a citizen of the United States? Agent Gallegos asked me.

Yes sir, I said.

Is she? he asked.

My heart raced. Before I could say another word, he asked us to produce identification. Fingers trembling, I passed along my driver's license. The agent waited while Mariazul took out her broken wallet and extracted a permanent resident card. Taking an ultraviolet LED flashlight off his belt, the agent examined our documents with a severe expression. Behind him, a second agent stood beneath a framed black-and-white photograph of a young, cleanshaven man in Border Patrol uniform and a cowboy hat. Beneath the framed photograph lay dozens of flowers, cards, and prayer candles. The agent standing under the portrait was a woman—the only one in uniform at the checkpoint—with pale skin and a diminutive face, her frizzy brown hair tied into a ponytail. She stood with tense focus, unaware of the traffic crawling through her station.

Agent Gallegos turned to her.

Agent Taylor, would you mind coming over here? he asked.

The woman known as Agent Taylor looked over at us. She stepped away from the shrine to inspect our IDs. She looked at Mariazul. All three of us waited.

Ms. Bautista's document appears to be authentic, Agent Gallegos said. A resident of Tucson, Arizona. Says here she was granted asylum more than a year ago. See anything wrong?

Agent Taylor took out a pair of mirrored sunglasses and covered her face. Agent Gallegos sighed. He returned our IDs.

Thank you, ladies. Drive safe.

I nodded. Exiting the inspection area, I reaccelerated to highway speed in slow, cautious increments. As the checkpoint disappeared around the mountains, I thought I could see Agent Taylor still watching after us.

Leaning against the window, Mariazul fell back asleep.

THIRTY MINUTES LATER, we were sitting on a picnic table in front of a truck stop outside the town of Van Horn. I smoked a cigarette, watching dark clouds gather in the sky, draining the redness out of the desert. Mariazul sipped from a bottle of water, wiping her lips, and looking back at the interstate traffic rushing along the dusty hills. Above us, the denuded branches of an oak tree stretched in a pantomime of shelter. Across the decaying highway stood an abandoned feedstore. We were seventy-four miles from Rosadero.

Mariazul rescrewed the plastic cap onto her water bottle. She tapped me on the shoulder.

Telephone? To write English.

I passed her my smartphone. She typed the question she must have wanted to ask since I picked her up in Hidalgo County.

Why are you traveling to Rosadero?

I let my cigarette burn, thinking about what to say. Mariazul jiggled her leg against the bench, waiting.

I told her the truth.

My brother is missing. His name is Jakob. He was last seen in Rosadero ten days ago. Nobody knows where he is. The police say he was kidnapped. I love him very much.

Mariazul sat with my words. She took a deep breath and transmitted something in return. Passing back my phone a final time, she looked away.

My brother is missing too. His name is Alejandro.

Neither of us spoke.

Finishing my cigarette, I communicated that it was time to leave. Mariazul and I returned inside my hybrid, buckling our seatbelts as heat recirculated throughout the interior. Turning on the engine, we began the final stretch of driving. The truck stop behind us appeared empty in the rearview mirror, inhabited by something realer than ghosts, but harder to name.

ROWS OF NAKED pecan trees stretched into the foothills of Jeff Davis County. Tucked behind the orchard, a freight train whistled and rumbled. On the other side of the highway, abandoned trailers popped out of grazing land. Forty minutes out of Van Horn, a sign announced the next town: Beauvoir, Texas—Population 98. Up and down the highway, Beauvoir seemed to comprise rusting trailers and sagging desert cottages. Not a single one of the alleged ninety-eight residents was in sight.

Halfway through the ghost town, a white cruiser with a green stripe sped up behind us, turning on its roof lights. I pulled over in front of an abandoned casita with a front door that had fallen off its hinges. Two withered magueys stood on either side of its entrance. Nobody, it seemed, had been home for years.

The Border Patrol cruiser screeched to a halt, kicking up dust like a plume of smoke. Out of the plume, Agent Taylor from the Sierra Blanca checkpoint jumped onto the road. She sprinted up to the passenger side of my hybrid, her frizzy brown ponytail bobbing behind her, her service weapon drawn. Tapping on Mariazul's window with her pistol, the agent ordered me to unlock the door.

I obeyed.

The agent pulled the door open and seized Mariazul by the arm, yelling for me to keep my hands on the wheel. The agent yanked Mariazul out of her seat, causing the seatbelt to burst out of its receiver, almost striking her in the eye. As Mariazul cried out, Agent Taylor forced the backpack off her shoulders, discarding it onto the dirt and gravel. Brandishing her pistol again, Agent Taylor screamed at me to keep my eyes straight. I complied, listening to the clink of handcuffs around Mariazul's wrists, seeing her in my peripheral vision led into the cruiser still flashing behind me. Agent Taylor slammed the door in condemnation. She looked at me with intensity and disappeared into her cruiser, screeching onto the highway before pulling a tight u-turn and speeding back towards the interstate.

The ghost town was silent.

For several minutes, I remained in a paralytic fog, my hands still clenching the steering wheel. Eventually returning to my senses, I looked out of the open passenger door. Mariazul's backpack still lay on the ground, along with the golden crucifix. Sometime during her arrest, her necklace must have broken away, sacrificed to the desert like so many anonymous articles of faith.

As I regained power over myself, I took out my cellphone. I had no signal. There was nobody I could call. All I had were Mariazul's last known possessions.

Stepping out of my hybrid at last, I walked around to the backpack and crucifix. Not knowing what else to do, I placed her belongings on her seat. Closing the door, I looked at the abandoned casita. Behind the open doorway, I could see a dim room. In a desperate pursuit for help, I stepped inside.

My eyes took a moment to adjust to the darkness. Slowly, the interior of the casita began to take form. Torn-up rugs lay on a primitive dirt floor covered in rodent tracks, defiled by guano and bird droppings. In one corner of the living room, a packrat nest glistened with urine. Plastic toy soldiers lay at angles they might occupy for a thousand years. On the walls, most of the coffee-colored paint had peeled away, revealing rough blocks of adobe. On either side of the fireplace hung two sepia-toned portraits, one of Benito Juárez, reserved and statesmanlike, the other Emiliano Zapata, youthful and determined under his sombrero.

Above, the tin roof began to reverberate with rain. I walked back to my car and resumed my place behind the steering wheel. There was nothing else to do.

Activating my left turn-signal, I rejoined the highway. A few yards from Beauvoir's southern edge, a green metal sign informed me I was leaving Jeff Davis County and entering Narváez County. Ten minutes outside the ghost town, I passed an unmarked white blimp moored to a circular runway, protected by razor-wire fence and flashing lights. Signs in English and Spanish warned away potential trespassers. Through an intelligence matrix I could not begin to understand, I believed the blimp had foreseen the entire course of my morning, monitoring my role in the young woman's passage from Lordsburg into the backseat of Agent Taylor's cruiser. Perhaps, the blimp had intercepted my phone signal, short-circuiting my line of communication to the Pacific Northwest. I would never know.

Blue slivers of light filled the sky. I would not encounter another soul for forty minutes.

BENICIO WASHINGTION IS waiting for me in a dim mahogany bar in downtown El Paso's historic Taft Hotel. Sitting alone in a booth, he raises a glass of whiskey to get my attention, though the gesture is unnecessary. With his athletic build and handsome face, he fills his olive-green Border Patrol uniform like a celebrity. The white cowboy hat he wears is immaculate. I place my audio recorder on the table, press the on-button, and shake his hand. I try not to blush as he looks into my eyes.

You must be Jakob, he says. Professor Ochoa told me you had pink hair. I'm Benicio, obviously.

Obviously, I say.

He nods.

Thanks for meeting me in El Paso. Sorry I can't get to Rosadero this week. I came straight from the field. Tomorrow, I'm spending at least fourteen hours in an office building. Thought I'd unwind between shifts.

It's no problem, I say as I slide into the booth. Hope you haven't been waiting long.

Not too long. I'm taking advantage of the opportunity to slow down. Don't get to do that very often.

I'll bet.

How do you like Rosadero so far?

I love it. It's so beautiful and quiet. I love all the postmodern art. And the people are so friendly. I'm still getting used to saying hello to my neighbors. They don't do that where I come from.

No kidding? I wouldn't assume Portland is big enough for people to be like that.

It's a Pacific Northwest thing. The unfriendliness is a holdover from Scandinavian settlers. Apparently, it's against Scandinavian etiquette to make eye contact and talk to people you don't know that well. It's considered intrusive, or something.

Or something.

I laugh, louder than I intend. Special Agent Washington smiles politely.

You grew up in Rosadero, I say.

He nods.

On the southside of town. My mother still lives in the house where I was raised. It's not too far from Professor Ochoa's home, actually. You've probably walked past it. For most of Rosadero's history, all the Mexican households were restricted to that area. Segregation has a long legacy.

I feel like we don't talk about segregation in the Southwest that much.

That's because we don't.

So, for the sake of accuracy, how do you define your ethnic background? Would Afro-Latino be accurate?

Sure. My people settled in Mexico sometime in the 1850s. They escaped a plantation near Beaumont and followed the underground railroad through Texas. The other underground railroad, that is.

The other underground railroad?

Mexico abolished slavery in 1829. The Guerrero Decree was the Emancipation Proclamation before the Emancipation Proclamation.

Huh. Really?

Really. Texas declared independence to hold onto slavery. Most people forget.

Yeah, I had no idea.

My people crossed somewhere outside Laredo. They ended up in Coahuila, in a village called Nacimiento. I still visit once a year to pay my respects to my ancestors. You ever hear of the Mascogos?

No sir.

Well, for your official record, my people are the Mascogos. They stayed over there for more than a hundred years until my parents resettled in the United States. That was in the 1960s, near the end of the Bracero Program. I was born and raised in Rosadero. But I've always felt Mexican.

How old were you when you joined the Border Patrol?

Not much older than a teenager. That was about a quarter century ago.

Did you go to college?

Tried to. Sul Ross State. But I don't do well in a classroom. I've always been something of an autodidact. Everything I learn, I learn on my own. It's a problem, more so than I'd like to admit, especially when it comes to working in a big law enforcement institution. Mavericks are always viewed as pathogens. Maybe that's why the union doesn't like me. Well, one of the reasons.

The union?

The National Border Patrol Council.

Why else wouldn't they like you?

Because I investigate corruption, mostly in the rank-in-file.

That would do it. Speaking of which, could you please state your exact title and the unit in which you operate?

Certainly. I am the Special Operations Supervisor of the Border Patrol's Internal Constabulary Division, which has existed for three years and of which I am the sole investigator. Always have been, and probably always will be.

How did the Internal Constabulary Division come into existence? What does it do, and why are you the only one doing it?

The I.C.D. came into existence after a string of corruption cases within the Border Patrol attracted national media attention. Some very dark, very high-profile stuff. Multiple agents in multiple sectors, caught acting at the behest of certain syndicates outside the United States. Some had even killed for their shadow employers. A lot of pressure came down from the politicians to do something. However, as you may already know, people who work in law enforcement tend to hold the line against outside investigations.

Yeah, definitely with police departments. So that's true with the Border Patrol, too?

Yes sir. The compromise struck by the command structure and the union was to create an internal investigating division, but to limit its scope by limiting its staff. As a result, my paycheck and field expenses represent the entirety of the I.C.D.'s budget. I'm the most hated agent in any sector I step into. But I also set the terms of the job. It's not too bad, all things considered.

Doesn't sound too bad at all.

Benicio smiles. He takes a sip from his drink, waiting for me to ask about the cases he investigates. So I do. He sighs, pondering what to tell and what not to tell.

The crimes I investigate are ordinary, he says, carried out by ordinary agents, acting on ordinary motivations, conducted by ordinary means. Human trafficking, weapons trafficking, drug smuggling. The cases I deal with are so unremarkable, it is almost immaterial to everyone but the victims whether they are solved. Now, I want to be very clear that this is not a statement of surrender, but a statement of experience. There is too much money being made for the serious operations to stop.

Serious operations? Like the cartels?

A little bit. But the way things are, illegal economics and legal economics are so interdependent, you can't prosecute the one without prosecuting the other. The system running across the border is neither clean nor dirty. The system is undaunted.

I'm stunned. A young waitress in a tuxedo approaches our table, setting down a pair of menus. She asks Special Agent Washington whether he would like more whiskey. He declines. I ask for a glass of water. The waitress nods. She leaves us alone again.

Special Agent Washington looks at me.

You're sitting in the most important metropolitan area in North America, he says. Did you know that?

El Paso? I ask.

He shakes his head.

Juárez-El Paso. Across the river is a city of one point four million. If Juárez were an American city, its population would be the ninth largest. And if you combine it with El Paso, you get the fifth largest, just behind Houston. And in truth, this is one city. Always has been. But with the border, two-thirds of America's fifth largest city is being laundered through Mexico. Economically, anyway. The border is a big lie, Jakob, but a lie with serious stakes. The illusion of separateness allows many other lies, more than any of us could comprehend.

We sit for a moment as Special Agent Washington's numbers hang in the air. In booths around the bar, I become aware that every other conversation is taking place in Spanish. From time to time, furtive looks are directed our way.

I'm sorry, I say.

Sorry for what?

I don't know. I didn't mean to…one point four million is a lot of people.

Special Agent Washington removes his cowboy hat and sets it on the table.

I spend a lot of time in Juárez, he says. Though I don't have jurisdiction there.

What do you do there?

Talk. Listen. Take notes and track down leads.

Where do your leads take you?

To networks. To quid pro quos, to transactions and balance sheets underpinning the cases that come my way. Every time I cross into Mexico, I learn something new. There is nowhere to hide anything. The violence is so far-reaching. Earlier this decade, in the same twelve-month period, Juárez recorded three thousand homicides. El Paso recorded five. This is not incidental. It is an expression of the power differential the United States wields over the rest of the world. Most Americans know nothing about it. The reality is too raw. Do you know why Juárez is so dangerous, even on a good year?

Why?

Because Juárez is a city hijacked. All for the United States. All for our needs.

At that moment, the waitress returns with my glass of water. She asks whether we would like anything to eat. Special Agent Washington places an order for a porterhouse steak, cooked medium rare. I order coffee. The waitress tells me she needs to put on a fresh pot, and that it will take about ten minutes to be ready. I tell her that's fine. As she walks away, Special Agent Washington places his cowboy hat back on his head, lost in thought. Our conversation is only beginning.

ROSADERO SLIPPED INTO existence as a series of blurred buildings, mostly beige or brick, some a pristine white, some decorated with Christmas lights and tinsel. Other than a silver water-tower and the ornate dome of the Narváez County Courthouse, there was nothing distinctive about the town. Nobody appeared on the sidewalks or in the streets. Aside from a few mud-splattered pickup trucks and luxury cars with European plates, the only other motorist I saw was a sheriff deputy sitting in his black SUV.

Red and blue lights appeared in my mirrors.

I parked beneath a speed limit sign where the last few yards of curb melted into shimmering yellow grass. In the distance, a broad monument of red stone rose out of the horizon. The deputy approached with a slow, heavy gait. He had gelled black hair and light brown skin. As I rolled down my window, he stopped in front of me, rubbing his hands to keep warm.

Afternoon, ma'am. I'm Deputy Ybarra. How are you today?

Doing okay.

Good to hear. Unfortunately, my radar clocked you at thirty-seven miles-per-hour. The speed limit here is thirty-five. I'll need to take a look at your license and insurance card, please.

I passed my documents through the window. Rather than taking the information back to his SUV, Deputy Ybarra lingered on the side of the road, surveying my license.

You drove all the way to Texas from Portland, Oregon? he asked.

Yes sir.

Wanted to be a tourist in the off-season, did you?

No sir. I'm looking for my brother. Jakob Tatevyan. He went missing ten days ago. Nobody knows where he is. He had been living in Rosadero while working on his master's thesis. The authorities seem to think he was kidnapped. I'm supposed to stay with a family around here while I'm looking for him. Do you know where the Celenia Inn is?

Deputy Ybarra looked at me.

Ms. Tatevyan, I am so sorry, he said. The Celenia Inn is just up the highway around that small hill. My sister is expecting you.

Your sister?

Angelica Ybarra. She's the one who agreed to put you up. Usually, she keeps the motel closed from November through February. The Celenia Inn has been in our family for a couple generations. I'm sorry about your brother. Now that I know you're in town, I'll call the sheriff. You'll be able to see him tomorrow morning. Is anyone else from your family in town?

No sir. I came alone.

That's a tough thing, driving that far by yourself. Tougher to travel alone as a woman.

Yes sir. It is.

Tell you what. Let me run your information through the system to see if you have any unpaid tickets or anything. If your record is clear, I'll let you off with a warning. Sound good?

I nodded. Deputy Ybarra returned inside his service vehicle. As he entered my data into his machine, I glanced at the backpack and crucifix next to me. I thought about what might come up if he entered Mariazul Bautista's name into his database, or Agent Taylor's.

Or my brother's.

Deputy Ybarra returned with my documents and a warning written on a pink slip. Before stepping away, he told me to ring the doorbell to the Celenia Inn's lobby. His sister was likely in the back office. He counseled me to be patient with her. She had a bad leg. Some days, the pain was so bad that she had to navigate the motel with a cane.

The deputy wanted to know if I had any more questions for him. I took a deep breath.

Deputy Ybarra—

Please, call me Arturo.

Deputy Ybarra, does the Border Patrol operate in Rosadero?

He nodded.

Technically speaking, the Border Patrol operates everywhere. They also claim the right to search any vehicle within a hundred miles of an international border, including coastlines. Most Americans live in the Border Patrol's jurisdiction. They just don't know it. But around here, the Patrol mostly sticks to ranch roads and remote spots down by the Rio Grande. You shouldn't have any trouble with them.

He tapped the roof of my hybrid, as though his statement had solved my preoccupations. I thanked him for his help. He stood back, allowing me to drive the hundred yards or so to the Celenia Inn. My hands were still trembling.

TURNING ON THE clock radio in my motel room, I collapsed onto the king-sized bed. The only items I brought in from my car were the backpack and crucifix, which I set next to me on top of the mattress. As a static-filled blues program played on Rosadero Public Radio, I took Mariazul's things into my arms, curling around them like a protective mother. My thoughts began to decouple from coherent order. Before succumbing to exhaustion, I unlaced my boots, letting them drop to the floor. My eyes closed. I breathed into the blanket, vaguely hoping my dreams could take me to a place of understanding about Mariazul's fate, or wherever my brother had gone.

When I woke up, I hoped I could tell myself the story of how I came to Rosadero.

· Two ·

Football Hero

SOMETIME THE PREVIOUS spring, Williamsburg, Brooklyn raised a new riverfront icon onto a warehouse of luxury condos. Popping out against the Manhattan skyline, a deep pink water-tower appeared overnight above lofts settled by professionals whose money never ran out. Captivating photographers and culture writers, Williamsburg's latest novelty attracted immediate speculation. Critics of certain insight determined the tower to be a scale replica of the one in Rosadero, Texas—which accounted for why the town's name appeared in bold black letters on its rose-colored façade. The beacon soon represented a point of aspiration for anybody who had come to Brooklyn to do more than ride bicycles and struggle to pay rent. Not since the installation of Justin Lehenwesen's site-specific displays in the West Texas landscape in the 1980s had there been such manufactured interest in Rosadero. In stunning numbers, hotel rooms were booked, flights reserved, and road trips planned by Brooklynites suddenly in love with the far-distant locale most had just learned about for the first time.

The pink water-tower proved to be a masterstroke in advertising.

Few of the dreamers taking inspiration from the vessel over the East River had ever heard of the Sierra Blanca Border Patrol Checkpoint. Fewer still had heard of extraordinary rendition, or could deconstruct the concept of due process, or define what it meant to be a lawful permanent resident. Perhaps only a handful of Brooklyn's up-and-comers could conceive of a person like Mariazul Lluvia Cenote Bautista.

Seeing her in every dream I had during my first twenty-four hours in Rosadero, I still could not conceive of her, either.

I STOOD IN the open doorway of my motel room the next morning—I had slept for the rest of the previous day—staring into the empty parking lot of the Celenia Inn. In the corner of the lot, the asphalt bled into gravel before passing into tens of thousands of square miles of high desert prairieland. A jackrabbit hopped into the tall yellow grass, silent and quick, like a creature gently bounding across the ocean floor. The memory of rain filled the countryside with the scent of damp hay. In the sky, the late November light was soft and metallic. I could see most of Rosadero from the motel's position atop a slight knoll. On the other side of a dried-out ravine, appliances and other consumer junk lay in the yards of crumbling casitas with tin roofs. American kitsch and Mexican knickknacks decorated the front doors of the more respectable dwellings. Mesquite trees and prickly-pears and agaves and intermingled with the properties, the reality of the desert insisting upon itself across every home.

It all looked so lonely.

I took slow, delicate steps over the asphalt to my car. Since yesterday, the toes of my black tights had ripped open. Between my crumpled-up shirt and unwashed hair, I must have looked like a victim of some kind, another young woman on the run. As I retrieved my suitcase and slammed the trunk shut, my ear took note of the immediacy with which the countryside swallowed the noise. Silence itself seemed to have stolen the people of Rosadero, as though the community were an aural phenomenon, able to be muted at any time.

I showered and dressed, attempting everything I could to pretty up the wear and tear of my marathon dash across the American West. After an hour, I reemerged in the parking lot, concealed in a faux-leather jacket, thick black leggings, and my black knee-high boots. Fake designer sunglasses covered my eyes. A braided ponytail and red headband brought order to my decaying blonde hair. As I stepped back outside, nobody else seemed to be around. For today at least, the motel assured total solitude.

Before meeting with the Narváez County Sheriff's Office, I needed a cigarette. Secluding myself behind the motel, I exhaled smoke, staring across the horizon of grass punctuated by yucca and ocotillo. In the distance, the rock formation I had seen from the highway erupted in a near-vertical slope of porous red stone, culminating in a flat island in the sky. A dark gray cloud hovered over the roof of the formation. The longer I stared at the rock, the more I could see a massive split running down its height, opening into a canyon. Somewhere in that monolith, another ecosystem resided.

A few minutes into my smoke break, a young woman approached me from around the corner of the motel. She was also holding a pack of cigarettes, out here with the same intentions. With black hair and heavy bangs, long black dress, black makeup, and black boots, she could have been my long-lost sister. Her ears were pieced by wide golden-hoop earrings, glinting against her cheekbones.

Hey, she said. Got a light?

I nodded, passing the lighter. She thanked me and ignited her cigarette. We stood side by side, like teenagers cutting class.

You must be Anna, she said.

Must be, I said.

She laughed.

My name is Sabana. My mom manages the motel. I hear you've already met my uncle.

Yeah, yesterday.

Sabana Ybarra took a long drag on her cigarette.

We tried checking on you yesterday, she said. You never answered your door. We were worried.

Sorry about that. I was sleeping.

The whole day?

Needed to.

I've had days like that. Not gonna lie, my mom sent me to see how you're doing. Happy to see you're okay. Just head's up, though, we don't allow smoking on the premises. Of course, it's the off-season, and these are difficult times. So don't worry about it, I guess. I'm not worried about it, obviously.

Thanks, I said.

Sorry about your brother.

Thanks, I said again.

Jakob was a great guy. Whenever he was in town, he used to come into the coffeeshop where I work. I always felt like I learned something new talking to him. Great sense of humor, too.

I said nothing. Sabana followed my gaze out to the rock formation. I checked the time on my phone, set my cigarette on the ground, and put it out with the heel of my boot before picking it back up.

Don't worry, I don't litter, I said.

I can take that, Sabana said. Is there anything else I can do for you?

I took another look at the horizon.

What am I looking at? I asked.

Sabana nodded.

The Zaldos Mesa. Named for the people who used to inhabit this land. It's a fascinating place. There's a stone pueblo at the entrance to the canyon. The whole thing is on private ranchland, though. I could take you sometime before you leave town. I know how to get there without attracting attention.

I nodded. Before leaving for the courthouse, I took out my smartphone so Sabana and I could exchange numbers. Then I returned to my car and drove into town. In the pocket of my corduroy skirt, Mariazul's crucifix necklace seemed to burn against the fabric.

SHERIFF DOUGLAS ALIRE'S laughter reverberated throughout the lobby of the Narváez County Courthouse. Standing beneath the interior dome and tasteful wooden walls, his heavyset body stretched his beige uniform beneath a rugged winter jacket. He had glaucoma in his right eye, which rested in milky complacency, and a thick, silver brush-shaped mustache over his jovial mouth. Deputy Arturo Ybarra stood at his side, smiling gently at whatever joke the sheriff had just told. Both men turned to look at me as I entered through the courthouse's elegant front doors. Their expressions sobered.

You must be Ms. Tatevyan, the sheriff said. I'm Sheriff Douglas Alire. Friends call me Deadeye. Thank you for coming down. I wish you were visiting Rosadero under kinder circumstances. Of course, you've already met Deputy Ybarra here.

Sabana's uncle nodded. I looked at Deadeye.

Sheriff, do you have any idea where my brother is? I asked.

Come with us, he said. We can talk in the conference room. Would you like any coffee? A pastry, maybe?

That's okay.

The sheriff and his deputy led me out of the lobby and down a short set of stairs into a quiet, dimly lit hallway. Only after we had passed several imposing doors did I understand that this building housed the county jail, too. We stepped into a glass-doored conference room, indistinguishable from what might be found on any college or corporate campus. On the cream-colored wall beneath the fluorescent lighting, a framed painting depicted five old, Anglo cowboys leading a massive cattle drive across the desert prairie, the Zaldos Mesa looming in the background.

We settled into office chairs around the oak conference table.

Sheriff Alire, I said, do you think there's a chance this…is there any evidence that this might be a hate crime?

He frowned.

Hate crime?

My brother's gay. His hair is dyed bright pink. He's never been ashamed of who he is.

Sheriff Alire glanced at Deputy Ybarra.

First off, I should tell you the investigation is mostly being handled by the Department of Public Safety, he said. They share with us what they can, but they haven't mentioned anything about a hate crime. And to tell you the truth…well, in Texas, it's only been a hate crime to assault a citizen on the basis of sexual orientation since 2001. Maybe a dozen such cases have been prosecuted with success. I doubt DPS would be spending much time on that thread.

Are you serious?

Yes ma'am. But the kidnapping and extortion elements are enough to give this case the highest urgency. The Texas Rangers are working it as best they can, keeping quiet so the media doesn't get involved. My understanding is that the Rangers have been in touch with your parents. Is that correct, Ms. Tatevyan?

My parents aren't here, I said. I'm the only one who came down. Who are the Texas Rangers assigned to his case?

Captain Winston Bryce Jr. is the lead investigator. His partner is Ranger Jackson Flores. They're based out of

Company E, out in El Paso. That's probably where they are right now.

Do they think my brother is in El Paso?

I don't know. The fact is, Ms. Tatevyan, the Rangers have taken this almost completely out of our hands. I'm happy to tell you what I can. But Deputy Ybarra and I are pulled in a number of directions right now.

Like what?

The sheriff cleared his throat.

Ms. Tatevyan, how well do you follow the news from this part of the world?

Why?

Earlier this month we had a shooting at a Border Patrol checkpoint out in Sierra Blanca. An agent by the name of Denton Pierce was gunned down in the middle of the night by unknown assailants. He was beloved by the community, a hard worker on his way to make rank. Before that, he was something of a star on his high school football team. He grew up in Fort Davis. That's about twenty-five-minutes from here.

Why are you telling me this?

The murder of Denton Pierce remains unsolved. You got law enforcement agencies all across West Texas putting in overtime on his case. Been about four weeks and nobody's any closer to knowing who killed him or why. Politicians are using his death to talk about border security. The Texas Legislature even held a moment of silence for him. I'm telling you this to say…the sheriff's office has a responsibility to public safety. When one of our own gets killed, it takes priority. We're doing the best we can with other cases, but we're a small operation. We're stretched about as thin as we can be.

I see. You're saying the death of some West Coast faggot doesn't matter.

Ms. Tatevyan, there is no need for that type of language. You are distraught.

Motherfucking right, I'm distraught. My brother's been missing for eleven days. Eleven days. If my parents don't pay his kidnappers the ransom, they will torture Jakob and kill him. That's what they said. Do you even know my brother's name? Do you even know how to spell it? J-A-K-O-B-T-A-T-E-V-E-Y-A-N. He's probably dead behind your bullshit. Where can I find the coroner's office?

I leaned onto the table, clutching my head, trying not to cry. My breath was shallow. Sheriff Alire leaned towards Deputy Ybarra and whispered. Deputy Ybarra stood from his chair and stepped out of the conference room. Sheriff Alire waited for my composure to return.

I'm sorry, Ms. Tatevyan, he said. I don't want you to get the wrong idea. Getting Jakob home safe and sound is a top priority. Deputy Ybarra is calling Company E to see about getting Captain Bryce and Ranger Flores out here to speak with you. They can probably be here as soon as tomorrow. You all can meet in this conference room. Does the sheriff's office have your permission to pass along your phone number so they may arrange the details with you?

I nodded. Sheriff Alire took out a miniature notebook with a short pencil and took down my number. He stood up, sighing as he lifted his substantial gait, looking down with something between with concern and unmoved pity. He told me to wait here while he and Deputy Ybarra confirmed with the Rangers.

Thank you for coming, he said. I hope for good news.

Sheriff Alire walked out of the conference room. Isolated beneath the artificial lights, I extracted Mariazul's crucifix necklace from the pocket of my skirt. I placed the necklace on the table, as though allowing it to come alive, to tell me what to do. By the time the sheriff and his deputy returned, I had returned the crucifix inside my pocket, a topic the light could no longer broach.

SABANA AND I lingered behind the backwall of the Celenia Inn, resuming our smoke break. In thirty minutes, she had her afternoon shift at Move Bricks Coffee, a coffeehouse located in a converted lumberyard. In late November, only a few tourists a day came in to order charcoal-activated horchata lattes. Sabana spent a substantial portion of her shift reading or working in her notebook. In college, she had studied journalism and creative writing, and had even interned at the offices of the *Texas Observer* in Austin. Though the difficult contours of her career had brought her back to Rosadero to work as a part-time barista—and, in the spring and summer months, to work at the family motel—she had not yet ceded her future. She was still shaping her story.

In a lot of ways, Jakob was doing exactly what I want to do, she said. An MFA at the University of Arizona. Earning a degree and getting all kinds of institutional support for a manuscript. Plus, I would love to live in Tucson, or a place like Tucson. Your brother used to tell me how beautiful the city is. Cheap, too.

I ashed my cigarette onto the gravel.

My brother is being held for two hundred thousand dollars, I said. Two hundred thousand. That's what his abductors are demanding. Tomorrow, I'm meeting with the Texas Rangers to see if there's any way he's going to make it out of this alive.

Sabana was quiet.

The Rangers have a rough history in this part of Texas, she said.

What do you mean?

Nothing. It won't affect you. Good luck with them.

That was all she wanted to say.

Our attention fell back onto the prairielands. Sabana asked me whether I had heard of the Rosadero Fireballs. I had not. The Rosadero Fireballs, she told me, were the primary draw for people who stayed at the Celenia Inn—on top of it being the cheapest accommodations in town. Ever since Rosadero's founding in 1880, residents and visitors alike had witnessed balls of pink light streaking across the plains east of town. They came only at night, bursting into existence and running across the earth before vanishing once again. Despite substantial eyewitnesses, as well as consistent photographic and videographic documentation, nobody had ever produced a credible explanation for the Fireballs. Perhaps, if I were lucky, I would see them during my stay at the Celenia Inn.

Sabana checked the time on her phone. She asked if there was anything else she could do for me before leaving for work. I took a deep breath.

Do people ever come through here who aren't supposed to? I asked.

What do you mean? Sabana asked.

I don't know. People who aren't in the country…border-crossers, I guess. We're close to Mexico, right?

Sabana nodded.

Yeah. About sixty miles down the road. You shouldn't be concerned about so-called cartels, Anna. That hasn't been a real thing in this part of Texas since the '80s, back when Pablo Acosta controlled Ojinaga. His reign is long over.

What about other kinds of people?

Sure. From time to time, people who cross the border without documents do pass by our motel. The mural seems to attract their attention. The one behind us, I mean.

The mural?

I turned around. For the first time, I noticed the luminescent painting of Our Lady of Guadalupe on the orange brick wall. Clothed in her pink tunic and starred, azure mantle, a golden cherub elevated the Virgin's body against the glowing rays of God.

Sabana touched the hem of the robe.

When certain people see the Celenia Inn, they see the Virgen and recognize this place as a sanctuary. Men, women, children. Refugees of violence and poverty. Survivors of horror you cannot begin to know, who the United States would not allow to enter otherwise.

She looked at me.

If you ever see anybody you suspect crossed over from Mexico, please call my uncle. I can give you his number. Or, if you feel like contacting the Border Patrol, there's a specific liaison who handles that sort of thing on behalf of the motel. I can give you his number as well. Would you like that?

I don't know, I said. It's just—I don't want to get into trouble.

Why would you get into trouble?

I don't know. What would happen if I picked up someone from the side of the road and gave them a ride? A border-crosser, maybe, who needed help? Would I be charged with anything?

Sabana put out her cigarette.

Honestly, yes, she said. Depending on which agency gets to you first, you could be arrested for human trafficking, no matter the actual context. We had a case like that in Jeff Davis County not too long ago. A prominent lawyer got put in jail for providing medical aid to a migrant on the side of the highway. That case got thrown out, but that's only because the lawyer was well-connected. An average citizen could get into a lot of trouble. That's why we have a specific liaison. His name is Benicio Washington. Your brother interviewed him a few times for his thesis, actually.

Sabana checked the time. She had to prepare for her shift at the coffeeshop. Texting me her uncle's and Special Agent Washington's numbers, she left for work.

Standing alone with the Virgen de Guadalupe, I took out Mariazul's crucifix, and tried to speak a prayer. All I could hear was the desolate breath of the wind.

· Three ·

The Spectators

WE STAND ON the rooftop patio of the Taft Hotel, looking south into Juárez. The city's lights form a gigantic grid dividing the nighttime desert into clear, linear order. Behind us, El Paso's mountainside star blazes like an incandescent signature. The air is warm and still, thick with smoke from Special Agent Washington's after-dinner cigar. In the bar downstairs, he had persuaded me to order the Chile Verde stew as we continued to talk, a lapse in my on-again off-again veganism. Most of our conversation compared growing up in small-town Texas to growing up in the urban Pacific Northwest. We then covered some early cases in his career, corruption cases that made headlines and made Special Agent Washington a pariah to his peers. Up on the roof, he is silent and reflective, as though stitching together his thoughts out of the expansive city before us.

He takes his cigar and points towards Mexico.

A century ago, during the Battle of Juárez, Americans would sit at vantage points throughout El Paso and watch the gunfights. One of the most popular venues was on top of a laundry facility in El Segundo Barrio. The war was prime entertainment. Marching bands would play, photographs were taken for postcards. The Americans claimed to support the insurrectos, but the truth is they supported the spectacle. The Anglos took it as an affirmation of their own civilization, and of the savagery of Mexicans. El Paso merchants made a handsome profit selling weapons to both sides of the conflict.

He looks at me.

Why are you writing about the border, Jakob? What story does a boy from Portland, Oregon have to tell about this place? And who benefits from your telling?

Special Agent Washington allows me time to cohere a response.

My interest sparked when Professor Ochoa visited my class, I say. She was giving a guest lecture on the bilingual creative writing program she co-founded, the one here in El Paso. The way she described the border as a form of objectification, an objectification that reaches into every aspect of the United States…I knew my thesis manuscript would have to come from here, especially since I was based in Tucson.

Benicio smiles.

Professor Ochoa led you to the borderlands within yourself.

She did.

Have you ever read Gloria Anzaldúa?

Not yet.

She was a friend of Professor Ochoa's. I'm sure she can recommend her works better than I.

I wouldn't doubt it. I've already learned so much from Juanita. She's really made me think about my own complicity in the power dynamics of the border—every American's complicity.

That's a good place to start. Complicity. Never forget, everything the Border Patrol does—and that Immigration and Customs Enforcement does—it does in the name of Americans like you. You and me and everybody else with citizenship.

Benicio taps the end of his cigar.

The truth is, Jakob, we are all either beneficiaries of the line drawn down here, or its victims. Think about all the borders you navigate every day. Housed, or unhoused. Insured, or uninsured. Wealthy, or destitute. Do you recall the Great Recession?

Of course.

The surge of violence in Juárez was a direct result. In the first year of the Recession, ninety thousand maquila workers lost their jobs. The financial crisis was created by Wall Street, not Mexico. At this moment of mass unemployment, the Sinaloa Cartel moved in to contest Juárez's trafficking plaza, hiring cheap soldiers from the ranks of the newly impoverished. These are not coincidences. They are the output of an interlocking system.

He checks the watch on his wrist. Special Agent Washington has been generous with his time. But he has to prepare for tomorrow.

We'll meet again soon, he says. Are you in Texas often these days?

I'm in Rosadero more and more. Professor Ochoa lets me stay in her guestroom. It's my preferred place to write, actually.

I'll keep that in mind. I'm interested to see where you take your thesis. Don't worry. I promise my critiques are fair.

He picks up his ashtray. He studies me for a moment.

When Professor Ochoa was setting up UTEP's bilingual MFA program, she quickly discovered that most of her students from Juárez suffered from trauma. Certain topics would come up in seminar and send her students into panic attacks. They had flashbacks, pain beyond description. She worked hard to create a classroom culture of support and compassion. Take every precaution with the story you aspire to tell. There are wounds everywhere, wounds no outsider should ever touch.

Special Agent Washington pats me on the shoulder and proceeds towards the stairs. Though he does not say so, he seems to understand that I will need a few minutes by myself.

I step towards the edge of the rooftop, watching Juárez. From somewhere far below, I hear a succession of loud pops, either from tires bursting on the interstate or from a city I will never know. After several minutes of listening, I am no closer to understanding what I've heard.

THE HOTEL JASPEADO loomed over Rosadero's town square like a prophecy. Pink and marbled, with a façade like glacial alpenglow, the hotel looked like a structure from a dream, though it had been out of operation for years. A slim door of dark glass comprised the front door, waiting for a reopening that may never come.

The hotel stood across the street from the centerpiece of the town's plaza: a colossal, teal-colored agave stretching its thick leaves across a plot of orange soil. A sign near a bench dated the plant to 1529, to the time of Cabeza de Vaca's wayward conquistadors, describing the maguey as the oldest and grandest in the Western Hemisphere. On the northern end of the plaza, the Narváez County Courthouse stood in resplendent classical architecture, where I would soon be meeting with the Texas Rangers. Art galleries and boutique fashion stores lined the other blocks around the square, their doors closed, their lights turned off for the season. Hardly anything in Rosadero seemed to exist beyond the narrow needs of haute-couture and postmodernism.

The streets were empty.

I sat down on a bench in front of the sprawling maguey with a pink cardboard box in my lap. Three dozen donuts from a bakery in Portland gleamed before me, a desperate gift for Jakob purchased before leaving for Texas. Since arriving in town, I had barely eaten. Aside from smoking and lying on my motel bed, I had barely done anything, in fact. With the Rangers due any minute, I picked up a donut—stale, filled with grape-flavored cream—and took a bite. I set the stiff, expired pastry down, picked up the next donut, took a single bite, and set it down, too. I continued like this with each donut, ruining them one by one. After twelve bites, I lit a cigarette, sprinkling my ash across the sugar-glazed treats. From behind my sunglasses, I studied the single stoplight in town, where Juan Sabeata Street, the east-west route carrying Highway 90, crossed Estevanico Avenue, the north-south state highway running all the way to the Mexican border.

A massive silver pickup truck with four-wheel drive arrived at the intersection from the east. Turning onto Estevanico Avenue, the pickup drove towards the courthouse, rumbling by the agave with profound self-regard. On the door was the insignia for the Texas Department of Public Safety, Ranger Division. Despite the tinted windows, I could perceive two men inside, wearing cowboy hats.

I closed the box of partially devoured donuts, put out my cigarette, and proceeded back inside the courthouse.

CAPTAIN BRYCE NODDED at his partner from his seat at the conference table. Ranger Flores turned on a small camera set up on a tripod beneath the painting of the cattle drive. The red light flashed on. He sat down next to the lead investigator, his relative youthfulness denoting his junior position. While Ranger Flores looked to be in his early forties, with a thick black mustache and dusky brown eyes, Captain Bryce appeared at least two decades older, with pale, roughhewn skin and severe light blue eyes. The Rangers each shook my hand, introducing themselves and their lengths of service for the Lone Star State. They said nothing about the camera, and I did not ask. My mind had only one line of questioning as I sat down.

Do you know where my brother is?

Captain Bryce sighed.

Ms. Tatevyan—

Do you know who my brother's kidnappers are?

Ms. Tatevyan, we are conducting this interview. Please do us the courtesy of letting us speak first. We're hoping for your cooperation.

I glanced at the red light. I began to understand.

Do I need a lawyer present? I asked.

That is your prerogative, Captain Bryce said. But that could make this conversation slow and complicated. When Sheriff Alire contacted our office yesterday, he gave us an impression of urgency.

It is urgent. My brother has been gone for eleven days. Why are you treating me like a suspect? I'm his sister.

You need to settle down, Ms. Tatevyan. I'm asking you once. Settle down.

I looked at Ranger Flores. His eyes bore into mine. I leaned back in my seat, crossing my arms, waiting. Captain Bryce nodded.

Let's establish a little about yourself. Please state your full name.

Anna Rachel Tatevyan.

How old are you, Ms. Tatevyan?

Twenty.

And what is your occupation?

I'm an undergraduate at Reed College in Portland, Oregon. But I'm taking the rest of the term off because of all this.

So, you're unemployed?

What? No. I'm a student. Just, not at the moment.

Do you work?

No. I'm a student. Taking time off.

Let's get to your brother. Ms. Tatevyan, in your experience, has Jakob ever espoused sympathy for the views of the Communist Party?

Blood rushed to the surface of my skin. Captain Bryce studied me closely.

Is that a serious question? I asked.

Yes ma'am.

Why on Earth are you asking me about the Communist Party?

Let me rephrase. Has your brother ever expressed allegiance to any political group invested in undermining the laws or security of the United States of America? Has he ever espoused an ideological point of view that could be characterized as extremist?

My fingers were trembling. I looked once again to Ranger Flores, silently pleading with him to serve as a counterweight. He continued his unemotional stare. I took the pink cardboard box of donuts from the table and placed it on my lap, as though to enlarge my personal space.

Jakob is a second-year creative writing MFA student at the University of Arizona, I said. He would come to Rosadero to write. He'd been living here for the last few weeks.

Were you aware that your brother was stalking and harassing a sitting United States Congressman?

What?

Representative A.P. Horne of the Forty-Fourth Congressional District. Were you aware of that?

I've never heard of A.P. Horne. My brother never mentioned him.

Do you stand by that answer, Ms. Tatevyan? Captain Bryce asked.

Yes. I do. Could you please explain what these bullshit questions are about?

Watch your tone, young lady. Let me illuminate something. Jakob was already on our radar prior to his disappearance. Your brother may have been a student, but he was also some sort of professional activist, too, as far as we can tell, and his activism led him to aggressively call and pursue Congressman Horne for several weeks. The Texas Rangers are charged with ensuring security for our state's elected officials. We know Jakob was close to a group of radical artists here in Rosadero, a number of whom are foreign nationals. We believe Jakob was on a path towards creating serious trouble on his own accord. Those who seek to cause trouble tend to find trouble visited upon them in return.

Captain Bryce waited for me to respond. I stared at the painting on the wall, the Anglo myth of domestication.

Do you know where my brother is? I asked again.

No, Captain Bryce said. We do not.

Then there is no reason for me to be here.

I took the box of stale donuts and stood up. The Rangers looked at me. I strode towards the door, trying to keep back my tears as I turned the handle. Against my better judgment, I glanced back at the cowboy-hatted men one more time.

Captain Bryce took the opportunity.

In our conversations with your parents, we advised that they wire the ransom, he said. It'll be a lot easier to recover the money than to keep your brother alive without a payment. Your parents have chosen to pursue other options.

You go to Hell, I said.

Has your brother ever expressed sympathy for human traffickers?

You go to Hell twice.

I raised the middle finger on my left hand—my tattooed hand—and held it high for the camera lens and for all the Rangers in Company E. As I stepped into the hallway, I could hear the Rangers murmuring. I did not care.

THE SILVER PICKUP truck backed out of its parking space in front of the courthouse before rolling towards Highway 90. I sat on the outdoor steps, my arms folded around my knees. Behind me, I heard bootsteps close in on me. A large body sat down at my side near the box of donuts.

Deputy Arturo Ybarra sighed.

How are you doing? he asked.

Been better.

I can believe that. My niece wants to treat you to lunch. She can be here in ten minutes. Should I tell here you're interested?

I don't think I've eaten an actual meal in days.

That's no good. I'm not trying to tell you your business, Anna, but you need to take care of yourself. Your brother doesn't benefit from your pain. There are ways to manage.

Without explanation, the deputy reached into the front pocket of his shirt and produced a thick, off-white business card. He passed it to me. On the front were the words The Naranjoven Gallery, followed by an address on Juan Sabeata Street, just two blocks away, right by Rosadero Public Radio's broadcasting station.

The man who gave me that card came by during your interview with Captain Bryce and Ranger Flores, Deputy Ybarra said. Told me his name was Javier and that he knew your brother. Told me that if you wanted to talk to come to his gallery during business hours. I'll be honest, Anna. I don't know much about the art scene in Rosadero. Maybe Sabana can tell you about the Naranjoven Gallery, whether this guy's legitimate or not.

Thanks, I said.

Deputy Ybarra smiled.

Before I take off, I gotta ask. Did you really tell the Texas Rangers to go to Hell?

I sure did.

Did you forget where you are?

Does it matter?

Ranger Flores is all right, Deputy Ybarra said. He's a local boy from Presidio. We've worked on a couple cases together.

What about the other one?

That's more complicated. Winston Bryce Jr. is the heir to one of the largest cattle dynasties in West Texas, a direct descendent of William Matthew Bryce, head of one of the so-called Five Families who settled this area in the 1880s. As long as there has been a Rosadero on Texas maps, the Bryces have been here. Their influence is more than you can believe. Same as the other Five Families. They have history. I won't say more.

Deputy Ybarra checked his watch. He had to go. I watched him descend to the sidewalk and walk to his SUV. Waiting for Sabana, I kept my eyes on the low clouds rolling over town. On Juan Sabeata Street, a navy-blue pickup truck with a cattle-guard pulled up to the stoplight, a horse trailer attached to the rear hitch. After a moment, the truck continued into the surrounding ranch country.

· Four ·

Boy Like an Opera

THE LAST FEW months my brother spent in the Pacific Northwest were at our family's apartment, staying in the bedroom where the interlaced consciousness of our childhood came together. In late nights and early mornings, the first stories Jakob would ever tell when we were children were told in cartoonish, sing-song voices. I would play his audience, waiting with rapt attention as he smeared our mother's makeup on his lips and cheeks and eyebrows, an auteur unbound by gender or plot structure. But between kindergarten and first grade, his one-boy burlesque turned disruptive: one evening, he decided our dining room table was the greatest stage of them all. That was the same evening our parents decided to enroll him in acting classes.

Early in the program, Jakob's teachers identified his talent for observing other children, watching and emulating the details of their expressions, testing out variations of their voices and cadences during performances, asking why they felt the way they felt. Above all, the teachers noted, my brother possessed preternatural passion, as though dramatic tension resided in his very limbic system, both a huge advantage and a hindrance. Tragedy colored mild setbacks: timeouts for excessive talking led to tearful pleas for forgiveness; failing to receive a role could set off red-faced screaming or speeches of startling articulateness and indignation. Friendship generated high comedy with the other actors and actresses, usually while waiting for their parents to pick them up. Jakob would laugh so hard he almost could not breathe. He was buoyant and turbulent.

He was a child who knew how to keep adults from ignoring him.

In his elementary school years, my brother did not consider any element of his life mundane. The views from our apartment's balcony in the Pearl District swept across forested hills, the shimmering promise of the Willamette River, the rusted intricacies of the Rose City's myriad bridges and trains. Clean, electric trolleys imbued the streets with futuristic kinesis. From our building's rooftop, Mount Hood's shroud presented itself with the morning sun, a brooding reminder of the continental scale of our world. Our neighborhood was a compromise between our parents: our father's affinity for the Pearl District's gutter grunge and post-industrial artists—our father, the self-conscious corporate attorney, forever pushing away from himself—and our mother's demand for an easy commute to Reed College, where she taught economics. Like all situations borne out of compromise, our household was a place of strain. Insults and accusations volleyed through the voices of our mother and father while my brother and I listened from behind our bedroom door. We knew too much, and we knew it too early, until my brother could displace our knowledge through his storytelling.

In the quiet worries of our early siblinghood, this was Jakob's gift to me.

Sometime at the beginning of my brother's adolescence, the clouds that brought the Pacific Northwest's rain over the western hills seemed to settle over his personality, cooling him into permanent introspection. By high school, notebooks had replaced theater as Jakob's refuge. He nurtured his self-creation through prose, extracting plotlines out of our overwhelmed household, maturing his perspective with the musculature of the written word. Aside from founding and leading our school's chapter of the Gay Straight Alliance, Jakob absolved himself from requiring the attention of others. He wrote for few to see but his family and first loves.

After high school, he moved slightly more than one hundred miles down the interstate to the freshman dorms of the University of Oregon.

FOR HIS FIRST two years in college, Jakob thought he might pursue a bachelor's in creative writing, until an ongoing crisis-of-expectations convinced him the job market would reward him better for a journalism degree. Upon graduation, he opted to stay in Eugene, working part-time at the YMCA while he sorted out where to take his talents. He was living in a house rented with five friends, a three-level craftsman bungalow within biking distance of every artisan pizzeria, smoke-shop, and lava butte in town. Writing in his closet-sized bedroom, Jakob homed in on the autonomy of longform fiction. Abandoning the pretense of his degree, he outlined and drafted several different novels, hoping to hook the attention of an agent before this thirtieth birthday. Though he labored without compensation, he declined to pursue basic reporting or editorial jobs, preferring to chase down a novel of consequence.

Three years passed in Eugene, three years of YMCA paychecks and unending revisions. Then came an acceptance letter from the University of Arizona, and the terms of the future began to set themselves. Before relocating to the Sonoran Desert, Jakob decided to move back into our apartment in the interim to save money. He secured a job at a streetwear clothing store to help finance the move to Tucson, easing the burden on our parents while they bankrolled my degree at Reed.

He was fired from his clothing job after three months. He departed for the borderlands not long after that, a full season ahead of schedule.

THE DIRTY PEARL Clothing Company occupied a corner on the periphery of Old Town and Chinatown, a place where cocktail bars mingled with social services, single-occupancy hotel rooms, and detoxification clinics. Pompadoured hipsters walked past sidewalk encampments, blue-tarp tents where torn-up men slept on cardboard and red-eyed women looked away. In this milieu, Jakob sold t-shirts and hoodies with designs by the West Coast's most subversive graffiti artists: giraffes drinking malt liquor, red roses tumbling out of the Japanese imperial flag, the Columbia Gorge greened by a thousand cannabis groves. Under the cash register, grotesque stickers and figurines sat on display amid glass pipes, vintage rap magazines, and autographed vinyl records. Most of the customers were white and spoke in Black accents. On a regular basis, some of the Dirty Pearl's patrons tried to convince Jakob to sell their mixtapes on the counter.

My brother worked at the store three to four days a week, from the early afternoon to the evening. The incident that would result in his termination occurred around 1:10 p.m. on a Monday—according to the police report—when a naked woman with a prominent ribcage, pale skin, and wispy black hair, sprinted through the front door, screaming, covered in sores and cigarette burns. With only one other employee present—a goth teenager named Marcus—Jakob was the senior man on the team. Directing his junior counterpart to lock the front door and call 911, my brother took the only measure he thought appropriate: he clothed the woman, telling her to stand still while covering her in a double-extra-large black hoodie and designer jeans. Once the woman was mostly covered—except for her calloused feet—my brother tried to ask her who she was and what had happened to her. With a sudden glare, the woman jumped up and shoved my brother as hard as she could, throwing him onto the hardwood floor. While Marcus continued to speak with emergency personnel on the phone, the woman ran out of the store, wearing over three hundred dollars' worth of merchandise. At 1:14 p.m., city police collected her moments before she would have collided with a streetcar. The entire episode lasted four minutes.

The merchandise would never be returned.

For the rest of the day, the Dirty Pearl was closed. After the police were done taking statements, the owner arrived to convene an emergency meeting. The owner was a heavyset, perpetually-sweating man from the Bay Area by way of South China, who dressed in basketball jerseys, athletic shorts, high-end sneakers, and gold chains, known to his employees only as Ziang. As details from the incident came into focus, the stress in Ziang's expression intensified to something like a low-grade fever.

He put a hand on my brother's shoulder.

You're a good dude, Ziang said. But you let yourself get played. Now the entire block knows they can punk you. Whatever your intentions were with that woman, I can't let you undermine the reputation of our business like this.

Then, according to my brother, Ziang pulled out a stack of hundred-dollar bills, peeling off five of them as severance pay. Biking up Davis Street to our building, my brother held back his tears until he was safely in our bathroom, standing under the sympathetic jet of the showerhead.

SITTING ON THE balcony in the evening sun, Jakob stared out at the city's northwestern hills, light burning across his face. I brought out a ceramic teapot with two sipping cups. Waiting for the spiced orange brew to cool, I sat down at my brother's side.

What are you going to do now? I asked.

I knew he had already decided.

I'm leaving for Tucson at the end of the week, Jakob said. I've been in touch with the guy who owns the place I'm renting. He says it's all right if I come down a few months early. Guess he couldn't get a vacancy through spring.

My brother shook his head.

When I was a kid, I had this story in my mind that all the people who lived on the street came from the forest, he said. They were survivors of a disaster that destroyed everything they knew. A flood, an earthquake, a wildfire. Some act of God forced all these people into the Pearl District's streets, like orphaned spirits. My little boy brain couldn't fathom that they were homeless because our society keeps an underclass by design. I still can't fathom it, I guess.

I poured the tea into the cups. Steam drifted from our mother's ceramic set. Jakob thought out loud, planning the logistics of the move: listing off everything he could fit in the back of the used, wood-paneled station wagon he had brought up from Eugene, speculating where he would apply for jobs, whether he would have to replace his driver's license. Aside from a few last family dinners together and a hike along the Columbia River, my brother seemed to have exhausted his interest in the place that raised him.

Will you miss it here? I asked.

He took his cup of tea, shrugging. We stayed on the balcony for almost an hour, silent nearly the entire time, watching light fill the luxury lofts that had gone up by the river since we were children.

THEN, IN THE very early hours of the weekend, Jakob's station wagon rolled out of our apartment building's subterranean garage, turning onto the predawn streets as though it were any other morning. Most of his belongings were clothes and books. He drove for two days.

CARLOS WHITEHEAD GREETS me from the porch of his off-white house in Dunbar/Spring, where he lives alone. Shining with perspiration, my new landlord is corpulent and young—younger than I am by several years—with a thin black mustache that could belong to a teenager. Dressed in a large white t-shirt, swimming trunks, and flip-flops, he looks as though he's on his way to a community swimming pool, if it weren't for the thick gaming headset around his neck. Today is one of his days off, he explains, and he's spent the entirety of it on a multiplayer role-playing game—the name of which I forget instantly—executing an elaborate campaign with his online friends. He asks if I play, and when I say no, I see self-consciousness seep into his expression. He moves on to a new subject.

So, you really drove here from Oregon, he says.

I nod.

Yeah. Wasn't too bad, actually. Got to spend the night at a circus-themed motel in Nevada. So that was fun.

Carlos peers at my car, as though certain there is somebody else hiding in the vehicle. Once the momentary scrutiny passes, he wipes the sweat off his forehead. He tells me that summer is Tucson's monsoon season. Flashfloods are a common occurrence on the city's streets. Arizona recently passed a law that fines drivers for poor judgment if they trap themselves on a flooded road. Though he never learned how to drive, Carlos emphasizes to me that navigating the city by car from June through September is far too risky, especially for a newcomer. He warns against it in all circumstances.

Well, I say. Good thing I brought my bicycle.

Carlos smiles weakly. He tells me to meet him out back while he finds the keys to my rental casita. Before I can say anything, he turns his large body around and shuts the mesquite door. I trot down the three steps off the porch and walk around the side of the house. Agave and prickly-pear brush against me. Yellow lizards scurry across the superheated driveway. The temperature is about 102 degrees Fahrenheit. The surface of the asphalt is at least twenty-degrees hotter. Somewhere in the neighborhood's paloverde trees, a white-winged dove coos in gentle melody.

In the backyard, I arrive at the casita, squat and lavender-colored, the size of a studio apartment, one room except for the bathroom and closet. Ten minutes pass before Carlos reemerges through the door to his kitchen, carrying a keyring as well as a packet of tenant papers. He unlocks the door to the casita and leads me to the kitchen. Aside from a red sofa—with a pullout bed, he reassures me—the only furniture is a stained coffee table. The tiled kitchen, complete with a short refrigerator, an electric stove, and a toaster oven, only has room for one person at a time behind the chipped counter. The bathroom is even smaller. The rolling closet gets stuck about two-thirds of the way open.

My landlord stands in front of the air-conditioner in the window of the dining area. In anticipation of my arrival, he made sure to turn on the unit to keep the space cool. I thank him as I review the terms of my rental. Unprompted, Carlos reminds me that I don't have to pay for electricity. His personal usage in the main house is so great he feels it's unfair to charge tenants for his excesses. Someday, he hopes to install solar panels on his roof to mitigate the damage of his lifestyle.

He reminds me that my water bill is my own, and to use the resource as sparely as possible. I nod, initialing and signing the contract in the places Carlos has highlighted. Once I pass back the finished documents, Carlos shakes my hand. He tells me that he spends most of his time in the main house—he's a computer programmer who works from home—but I should feel free to knock on his door whenever I have an issue, in case I ever encounter a scorpion or black widow or something. I thank him for his diligence.

Welcome to the Old Pueblo, he says. We should grab a beer sometime.

Sounds good, I say.

Carlos looks away, as though he's made a mistake, and says nothing more. Then he leaves me alone to settle into my new home. I kick off my shoes and lie down along the red sofa, closing my eyes. A few hours later, I wake up in the dark.

The Sonoran Desert has cooled. In the blue desert light, I begin to unload my station wagon, box by box. From behind the living room window of the main house, I can see Carlos' computer twinkling like a city unto itself.

ON MY FIRST full day in Tucson, I wake up early. Setting out on my bicycle, I pedal down the wide, potholed streets of Dunbar/Spring. Turning onto Sixth Street, I pass a rundown piñata factory with a gigantic paper-mâché skull sitting in its lot. Crossing into the Fourth Avenue neighborhood, I encounter my first Joe Pagac mural on the side of a converted factory: a young, bare-skinned woman, her features flush with wisdom, an agave growing out of her black-haired scalp, flowers in her hair, prickly-pears floating around her like sprites, saguaro cacti at her sides like companions.

These, I realize, are the guardians of Tucson.

Fourth Avenue itself is the type of bric-à-brac retail canal requisite to every university town: dive bars, secondhand clothing stores, Mexican joints, at least two bookstores: commercial enchantments for the energetic and creative. As I lock my bike by a trolley station, a pickup truck full of hooting and shirtless frat boys rolls down the street, testosterone at its most inept. I step into the food co-op, hoping to secure breakfast. The co-op is well-stocked for ethical diets and back-to-the-land practices. Purchasing a plate of vegan nopal enchiladas from the hot bar, I speak with the manager, who happens to be my checkout clerk, about working part-time. Over my meal, I fill out a job application, submitting it after dispensing my upcycled fork into the compost container. The manager shakes my hand and tells me to wait for a call.

By the end of the day, I'll have the job.

Unlocking my bicycle, I'm off.

The goal of this ride is to commit Tucson to muscle memory, weaving the topography of the city into my moving legs. I pedal through downtown and into Barrio Viejo. Amid minimalist, pastel-colored pueblo houses, I pause at a wishing shrine, a Wailing Wall in miniature. Hundreds of slips of paper are tucked between rough adobe bricks, pleas to dead ancestors and higher powers, pleas for survival. Candles, rosaries, and family photographs collect by a shrine to the Virgen de Guadalupe. I close my eyes and whisper a Hebrew prayer. Then I drink from my water bottle, a prayer of another kind.

Twenty minutes later, I chain-up my bike at the base of Tumamoc Hill. Spraying myself down with sunscreen, I survey the saguaro-studded incline, a three-thousand-foot elevation fortified by centuries-old columns of thorn and fire-resistant flesh. Hiking up the well-paved switchbacks, I wind higher and higher above the Old Pueblo, pausing to catch my breath. White retirees pass by effortlessly. Women exchange tips for the best methods to xeriscape their cactus gardens. A grinning, middle-aged man trots upwards without a shirt, his rippling abs sunburnt and accented by a layer of loose flesh. Chicano couples push baby-strollers, speaking to their infants in English and Spanish, delighted by every bilingual vowel to emerge in return from their darlings. Near the peak, signs warn hikers against straying into the boulders where horned lizards and Gila monsters sun themselves.

On the summit of the Tumamoc Hill, I survey the valley floor, the urban core and patchwork of suburban subdivisions, and strip-malls of Pima County. Mountains wall off the metropolitan area; sharp ridges sculpted by storms. In the sky, clouds linger at a surreal standstill, as though fixed in permanent positions. I want to have a conversation with everything I see.

I RETURN TO the mural by the train-tracks. A procession has taken over the road: community activists, religious leaders, and students, their fists raised, their voices angry. The demonstration appears to be impromptu, devoid of the banners and signs customary of premeditated assemblies. Sixteen black coffins float over the crowd, levitating with moral fury.

Sixteen block coffins, with over one hundred pallbearers.

I walk my bike over to a mustachioed Mexican-American man near a fire hydrant. The man—dressed like a mechanic—nods at me, scratching his unshaven neck. We stand side by side, occupying the same point-of-view.

Who were they? I ask.

The man wipes his brow with a rag.

¿Quién sabe? Teenagers, maybe younger. Robbed before they were left to die. We know they are being sent home to El Salvador. There are many more. This protest happens a lot.

Are those coffins real? I ask.

The mechanic steps off the sidewalk, joining the impassioned throng. A couple blocks ahead, a stalled freight train blocks the funeral's path. We all have to wait. As the marchers temper their energy, somebody begins to yell about why these boys died: the funneling of migrant routes by the Border Patrol into the wilderness, the imperial coups overseen from Washington, D.C., the endless horror show of gangs and death squads in their home country.

Though I have just arrived, I understand that I, too, have a place in the death of these boys.

· Five ·

Women Who Stay

KIKI OCHOA SAT at a table in the corner of Adelitas Burrito, scribbling out equations on graphing paper in the restaurant her grandmother ran out of their large house. The twelve-year-old girl did not seem distracted by the hissing and clattering of the kitchen, where Juanita Ochoa prepared foot-long burritos on handmade tortillas. The walls of the small dining area were painted in homage to the eatery's namesake: battalions of women warriors who fought in the Mexican Revolution, also known as Las Soldaderas, famous for their bravery. Dressed in sombreros and petticoats and long skirts, they carried sabers and rifles, their bodies clad in heavy magazine clips like Pancho Villa. The Adelitas' missions included ferrying water to soldiers, scouting for critical intelligence under the cover of night, participating in firefights, and protecting children from atrocity.

In her puffy black jacket, jeans, light blue sneakers, and braided black hair, Juanita Ochoa's granddaughter was working in the legacy of her forebearers.

Sabana placed an order at the half-door to the kitchen. Juanita responded in cheerful Spanish. She asked Sabana who I was—I could tell—gesturing in my direction. I stepped away as my companion explained my connection to Jakob. At my brother's name, Kiki Ochoa's eyes lit up. She looked over as I sat down near the communal bowl of house-made salsa verde. I nodded at her. She returned to her homework, saying nothing. In the late morning, we were the only customers.

Give me six minutes, Juanita Ochoa said.

Sabana paid in cash, then went over to Kiki, giving her a hug, and briefly checking over her homework before sitting down with me.

Professor Ochoa wants to meet you, she said. Are you okay if she comes over?

I nodded.

She also wants to show you your brother's writing studio, Sabana continued.

I didn't realize she ran a restaurant, I said. I thought she was a creative writing professor.

She's a retired professor, yeah. She mentored Jakob because she liked him. But she opened this burrito operation to help with the bills when she became Kiki's legal guardian.

Sabana leaned over the table.

Kiki lost both her parents, she whispered. Narco-violence in Nuevo Laredo. Hasn't been back since immigrating. She and Jakob got along great, from what Juanita tells me. Sometimes, he would help with her English on writing assignments.

Tears broke through me at last. Burying my face in my hands, I listened as Sabana left the table and returned with a glass of water for me to sip. She waited with practiced empathy. I could tell she had done this before.

How did it go with the Rangers? she asked.

They're going to let Jakob die, I said. I don't know what's going on. I don't know how my parents will be able to negotiate this—none of this makes sense.

Anna, I'm so sorry, Sabana said.

You told me the Rangers have a rough history around here, I said. What did you mean?

I don't know. They have…there's a deep history of anti-Mexican violence with them.

What?

Nothing. This doesn't have anything to do with your brother.

No, tell me.

Sabana sighed.

About a century ago, they were involved in a lot of lynchings. A lot. Mobs acted with their permission, their guidance. For decades, they broke the backs of striking farmworkers, keeping them in line. I'm sorry…I don't want to concern you. But the Rangers hide behind their own mythology, and I just…I'm sure they'll handle your brother's case just fine. Forget I said anything.

I shook my head. I studied the cowboy hats mounted on the ceiling like trophies: torn-up, dusty, retired from the hard, seasonal work on the estates surrounding town. Among the cowboy hats, Juanita Ochoa had also mounted a jalapeño-green hat for the Customs and Border Patrol.

Do the Rangers have a decent record responding to kidnappings, at least? I asked.

I'm not an expert, Sabana said. But back in the nineties, my aunt…this is a tough story for me to tell. Please don't mention this to my mom or uncle.

I nodded. Sabana closed her eyes for a moment before beginning again.

When she was a young woman, my aunt, Celenia Ybarra—the motel is named after her—used to be the most elegant dancer this town has ever seen. From when she was a teenager to her late twenties, she danced for hours in front of the gigantic agave in the plaza, practicing outside even after she became an instructor at the school. During the warmer seasons, she would teach her students there, too. The whole community would come to watch, in all weather, at sunrise, sunset. On comfortable afternoons, dark nights…

I listened. Sabana continued.

One day, Tía Celenia got abducted. Nobody knows who took her. It was winter. She had danced until dusk. Somewhere on the walk home, she disappeared. The sheriff's office got involved pretty quickly. So did the police department, back when Rosadero had one. Even the justice of the peace came out. But then the Texas Rangers took over the case. And the case…went nowhere.

She took a sip from the glass of water she had brought for me.

Three and a half days after her disappearance, my aunt wandered into town from the prairie, Sabana said. She was bruised and cut. Her clothing was torn so much she was almost naked. She could not tell us who had hurt her, or where she had been. All she did was cry. It was the worst sound any of us have ever heard. Celenia Ybarra never danced in front of the agave again. Eventually, we sent her to live with my grandparents in El Paso. She passed away last year. Nobody was ever arrested.

Sabana sat back in her seat, suddenly exhausted.

Did…did Captain Bryce have anything to do with the investigation? I asked.

Sabana nodded.

My uncle has never been so furious. You wouldn't believe it. He did some investigating himself—off the books. He did it with a friend of his in the Border Patrol, Special Agent Washington. I mentioned him to you.

Yeah, I remember.

Well, they didn't find an official record on Bryce or anything. But they did come into some information that raised their eyebrows.

Like what?

Well. I told you Ojinaga used to be a major drug-trafficking point in the 1980s. Pablo Acosta used to run the market with the blessing of the Mexican military. He was a gangster of an old kind. He had a paternal, almost protective view of his community. Anyway, part of Pablo Acosta's notoriety came from the rumor that he had a network of cooperators among Texas ranchers. After Acosta went down in a hail of bullets, the

FBI did some accounting. They brought in Winston Bryce Jr. for an interview at their office in Alpine. Apparently, some of Acosta's smugglers were found with keys to the Bryce Ranch's gates, along with detailed maps of the trails on the property.

Are you serious?

Very. In Mexico, smugglers tried to claim that Winston Jr. was one of Acosta's chief partners. He denied everything, and his family lawyered up quickly. Nothing came from the inquiry, but it's a hell of a find. Don't tell anyone I told you this. Especially my uncle.

I nodded. From the kitchen, Juanita Ochoa plated two enormous burritos and set them on the half-door, ringing a bell to alert Sabana to the order. Sabana walked over and brought them to the table. At least twelve inches long, each burrito was weighed down by generous helpings of scrambled egg, cheese, potatoes, and refried beans. I did not know how to begin.

As Sabana drenched her plate in salsa verde, I thought I would try to resolve another problem working through my thoughts.

Who's A.P. Horne? I asked.

Sabana laughed.

Oh god. Representative Augustus Prescott Horne is the esteemed delegate for the Forty-Fourth Congressional District, which covers most of the border from El Paso down to Laredo. He's one of the most notorious immigration hardliners Texas has ever produced, and that's saying something. Before that, he was the Director of the Department of Public Safety, a posting from which he somehow attracted a political base. He's a total embarrassment, like an idiotic cartoon of what everybody else thinks Texans are. Why?

Captain Bryce accused my brother of stalking and harassing A.P. Horne, I said.

Sabana frowned. She took a bite of her massive burrito, chewing thoughtfully. Before we could pursue the topic any further, Juanita Ochoa emerged from the kitchen. She switched the sign on the door from Open to Closed and came over to our table. She looked at me with mournful eyes, gesturing for me to stand up. She was a small woman with short silver hair and thick glasses. For work, she was dressed in an apron, with a maroon sweater and black pants and sensible, teacher-style shoes. Though she was a septuagenarian, in some ways, she reminded me exactly of my mother.

Jakob must have seen the resemblance, too.

I am so, so sorry, Professor Ochoa said. Jakob is a very sweet boy. He deserves so much better.

She embraced me in the tightest of hugs, murmuring reassurances and affections to a young woman she had just met. Over her shoulder, her granddaughter, Kiki, watched me with caution. For a second time, I felt Mariazul Bautista's crucifix burning in the pocket of my corduroy skirt.

PROFESSOR OCHOA WALKED me to the nook in her house where Jakob worked on his thesis manuscript. An electric typewriter sat by a stack of clean white paper on the desk beneath a window. Outside, the dark yellow prairielands rolled into the winter sky. On the other side of the nook, a twin-sized bed stood against the backwall, its vivid serape blankets tidy against the pillow. On a bedside stand, my brother had set up his customary shrine, a consecration of his creative space: a brass menorah salvaged from Poland in 1939, complete with scented candlesticks; a stone khachkar crucifix our father brought back from a pilgrimage to Yerevan; an enameled burgundy rose from our hometown; a collection of Alaska cedar pinecones; and an ancient coin bearing the Arevakhach, the Armenian symbol for eternity and rebirth.

All my brother's pieces, interdependent and necessary.

I sat down on the twin-sized bed. Juanita Ochoa stood over the wooden chair where my brother once wrote, contemplating his vacancy.

I withdrew the crucifix necklace from my pocket, as though allowing it to photosynthesize. Professor Ochoa turned. She looked at the golden object glinting against my palms.

¿Qué es esto? she asked. What is that, dear?

I surrendered the necklace.

It belonged to a woman I saw get arrested, I said.

Professor Ochoa held Mariazul's crucifix up to the light.

Border Patrol?

I nodded.

She sat at my side. She put her arm around my shoulders and spoke a prayer under her breath, crossing herself afterwards. Returning the necklace, she watched as I pulled out the thick business card Deputy Ybarra had given me on the steps of the courthouse.

I was told I should speak with someone named Javier Galvenez, I said. Who is he?

Professor Ochoa took the card. She smiled sadly.

He's an artist, she said. He and your brother were in love. Pure delirium. That's what they had. Javier is worth talking to. I'm surprised you don't know about him already.

Professor Ochoa and I stayed on the bed until Sabana came looking for us.

THE NARANJOVEN GALLERY stood in a white converted dancehall on Juan Sabeata Street, accessible by a heavy colonial door with tinted glass and a wrought-iron handle. Wrenching open the door, I was immediately greeted by a huge glass portrait of a handsome black man wearing a cream-colored trucker hat, the name Naranjoven stitched above the bill in distinctive orange lettering. After a few seconds, I realized man under the trucker hat was Lakeith Mercy, the avant-garde R&B artist from Houston whose debut album Jakob worshipped. The composition of the photograph was so radiant, the subject appeared almost like a stained-glass painting.

Slowly, I began to understand the miracles Rosadero held for my brother.

A young, light-skinned woman standing by the front desk looked over at me. She had brown hair and heavy bangs and wire-rim glasses. She wore an orange blazer, denim jeans, and black heels. Her name was Alyssa, according to a silver nametag pinned to the lapel of her jacket. On the computer monitor, Alyssa appeared to be studying the designs of an upcoming exhibition.

Welcome to the Naranjoven Gallery, she said. Have you been here before?

I took out the business card.

I'm here to see Mr. Galvenez, I said.

She took the card.

Javier is not available, she said.

My name is Anna Tatevyan, I said. Jakob Tatevyan is my brother. I can wait until Mr. Galvenez comes in.

Alyssa nodded, betraying no recognition at Jakob's name. She told me she would make a phone call, and in the meantime, invited me to sign the guestbook and take a look around. As a nonprofit organization, donations were a critical part of the Gallery's revenue stream. I was encouraged to contribute.

Rather than take out my wallet, I drifted over to a doorway hidden behind a black curtain. On a nearby wall, a column of text deconstructed the multimedia presentation inside.

The exhibition was titled: The Hall of Narcoliberals.

I slipped behind the curtain into the darkness. Neon sculptures lined the black walls, two sets of nine, one set depicting Mexican Presidents as Jesús Malverde—the drug icon in faint green regalia—the other depicting American Presidents as Nuestra Señora de la Santa Muerte, dressed in purple robes, wielding scythes and globes in their skeletal hands. The sculptures represented every set of Presidents since the dawn of the War on Drugs, beginning with Luis Escheverría and Richard Nixon. At the end of the hall stood two older, grander idols: President James K. Polk and Brevet Lieutenant General Winfield Scott, the so-called heroes of the Mexican-American War, glowing in purple and green. Though they did not inhabit the form of the Narcoliberals, they inhabited the same auras.

A projector hung from the ceiling, casting a video likeness of President James Monroe against the wall between Polk and Scott. I stood before the image, waiting. Then, as though sensing my ambivalence, the video cut to an antiquated countdown sequence, terminating with a black title contrasted against a white background:

The Monroe Doctrine, Exploded.

Before I could prepare my senses, the screen detonated into a violent video montage. Gunfights erupted between cartels and Mexican security forces, mixed with the desperate cries of children screaming for their mothers, mixed with drone strikes in the Middle East and footage of migrant camps. Complementing the montage was an atonal synth orchestra, a reverbed amalgam of patriotic anthems unspecific to any country.

The video stopped. The music cut out as the lights all turned on.

Javier Galvenez pulled back the curtain.

With his deep brown hair tied in a ponytail, flashing gray eyes, and a beard like desert scrub, he accented his natural complexion with a plain orange t-shirt, pink cowboy boots, and torn-denim jeans. His silver belt-buckle depicted seven intricate caves surrounding the word Chicomoztoc, a creation myth rendered in fashionable hieroglyphics. CDMX was tattooed in black on his left knuckles.

We eyed each other from across the room.

So, you are Anna, he said.

I nodded.

Do you know where my brother is? I asked.

No, he said. Do the Rangers suspect I am his kidnapper?

Not at all, I said. The Rangers say they don't have a suspect at all. Do you?

Javier Galvenez bit his lip.

You are heartbroken, he said. So am I. Thank you for coming in. I wanted to speak with you, but I wanted you to visit me of your own volition. I do not know where our beloved has gone. But I thought I'd share with you the parts of Jakob you may not know, the parts forged in Tucson. This is the man who was stolen.

I agreed to stay and listen. Javier called out to Alyssa—whom he formally introduced as his assistant—informing her that he and I would need privacy in his office through the afternoon. Alyssa nodded. As Javier and I stepped out of the Hall of Narcoliberals, he began to detail the unlikeliest of journeys that brought him into my brother's heart.

We met in Arizona, Javier said.

· Six ·

Santuario

*O*N THE STEPS *to the 1904 Santa Cruz County Historical Courthouse in Nogales, Arizona, a young man with ponytailed hair takes to the podium above a gathering of protestors. Raising his fist beneath the vaulted monument to Classical Revivalism, the speaker commands the aesthetics of dissent. The structure behind him sits atop a hill overlooking the city and its counterpart in Mexico, unseparated twins upon whom the rusted international fence seems a trick of shadows. Though the courthouse still hosts a few administrative offices, the actual Santa Clara County Superior Court is located in in an unremarkable beige building on the other side of town. In contrast, Nogales' initial seat of justice proclaims its significance with terraced gardens, stones, and columns, its dome topped by a* *statue of Lady Liberty. When thunderstorms gather over these twin cities, this hill is one of the first places lightning strikes.*

The speaker on the stairs heats up the crowd with impassioned Spanish, occasionally switching into a second language I don't recognize—possibly Mixtec, maybe Nahuatl. Then, with a wink, the ponytailed man delivers the only words in English I have heard him speak since I wandered into this scene.

Here, in this mountain pass between Arizona and Sonora, we declare the right of all peoples to enjoy unrestricted passage across the hemisphere, he says. Here, where Juan Bautista de Anza's ancient trail meets the southern terminus of the CANAMEX free trade corridor, we demand the free movement of labor. While capital knows no bounds, the walls of nations harden against workers, pitting the Global South against itself, pitting Americans against their sisters and brothers beneath the Rio Grande. The only true justice is the justice of migration. ¡Sí, Se Puede!

More applause, more raised fists, more shouts and cheers. The speaker returns to Spanish, and my comprehension falls off once again. Though I have lived in Tucson for almost ten months, my gains in the city's first European language are limited. While I listen from the sidewalk, a short-haired Latina woman in neon yellow shorts, a tank-top, and running shoes approaches me. She passes me an orange slip of paper. On the back, a bilingual paragraph explains the purpose of the rally, details I will absorb later in a quieter place. I turn the paper to its front side, taking in the slogans and sponsors of this rally:

¡El Pueblo Unido Jamás Será Vencido! ¡Todos Americanos Son Fronterizos!

El Colectivo del Naranjoven

CDMX

Before the volunteer moves on, I point up the steps.

¿Cómo se llama ese caballero? I ask.

My Spanish is still too formal. The volunteer laughs but does her best.

That gentleman calls himself Javier Galvenez, she says. *He is a journalist and an artist. He journeyed the migrant trails from Central America to the United States and wrote about it. This rally is to bring attention to the struggles of his fellow travelers, who are in a detention center awaiting trial for unauthorized entry. More information can be found if you follow the URL printed on the bottom of the flyer.*

I thank the volunteer. She moves through the crowd, disseminating information and engaging in more brief conversations. From time to time, purple cruisers for the Nogales Police Department circle the block, monitoring the lawful assembly with unimpressed stares. I check the time on my phone, deciding I need to walk back down the hill towards the Morley Gate, the pedestrian crossing where my landlord will be returning to the United States.

Descending into the shopping district, I return to pastel-colored storefronts with midcentury neon signs: department stores, appliance outlets, clothing vendors. Earlier in the day, my landlord, Carlos, requested I meet him at the bus stop near the port of entry rather than the port of entry itself, fearing what may happen if the Border Patrol observed me loitering too close to the international fence. Rather than contest Carlos' anxieties, I acquiesced. Standing in the dusty outdoor shelter, I am the only white face among the throngs of shoppers, conspicuous but mostly ignored. Passing the time, I notice a black advertisement with white text. The message is brief, printed behind scratched and graffitied glass:

Wars need soldiers to fight.

America, call home your drones!

I wait for my landlord.

Five minutes later, Carlos Whitehead arrives, carrying a large paper bag with a red helium balloon tied around his wrist by a ribbon. He tells me the balloon comes from his cousin's sixth birthday party—a cousin Carlos has just met for the first time—and the paper bag is packed with leftovers, mostly machaca tacos prepared by his aunts, his mother, and his grandmother. Half of the leftovers are supposed to be for me, despite being full of rehydrated beef.

I tried to tell my family you don't eat meat, Carlos says, but they thought I was joking. Sonorans are like Texans. Anyway, everyone wanted to pass along their gratitude for driving me down here. They hope to meet you next time. Also, they wanted to compensate you for gas money, even though I already covered it. Here you go.

Carlos reaches into his pocket, taking out a wad of pesos.

That's all right, I say.

This is how my family shows respect, he says.

I nod, accepting the pesos in my pocket. My landlord and I walk up the street to my station wagon. On the way, I ask Carlos whether he's ever heard of the Naranjoven Collective, or an activist by the name of Javier Galvenez. Carlos shakes his head, dismissing these names without asking why I bring them up. He switches the subject to the Border Patrol checkpoint on the northbound interstate to Tucson. Though he insists everything will be fine, he also tells me to be prepared to have my vehicle searched and for both of us to be interrogated.

Despite his warnings, we return home an easy ninety minutes later.

SINCE I MOVED into his backyard casita last year, Carlos and I have cultivated a relationship somewhere between neighbors and roommates. Most of the week, we do not see each other. I bicycle over to campus, participate in workshops and critique groups, meet with professors and my thesis adviser, and do most of my homework in the University of Arizona's air-conditioned poetry center. I attend readings by my peers, hike when I can, and take three or four shifts a week at the food co-op, usually in the evenings or early mornings. In contrast, Carlos spends almost all his time in the living room of the main house, of which he remains the sole occupant, despite having at least two spare bedrooms. He codes, he takes conference calls on his headset, he watches videos, he games. Dinner comes almost exclusively from a rotating cast of deliverymen, hauling heavy plastic bags up the front stairs. Though we are friendly, Carlos never asks about my life, and doesn't provide any specific answers when I inquire about his. We mostly cross paths in the driveway when I'm walking my bicycle to the casita and he is retrieving the mail. For at least the first four months, I did not set foot in the main house.

Then, one day, he knocked on my door. His computer was updating itself, and in the meantime, he wanted to know if I would like to come into his abode and enjoy a movie night. Despite the coolness of the evening, he was sweating more than normal.

I accepted the invitation. This became a weekly tradition, mostly on Thursday nights—the co-op has me on Fridays—the mainstay of our time together. My landlord loves science fiction and fantasy, especially superhero movies. Our selection process consists of Carlos presenting three options and asking me to rank them from most interested to least interested. I do not dispute his system. In a strange way, I am comforted by how much thought he has put into the experience. He always has popcorn ready. I brew myself tea in his kitchen.

Nobody else, as far as I can tell, ever comes to visit Carlos in his home.

As a consequence of his hermitage, Carlos' house is a dumping ground: wrappers on the floor around his desk, a layer of dust on every surface, overflowing garbage cans, a permanent pile of dirty dishes in the sink. One week, I broached the uncomfortable topic in the form of a transaction: if he was willing to knock back a hundred dollars from my monthly rent, I would clean his home on a weekly basis, with a deep-clean at the end of the month.

Carlos, who had thought about hiring a cleaning service anyway, loved the idea. In the course of my dusting, vacuuming, and dishwashing, I learned about his parents: how he was raised in Tucson by a white father, how his mother stayed in Sonora with her extended family. Carlos does not talk about his parents in detail. His mother is a nurse, and his father was a journalist. His father, Edward Whitehead, passed away a few weeks after Carlos began his freshman year at the University of Arizona.

His family in Mexico did not attend the funeral.

His Mexican relatives refuse to come into the United States, Carlos explained one evening. They are all too scared of the Border Patrol. And, after the 2011 massacre in Casas Adobes that killed six people, including a federal judge and nearly a Congresswoman, his family decided the violence in El Norte was too extreme. Despite their immense pride for their college-educated programmer—who earned his computer science degree on a full-ride scholarship and purchased his home a year after graduating—the security conditions in the United States are too unpredictable.

I pointed out the irony in this, given the massacres taking place in Mexico every day. Carlos looked confused when I said this. He admitted he does not pay attention to the news and does not know much about the Drug War, except for what his relatives report. Sonora is far safer than neighboring states, he has heard. The trafficking corridors to Arizona are less lucrative than those that lead to California or Texas. But from the position his family enjoys in Nogales, the regular mass shootings in the United States leave the impression of a primitive, ungovernable nation.

Do you ever visit Nogales? I asked.

Carlos sighed. He used to, but the bus ride is an all-day affair, and the Border Patrol has pulled over every bus he has taken home from Mexico, the agents inspecting every passenger's documents one by one.

I told him I would be happy to take him to the border if he was willing to deduct the gas money out of my rent. My landlord looked overwhelmed with joy. The Saturday when I encounter Javier Galvenez is the first of many trips Carlos and I will take along I-19 so he can spend time with his family.

After our first sojourn with the border, I settle down onto the sofa of my casita to read the back of the orange flyer. By the end of the passage, I know I must reach out to Javier Galvenez to talk about his journey, his activism, his art, and his writing.

Within two months, I will be bringing him home.

HE DESCRIBES HIMSELF as a Chilango: born and raised in Mexico City. He has since wandered far from home, all up and down North America. The initial autobiography Javier presents is almost identical to what I've already read online: the renegade son of a wealthy banker, who studied art in New York City, whose network of family connections assured him an instant O-1B Visa—

for individuals of extraordinary ability in the arts—who took his visa and went the other way, decamping to the mountain communes in Chiapas near the border with Guatemala.

Embedding himself among the Zapatista guerilla movement, Javier Galvenez immersed himself in the Indigenous resistance to what he calls the Imperial Economy. As Mayan campesinos seized and worked the land of old feudal lords, they rooted their new way of life in education, medicine, and agriculture. The distillation of the Zapatista creed could be found in the curriculum of the community schools: the reconstruction of lost languages, the abolishment of hierarchy, the autonomy of local food systems, the primacy of women. Though the communes eschew conventional leadership structures, a ski-masked man known as the Subcomandante serves as the liaison both to the press and to the Mexican government. Dressed in military fatigues, the Subcomandante frequently appears with an authoritative pipe in his mouth, riding a horse down from the mountains into San Cristóbal de Las Casas to grant interviews to the press and negotiate with the governor. Armed but peaceful, the Zapatistas have been granted autonomy, based on a provision in the Mexican Constitution permitting Indigenous self-rule. They have thrived in the mountains for over a quarter century.

The Subcomandante inspired Javier Galvenez to travel the migrant trails, to document them in journalistic dispatches, and to raise hell once he crossed back into the United States. He has done so in partnership with the Naranjoven Collective, based in the Mexico City barrio of Tepito. The Naranjovenes—roughly, the Orange Youths—disseminate their ideology of postmodern post-Marxism—Javier's phrasing—across the capital in pamphlets and posters. They stage creative disruptions in front of the National Palace with massive puppets, choreographed dance-offs, and smoke-machined theatrics. The story of Mexico, Javier tells me, is the story of a nation whose autonomy has never been guaranteed. By every means available, the Naranjovenes seek to reclaim public spaces for the common good, not the narcos, and not the elites.

A commune across a continent.

Javier's journalistic account of the trails brought elevated attention to the Naranjovenes, as well as to the plight of refugees. Trekking from their smoking homes in El Salvador, Guatemala, and Honduras, a group of twenty-one young men permitted Javier to document their remote hikes, violent train rides, and negotiations with coyotes and corrupt police as they hurtled to Arizona. Written with an ear for poetry, the articles circulated through humanitarian and literary communities adjacent to the corridors of power. The group of twenty-one—Grupo Veintiuno, as Javier named it— crossed into America near the town of Sasabe. Marching into the Tohono O'odham Reservation, the young men were footing it without a coyote, convinced they could save money and find their way to the interstate without guidance.

They almost succeeded.

Though they stayed the course—they were quick and stealthy, they were courageous, they did everything right, almost everything—their water ran out. To their shock, to their horror, it was water that betrayed them in the desert.

They slowed, and slowed, and slowed.

Until they were stranded.

They were saved by water jugs left by activists, but the salvation did not last.

Ground temperatures soared, and soared, and soared.

Two fears took hold: one of heat stroke, the other of a mass kidnapping. Bajadores were well-known in those parts, loading unlucky groups into vans at gunpoint and taking them to extortion houses in Phoenix.

Most of the group was near death when Javier and three others scouted out an emergency beacon, pressing a button for La Migra to rescue them from a remote valley. Four almost died during the Border Patrol's attempts to hydrate and cool them off. Almost all were convinced they had been abducted by bajadores, even after arriving for booking at the Border Patrol station.

They lasted fewer than thirty-six hours.

Javier wrote it all down. After posting bail for a misdemeanor civil offense and speaking with his family's attorney, Javier sent his Spanish language account to the Collective's headquarters in Tepito, which soon published it online. Though Javier's case has already been thrown out—his family's attorney is highly persuasive—his twenty-one companions languish in a private detention center outside Nogales. Though they have applied for asylum, deportation is the most likely outcome. In the buildup to the trial, Javier has dedicated himself to rallying civil rights and religious organizations in Southern Arizona to the cause of the Nogales Twenty-One. Though the Galvenezes' high-powered attorney has agreed to represent the refugees, justice in America is obtuse and cruel. Javier believes he is nearing the terminus of what he can achieve. Above all, he needs a wider audience.

In the course of our correspondences, I agree to help edit the English translations of his articles. His goal is to develop them into a book, a bestseller that creates urgency in his readership. My assistance is pro bono, and after providing several weeks of volunteer labor, I propose modest compensation: that Javier come to Tucson and speak to my MFA cohort.

He agrees, on the conditions that I provide transportation, as well as a place to stay.

I run this by Carlos during movie night, asking if Javier can stay in the casita. After some nervous mulling, my landlord agrees. I call Javier and tell him we will pick him up on Saturday evening. I hope he is all right sleeping on a sofa. Javier is delighted and gracious.

My heart is pounding.

HE DOES NOT remember the last time he slept on a soft surface. Since his arrival in Nogales, Javier has been sleeping in the pews of a church, a church outside of which Carlos and I wait as dusk falls over the city. The congregation has come together for one last prayer. My landlord and I do not feel right joining them.

Javier emerges from the church doors with a dusty brown duffel-bag over his shoulder. He embraces me with a hug and shakes Carlos' hand. Tossing the duffel-bag into the back of the station wagon, our guest sits in the front passenger seat. Before we leave town, he wants to treat us to raspado. The day in Nogales has been scorching. Carlos and I are on board.

With Javier's meticulous directions—he estimates he has walked every street in the city—I drive us to a residential neighborhood beneath a lush hill. We pull in front of a house with a metal door, cumbia music booming from the windows, a string of lights hanging from the roof. On the outer wall, ceramic tiles honor Saint Martha. She stands on a field in the South of France with a flaming torch in her hand, the tamed Tarasque behind her: a black, six-legged beast with a massive tortoise shell, the tail of a scorpion, and the head of a lion, a grin of sword-like fangs. Behind its patron saint, the interior of the raspado joint feels like any ice cream shop in the country. Buckets of shaved ice sit beneath a clean glass barrier.

The bald, grinning purveyor greets Javier in Spanish. He nods at Carlos and I, asking for our orders.

My landlord and I don't know what to do. Javier takes charge.

Tres raspas de horchata, por favor, he says.

Javier pays in cash. He and the vendor have deep rapport. They exchange laughter and rapid conversation, then hug and slap one another on the back. We receive our cups of cinnamon-flavored hielo, then return to the car. Sitting with the air-conditioner running, we consume our treats. We don't need to be anywhere else right now, doing anything else.

The moment is a simple gift, I tell Javier.

Carlos says nothing. In the rearview mirror, I can see his lips trembling. He wipes his face, then resumes eating with the small plastic spoon. Consuming only half my portion, I set the rest in the cupholder. I drive us back up the street to the highway out of Nogales. Before reaching the interstate, the sun sets over the mountain pass, the horizon falling into melancholy blue.

BEFORE REACHING TUCSON, we take one more detour, this one to the San Xavier Indian Reservation. Javier would like to pray. Under a night sky incandescent with stars, we drive along remote desert roads, winding towards the Mission San Xavier del Blac. The church lights up the black landscape with singular intensity: two rising bell-towers illuminated from below, a façade of ornate adobe, an expansive complex of schools and museums surrounding the cathedral. We have come to the White Dove of the Desert, a community and a beacon since 1692, more than two centuries older than Arizona itself. We are alone, the only worshippers on this warm night. Cottonwood trees, saguaros, and a grove of towering palms are our only visible companions.

I park in a space reserved for tour buses. The three of us step out near a series of empty frybread stalls. Secular visiting hours end at sunset, but the chapel remains open to whomever needs to make contact with the Holy Trinity. No matter the hour, Father Kino's holy undertaking will not be denied.

Before Javier and I walk into the chapel, Carlos lets out a choked sob. Overcome, he excuses himself for a pilgrimage. Moving more quickly than I've ever seen him, my landlord ascends a hill rising to the side of the Mission. At the top of the trail, a white statue of the Virgin of Guadalupe stands in a cave behind a set of protective metal bars. Carlos gets down on his knees and breaks down crying. Javier and I leave him alone until he comes down. My landlord does not want to talk. He waits in the station wagon while Javier and I enter the darkness of the chapel.

Inside, Javier and I stand in silence. Intricate paintings of saints and martyrs flicker above votive candles.

Our fingers touch.

IN THE CASITA, Javier and I hold each other while the air conditioner cools our sweating skin.

· Seven ·

Places of Absence

TEN MILES ALONG the highway towards Alpine, Javier told me to pull onto the side of the road, identifying the exact fenceposts in the polymer barrier where the sheriff's office found Jakob's car. I parked and turned off the engine. Javier and I stared into the fog-drenched countryside, neither of us speaking. The Zaldos Mesa loomed in and out of the suspended moisture. We were close enough to see the pueblo at the base of the canyon.

This is where they stole him, Javier said.

He did not elaborate.

No trucks or other cars were on the highway. After the Texas Rangers canvassed the scene, they impounded my brother's station wagon to El Paso. Since then, nothing in this spot had provided any hints of who took him, or why.

I turned the engine back on, unable to stand it anymore. Javier and I had spent most of the afternoon together in the office, talking about Jakob, and everything else. Though our time was almost up, he requested I take him to one more place in town before dropping him off at the Naranjoven Gallery.

In the near-invisibility, I drove us back to Rosadero.

VICTORIAN TURRETS STOOD guard over the street where the wealthiest residents of Narváez County made their homes. Oak trees shaded the wide, empty sidewalks. Iron gates and immaculately trimmed hedges assured the privacy of Rosadero's elites. We were in the town's northeastern neighborhood, a place populated by properties so expansive their true shapes were indiscernible.

Javier did not explain why he had asked me to come here. I kept the engine idling.

Do you know about the Five Families of Rosadero? Javier asked.

I nodded.

One of the Rangers investigating Jakob's case is a descendent of the Bryce family, I said.

Javier laughed.

That's right. Bryce, Peale, Ogle, Riggin, and, of course, Hollis. You know the name Hollis?

I shook my head. Javier pointed at the ash-colored mansion to our right.

This is the Hollis residence, he said. Miriam Hollis is all that's left of their dynasty, the widow to John Rodger Hollis the Fourth. The original John Rodger is considered Rosadero's Great White Father, the one who rallied all the others here. He and the rest of the Five Families all came from Maryland, from the colonial aristocracy, trying their luck on the Texas frontier. Most of this neighborhood's current inhabitants are widows. But power does not decay quickly. Not the type of power the Five Families wield.

Javier directed my attention across the street, pointing at a colonial home that looked almost like the White House. Two small security cameras watched the front door.

And over here, we have the residence of one Augustus Prescott Horne, Javier said. Well, one of his residences. When the Congressman for the Forty-Fourth District isn't gallivanting around his Georgetown townhouse, he primarily spends his time at a huge estate outside Laredo. Have you heard of Congressman Horne?

Why was my brother so interested in him? I asked.

Javier sat as though he had not heard my question. Finally, he put his words together.

Before his abduction, Jakob had tapped into something dark and true about the United States. He had locked not only onto Congressman Horne as a subject, but the people around Congressman Horne, and the people around the people around Congressman Horne. Your brother used to tell me he was mapping out a river system, all the creeks and streams and tributaries leading to the final current of American power. This was the vein of his project. And it's the reason he disappeared.

Javier opened his door. He stepped onto the sidewalk, apparently planning to walk the rest of the way to the Naranjoven Gallery. He looked at me with worried eyes.

The less you ask, the safer you will be, he said. The less you ask, the safer Jakob will be, too. But we should continue this conversation. I'll see you tomorrow, Anna.

He waited for me to reply.

See you tomorrow, I said.

Closing his door, Javier turned around and proceeded down the sidewalk, his hands tucked into the pockets of his jacket. I watched him in the sideview mirror until I noticed a rustling in the curtains in the Hollis mansion. Executing a three-point turn, I passed by Congressman Horne's property. The security cameras swiveled, following my car with their blank lenses.

THE FBI HAD dispatched a team of crisis negotiators to Texas to secure Jakob's release, working alongside Captain Bryce and Ranger Flores. Over this entire ordeal, the kidnappers had only called once, reaching my parents in an untraceable cyborg voice to make their initial demand. Somehow, the FBI's team was now in touch with the kidnappers, though they had not established any credible identification yet, or a location for where my brother was being held. The phoneline used by the kidnappers was a spoof, or something, routed through several layers of encryption. Whoever was holding my brother was savvy; whoever was holding my brother was also open to negotiation: the two hundred-thousand-dollar ransom had been reduced to one hundred thousand.

According to my father, this was progress.

Jakob had apparently spoken with the negotiators over the phone, shaken but alive. My father listened to a recording of the call from our apartment in the Pearl District, tentatively verifying the authenticity of his son's voice—though he was not sure. This all happened a few hours ago, while Javier was telling me the story of how he and my brother first met.

I was lying on the bed of my motel room, video-chatting with my father. Since this nightmare began almost two weeks ago, my father had taken an indefinite leave of absence from his law firm, spending most of his time on the phone and, as he explained to me, pushing the Rangers for the involvement of the FBI.

My mother continued to work. She divided her time between her office and a seminar room at Reed. She and I had not spoken since I left Oregon.

Where's mom? I asked.

My father looked at me with a drawn expression, his dark Armenian features paled by uncertainty, regret etched into his features. He looked over his shoulder—I could tell he was in the apartment's dining room, looking down the hallway to the bedrooms—before answering.

Your mother's taking a nap on Jakob's bed. She spends a lot of time there now. Say, sweetheart…

Yes, dad?

When are you coming home?

I don't know, I said. I'll come home when I'm done here.

But, sweetie. What is it that you're doing down there? You're not looking for Jakob yourself, are you?

No, dad. Nothing like that.

Well what, then?

I'm not sure yet. Retracing Jakob's steps, I guess. Seeing the place where he lived for the last month that he was alive.

Anna, listen to me. The FBI's Crisis Negotiation Unit has a ninety-seven percent success rate. Jakob is going to get out of this. We need to keep an open mind about potential outcomes. Especially positive outcomes. Okay?

Okay.

Positivity is all I ask. For your sake as well as your brother's. Hey—what's that you're holding there, sweetheart?

Mariazul's crucifix had appeared over my collar. I did not notice its placement until my father pointed it out.

This came from a woman who got arrested by the Border Patrol, I said. It was the strangest thing. She got through a checkpoint no problem, with a verified green card and everything. Then, one of the agents followed her and arrested her about thirty miles later. It was a violent arrest, too. Like an assault.

This is a story you heard? my father asked.

It's something I saw, I said. Do you know anything about immigration enforcement law?

Not at all, sweetie. Frankly, that sort of thing is not on my mind right now. Listen, Anna…your mother and I need you home. I know you feel helpless here in Portland. But it's important we stay close. One of our children is already in jeopardy. I know it's been tough getting along with your mom. She handles stress in a very reactive way, I'll admit. But I don't know what we'd do if you got yourself into a situation, too.

Dad, stop catastrophizing, I said. I'm staying safe. I'm not looking for Jakob myself. I guess…I guess I'm here because I needed something tangible. I don't know.

My father said nothing. We shared a quiet moment together, simply sitting in one another's attention. Then my mother emerged from her nap, and the videocall was over.

THE YBARRAS INVITED me to dinner that night, and I accepted. A dining room table had been set up in the back of the Celenia Inn's front office in the makeshift apartment where Angelica Ybarra spent most the tourist season. She embraced me in a warm hug. Her brother, Arturo Ybarra, waved at me from the kitchenette, presiding over the distribution of dinner with winking contentment. Despite the autumnal chill, he was dressed in a yellow Hawaiian shirt, shorts, and flip-flops. He and his sister had spent most of the day preparing the elements of the meal at his house: a rich stew of chorizo, tomato, and hominy, supplemented with handmade tortillas, empanadas, and guacamole.

As Sabana and I set out the plates and dishware, three more guests arrived.

Two twin men walked into the apartment, dressed in button-down plaid shirts, khaki pants, and polished brown shoes, as though arriving for a job interview. Plump and short— they must have been five feet tall—the twins appeared to be Central American. They were nervous, giving familiar nods to Arturo and Angelica, but not speaking. They were unable to make eye contact with either me or Sabana. They stood in place, waiting for the third member of their party to arrive.

Benicio Washington came into the room, still in his jalapeño-green uniform. He presented his hosts with a bottle of red wine from a vineyard in the Texas Hill Country, an award-winning sauvignon which elicited snickers from Arturo and gratitude from Angelica. Removing his white cowboy hat, Benicio kissed Sabana's mother on the cheeks before directing the twins to sit at the table. He spoke to them in a language I had never heard before.

Benicio looked at me from across the room. He came over, holding out his hand.

You must be Anna, he said. I'm Special Agent Benicio Washington. It's an honor to meet you. I knew Jakob well. I'm so sorry about all this. If you need to talk, please reach out. Sabana told me you already have my number.

I shook his hand.

Pleasure to meet you, Special Agent Washington, I said.

He gestured at the twin men.

Allow me to introduce my guests. This is Babajide Canul and Cadmael Canul. They've come all the way from Guatemala. This is their last night in Rosadero. Unfortunately, they don't speak any English, and they only know a little Spanish.

What do they speak? I asked.

Q'eqchi'.

Oh.

He laughed. From the stove, Arturo encouraged me to take a seat while he and his niece served everybody. Sitting down with the Canul brothers, I gave a wave and a strained smile.

Hello, I said. Yo soy Anna.

The twins blushed. Sabana smiled at my Spanish and rolled her eyes. I blushed, too. From the kitchenette, Angelica Ybarra took command of the dinner operations, ordering her brother and daughter to plate the food. After the stew and appetizers were set, Angelica checked her blood sugar on her glucometer, announced a good number, and invited us all to eat.

Several minutes of laughter and slurping and chatting went by, though neither I nor the Canul twins had much to say. We were pained by memories, and silenced by them, hiding ourselves within trenches deeper than linguistic or cultural barriers.

But for a single meal, we all had a family again.

Sitting down with his second serving of stew, Arturo Ybarra looked at me from across the table, mischief in his eyes.

So, Anna. What's the deal with the vegan thing?

I raised an eyebrow.

I don't know. I'm not vegan. Why?

Well, I'm just asking because you're from the Left Coast, he said. You're in Texas now. Just wondered if you had any thoughts on the subject, given we're dining on delicious pork sausage that's been simmering in my kitchen all day.

Angelica pinched her brother on the arm.

He doesn't mean to be a jerk, she said. I've thought about trying the vegan diet. I hear it's good for people with diabetes.

I hear that, too, I said. For a lot of people—where I come from, anyway—veganism is about reducing the worst effects of industrial animal farms, not only greenhouse gases, but all the water they require. It's about stewardship of the land.

Silence fell over the table. Arturo burst out laughing. He pointed at me with his fork.

This is a brave woman here, he said. First, she comes to Texas and trashes the Rangers to their faces, then she trashes the ranchers. I respect the huevos, señorita. You don't buckle for anyone, do you?

I shrugged. Benicio wiped his mouth, lost in thought.

It's fascinating how food systems are a form of social power, he said.

Here we go, Arturo said. Professor Washington, about to give a lecture.

I'm serious, Benicio continued. How we consume our food is like a mode of citizenship. When the hands of poverty pick our crops, we are, in a sense, saying yes to that poverty. With a big cattle ranch, you have a core of prosperous owners and a handful of dependent seasonal laborers working the herd. Nobody who partakes in that model can provide for themselves independently. It's very much the opposite of the small, yeoman farmer, who, as I will remind you, was Thomas Jefferson's ideal democratic citizen.

Thomas Jefferson, Arturo said. Really?

Benicio nodded.

Food is everything to a society, he said. Think about what the destruction of the buffalo did to the Plains Indians. From the Comanches to the Lakota, the United States Cavalry knew the tribes would see their political power annihilated with their herds. And that is exactly what happened. The Cavalry didn't kill their buffalo to integrate them into our society. They killed their buffalo to render them stateless. The American Indian was a political orphan until 1924, when they were finally granted citizenship. That was less than a hundred years ago.

Arturo Ybarra served himself another bowl of stew. Benicio kept thinking. Sabana and I could not take our eyes off him.

That's what the Civil War was fought over, too, Benicio said. The conflict was as much about citizenship as it was about slavery. You can't emancipate a caste of people if they aren't citizens. Hence, the naturalization clause of the Fourteenth Amendment. Americans have shallow memories.

Sabana raised her glass in a toast. Arturo took an unimpressed bite out of an empanada. Angelica looked around the room, checking everybody's expressions. She exchanged brief smiles with Babajide and Cadmael.

I looked at Benicio.

It worked that way in Nazi Germany, too, I said. The first step the regime took to persecute the Jews was to toss out their citizenship. It's worked that way in other genocides, also. In the Ottoman Empire, Armenians and other minorities were put into a second-class system behind Muslims. The sultan would not have been able to orchestrate the death marches otherwise.

Benicio nodded.

Arturo pointed at his sister.

Remind me to never bring up veganism ever again, he said. Next thing you know, the conversation will turn to genocide.

Angelica kicked her brother in the shin beneath the table. Most of us laughed. Babajide and Cadmael Canul looked around in uncertainty. Benicio leaned into them, translating the conversation in Q'eqchi'. The rest of us listened as though he were reciting a hymn.

SABANA AND I smoked our cigarettes behind the motel while Arturo and Angelica prepared a desert of cinnamon rice pudding. In the distance, pink flares lit up and streaked across the boundary of earth and sky like heat lightning: the Rosadero Fireballs, the town's signature phenomenon.

I used to be so scared of the desert at night, Sabana said.

How come? I asked.

It started during the femicides in Juárez. Hundreds of women were getting abducted outside the maquiladoras where they worked. Their corpses were found in the streets the next day, raped and mutilated. These women spent their lives toiling in factories, only to be killed by men. I could never overcome that idea of how they disappeared. Gone forever, just like that.

Sabana finished her cigarette. She stomped out its remains under her boot, then picked the flattened butt and kept it in her palm. She picked at it, thinking.

Do you know anything about the slave trade in this part of the world, Anna? she asked.

I shook my head.

New Spain's economy was all about slavery. Indigenous peoples and mestizos were the victims. Debt peonage and the usual Christian brutality took the place of the whip. As the centuries wore on, coerced servitude continued as a legal activity, even in the United States, even after chattel slavery. Most servants, as they were called, performed domestic roles, hidden from society. Slavery out here relied on anonymity. People disappeared, stolen. Still happens to this day.

Sabana took a rock from the ground. After tossing the rock from palm to palm, she wound up and pitched it into the night; a gesture repeated by forced hands all over the world.

In a few days, Benicio and my uncle will take the twins to El Paso, Sabana said. They've been staying at the motel, a few doors down from you. Once they're in El Paso, my grandfather will provide job training for them at his bakery in El Segundo Barrio. My grandparents will provide them with housing, too. Most important, they will connect them with immigration lawyers. Most refugees don't understand their rights. My grandmother is something of a community leader, a priestess too. Her life's work is to counterbalance the weight of injustice.

Before I could say anything, a deep and menacing sound cut through the blackness. An engine roared through the ranchlands. We listened as an all-terrain vehicle rolled through the countryside, driving with its lights off. The vehicle cut its way out of the backcountry and onto the highway, its sound receding into the ambience of the plains. Several seconds later, the feeling of surveillance still lingered in the air.

Somebody was out there, I said.

Somebody is always out there, Sabana said.

· Eight ·

Love in the Old Pueblo

*T*HE NEW MATTRESS *lies underneath the kitchen counter on the dining room floor. Wrapped in shimmering plastic, the California king-sized bed looks wider than my station wagon, copious in volume and buoyant in texture. With the air conditioning running, the gift occupies a corner where the heat of early summer has no power, where the body can be active without punishment from the Southern Arizona furnace.*

As I step into the casita, Javier is crouching over a new record player on the carpet by the sofa. He stands up when I close the door, holding a vinyl album in his tattooed fingers: Ultracedar *by Lakeith Mercy. On the backside of the album, the brooding male siren of Houston R&B looks at the camera, sweat glittering on his skin, his purple du-rag lustrous. I'm so distracted by the album, I fail at first* to notice the mattress. When I do see it, I just laugh as though it were a punchline.

Javier smiles.

Welcome home. How was the co-op?

I set my backpack by the door.

As good as something like that can be. What's all this?

A friend from home sent me a care package. She included my all-time favorite record. I thought we could listen to it tonight. Do you know this one?

He holds up Ultracedar *as though it were encrusted with jewelry. On the cover, a biblical tree from Lebanon is engraved onto the hood of a pearlescent Cadillac. Lakeith Mercy sits in front of the bumper in his driveway, melancholic but luxurious, his designer clothes soaked from riding through a rainstorm: a baptism in the Fifth Ward.*

That's my favorite record, too, I say. Put it on.

We kiss and caress. Javier returns to the floor, takes out the black disc and sets it in the record player. The opening strings and basslines of the first song float into the casita, creating a pillow for the artist's soulful falsetto. A tale of heartbreak told through bicurious melody flows through us. I hold Javier tight, thanking him. Coveting him.

I lean into his ear and whisper.

And what is that?

We look over at the California king bed.

Gratitude, Javier says. You have been a generous host, more than I ever could have asked for. I thought I'd give you something.

You can give me a whole lot more than that, I say.

We kiss and make love until midnight. Then we lie in childlike lucidity. We are eager about every possibility the two of us could share. We conjoin ourselves without self-consciousness, without a need to know about tomorrow. Our sleepover does not have to end.

THE FIRST MONSOON of the season bursts over the city around 4 a.m. Two inches of rain fall in nineteen minutes. We listen to the drops cascading against the window, beating against the metal of the air conditioner, roaring across the roof. Every now and then, the lashing torrent is illuminated by lightning. Thunder rolls over Tucson. In the aftermath of the storm, birds and insects cry out in a sweeping crescendo before quieting again. A car alarm bleats until its owner shuts it off. Runoff pours through gutters and drainage pipes. Dips and tunnels are flooded, but the early hour guarantees few cars will be stranded. The dry washes are canals christened with rainwater. The inundation creates a city of inland harbors.

Tucson is perfect, Javier says.

I kiss him on the forehead. When we realize we won't be able to go back to sleep, I stand up. Crossing the room to the record player, I take out the chopped-n-screwed Swishahouse remix on Ultracedar's second vinyl disc, this one translucent purple. Lakeith Mercy's voice, mournful and resonant at the lower pitch, scratches and repeats itself over and over. I lie down with Javier. He nestles up to my side, his stubbled face on my chest.

We listen to the remixed album twice. We fall asleep, staying in bed until midday.

HE STANDS BEFORE my cohort, reading from notebooks rather than his laptop or printouts of his stories. This is the uncut dope, he jokes, the raw scribblings taken from the migrant trails. This is the most authentic version of the story he seeks to tell, perhaps in a manner antithetical to the MFA pedagogy. Everyone is listening with single-minded attention.

Javier tells the story of Grupo Veintiuno, now the Nogales Twenty-One. He names the slums in Honduras, Guatemala, and El Salvador from which the Veintiuno hail. He describes the plantation economies of their homelands, names the multinational corporations who fulfilled the Antebellum dream to conquer the Golden Circle across Latin America. He identifies the gangs who terrorize the Nogales Twenty-One at home, deconstructs how these gangs recycle the techniques of death squads trained by the United States.

He pauses, making sure we hear what comes next. Disposing with history, he describes the sensory horror of his travels, day after day, night after night. Lost limbs riding the freight trains through the mountains; bullets flying out of the guns of narcos; beatings by angry townspeople and ranchers.

Then, there is the desert: the searing maelstrom, social control in the form of hyperthermia. Holding back tears, Javier does not devote much time to this topic. While he has been able to articulate what he has witnessed, few are so lucky. Out of these horrors, twenty-one distinct human beings hold onto the dream of survival.

These boys are sparks of humanity, he reads, living on the conveyor belt of organized cruelty. Seceding from the spiritual nourishment of home, they endure exploitation everywhere from the Río Suchiate to the Río Bravo. They do not know the violence they flee has its origins in the United States. They do not know that the violence is in the service of El Norte's luxury malls, supermarkets, car dealerships, warehouses, electronics stores, motels, and hotels. They do not know that materialism is nihilism exchanged into dollars. Thank you.

Every member of the MFA cohort rises to their feet, standing in ovation. Something important has taken place here, they agree. Before he takes questions, Javier invites me to stand with him at the podium. Blushing, I join him. Javier details how vital my editing has been in bringing his translated story to the University of Arizona. He takes my hand and raises it, declaring ourselves champions. In their hoots and whistles, my cohort agrees.

The next act of my creative writing career begins.

WE DINE WITH my new thesis adviser at El Charro Café, joined by another guest lecturer, a professor named Juanita Ochoa, recently retired from the University of Texas, El Paso. My adviser is an intense man named Milos Erickson, renowned essayist and poetry anthologist, an immigrant with a Scandinavian father and a Serbian-Cuban mother. He is the son of Havana intellectuals, with black curly hair and thick eyebrows, perpetually dressed in blazers. Though Professor Erickson is something of an anarcho-communist, he has a soft spot for bourgeoisie restaurants. He is patient with his students when he needs to be, and openly frustrated with trends in autofiction and the hyper-personalization of literature. This is why I have been assigned to him: after toiling away at an unsuccessful piece of autobiographical fiction, I have connected with a man with sympathetic values.

You and I think in systems, Professor Erickson once told me. The great task as author is to find our place in the system, to measure our distance from the center to the margins of the oppressed. The borderland is the physical revelation of this.

Bringing Javier Galvenez to Tucson has proven my credibility. Now comes the work.

Professor Ochoa, who has also given a lecture to the cohort today, listens as I tell her about my upbringing in the Pacific Northwest. She is fascinated by the Pearl District's intersection of gentrification, vagrancy, post-industrialism, and fetishism of authenticity. She speculates about how this milieu will inform my senior thesis and wants to know where I may take my work. I tell her I want to build on the ideas represented by Javier's reading. Professor Ochoa rests her chin in her palm, listening.

You want to layer a new consciousness onto yourself, she says. Self-aware, anti-colonial. One that can take clear-sighted inventory. Do I have that right?

Around the table, we all laugh, not expecting the intensity of Professor Ochoa's remarks. She joins with self-aware amusement.

Something like that, yeah, I say. But I don't know how to begin. I don't have the language yet. But I do know I want to embed the story the power relationship between the United States and the Global South. The U.S.-Mexico border seems like a good place to start.

An essential place to start, Professor Ochoa says. Everything you need to know about the Western Hemisphere is down the road. You must let me introduce you to a friend of mine. He's a special agent with the Border Patrol. He isn't like the rest of the Migra. He specializes in investigating agency corruption. He has a lot of enemies in the CBP. His name is Benicio Washington. He's based out of El Paso, a few hours from here. We come from the same small town in Texas. My family has known his family forever.

Professor Ochoa asks if I've ever heard of Rosadero. It's a unique place, she tells me, a Far West Texas cowtown turned postmodernist art haven, with a population around nineteen hundred. Though the majority of Rosadero is poor and Chicanidad, it has been commodified for mostly white and wealthy tourists. The trend began in the 1980s with a man named Justin Lehenwesen—scion of a notorious Philadelphia banking family—who converted the ruins of the Fort Rosadero Airbase into a sprawling piece of landscape art, rearranging the light and angles of the grasslands with massive geometric objects.

The art itself is consciousness-raising, Profess Ochoa contends, a reconstruction of industrialism and the ever-shifting tones of the sky. But the history of this part of America is that of land-holding elites displacing the poor. All the subsequent artistic spaces opened in Rosadero are by wealthy outsiders. This is Justin Lehenwesen's legacy. It is a shame, a squandering. But we appreciate the money brought in by visitors.

Javier's eyes have been alit since hearing the name Rosadero. He leans across the table, asking Professor Ochoa if she is familiar with the white dancehall on Juan Sabeata Street near the radio station. She knows the dancehall well: before it closed a few years ago, the Rosadero Independent School District held all their extra-curricular events there.

Why? she asks.

Javier beams. The Naranjoven Collective has purchased the dancehall and is in the process of converting it into new kind of art gallery. The gallery will serve as a foil to depoliticized spectacles favored by the mainstream. His own exhibition will be the first, brought in from Mexico City. He describes the project as neon-emancipationism.

Professor Ochoa claps her hands with excitement. She invites us to visit her home in Rosadero whenever we like. Though she moved back for retirement, she is now raising her granddaughter there, a refugee from the Drug War in the state of Tamaulipas. Her home is too large for just an old lady and a young girl, she says, and though she plans to convert part of it into a hole-in-the-wall restaurant, she has plenty of nooks for an aspiring writer to work.

Professor Erickson encourages me to take Juanita up on her offer. I thank Professor Ochoa with gratitude. As we raise our pints of Mexican beer, the waiter appears with saucers overloaded with enchiladas of the richest qualities. We remember our surroundings, the grand house where generations of Tucsonans ordinary and illustrious have shared plates. Portraits of mariachi musicians, movie stars, and desert flora decorate the walls. Clinking glasses, conversations, and aroma bind us together.

At the end of dinner, Professor Erickson picks up the check. On the steps outside, he shakes our hands, confident in the work we are all about to do. Professor Ochoa kisses Javier and I on the cheeks, then walks with Professor Erickson to his parked luxury sedan.

Under the cool evening sky, Javier and I begin our walk across the train-tracks to Dunbar/Spring. On the way, we cannot contain our desires. He grabs my ass, and I grab his front. Across the street, a group of young women howl their approval, and attraction. Tonight, the pastels of Tucson's barrios are painted in seduction.

WE DO MOVIE night with my landlord in his living room, integrating our new romance into the routine I have with Carlos. When the sci-fi spectacle ends, Javier and I sit up from the couch. We have a proposal we'd like to make about adding Javier as a long-term guest in the casita. Carlos listens from his recliner. Javier volunteers to pay rent, pay utility bills, assist in my regular cleanings around the main house, and even cover the costs of Carlos' weekly visits to Nogales. My landlord laughs, agreeing only to a modest increase in the monthly rent payment, but dismissing the rest. Javier is more than welcome to stay.

The evening, so far, has been a series of blessings.

It's exciting, actually, to have a couple of intellectuals living here, Carlos says. You guys kind of remind me of my dad. Speaking of which, I have something of his I'd like to share, if you don't mind. From one deceased writer to two living ones.

As Carlos retreats to his bedroom, Javier and I exchange amused looks, unsure what to expect. Our landlord returns with several wide leather-bound albums. The look on his face is between chagrin and pride.

I was a sanctuary baby, he says. I don't know if you knew that already.

Neither Javier nor I know what this means. Carlos passes us the archives. Immediately, we understand that he has been wanting to share this for a while.

We open the first leather-bound album. Inside are a series of laminated newspaper clippings from the Tucson Citizen, *shuttered for over a decade. Edward Whitehead is pictured in a vest and wristwatch, hiking boots and shorts. He is masculine and grizzled, a man who has embedded himself among narcos and border agents, who can speak the language of victims and victimizers, a chronicler of the violent entropies undergirding society. He was a close peer and confidant of Charles Bowden, passing many hours at the wine-fueled salon in Bowden's famous backyard garden. For decades, Edward Whitehead was the most important columnist in the* Citizen's *pages. In the early 1990s, he journaled about the struggles of his own family. In a Pulitzer-prize winning series, he documented the months his newborn American son spent living in a church in Barrio Hollywood with the mother of his child, an undocumented Mexican national seeking sanctuary. Baby Carlos' crib was kept beside the pew where his mother slept. He was bathed in a makeshift tub in the church's basement. In solidarity with his lover and child, Edward Whitehead lived in the church too, writing the story with coarse, first-person insight.*

A judge resolved that Carlos' mother may return unmolested to Mexico, her violation expunged from the record. She was allowed to apply for reentry the legal way to be with her new family, perhaps to marry Mr. Whitehead. But by this time, the relationship had dissolved. Carlos' mother was escorted to Nogales by state police, and never crossed back.

Edward Whitehead became the most famous single dad in Arizona. He stayed that way for almost two decades. The Tucson Citizen *shuttered in 2009, taking the record of Mr. Whitehead's journalism with it. What Carlos shares with us represents the only comprehensive collection of his father's work. He hopes to someday find a publisher to compile it all in a book, though he has not tried.*

Javier looks at our host, stunned.

My goodness, you've been through a lot, Javier says.

Carlos looks away, tears in his eyes. He excuses himself to the restroom. We wait for him to return before we retire to the casita. We wait for some time.

THE NEWS BREAKS before dawn: the Nogales Twenty-One will all be deported to their home countries. The Galvenez family attorney calls Javier early in the morning. He apologizes for his failure. Javier does not say anything on the subject for about a week.

· Nine ·

Alone in Suites of Marble

JOHN RODGER HOLLIS stared with severe eyes out of sepia photographs hanging on the pink walls of the empty Hotel Jaspeado. In every monochromatic still, he stood in a dominating, wide-legged posture, dressed in classic cowboy attire: spurred boots, denim pants, fur-lined denim coats, a large cowboy hat, a flaring belt-buckle. Posing with business partners, or with his extended family, or at the head of a cattle drive, the Father of Rosadero was a man who looked like he owned everyone around him. His proprietorship over the plains of Texas could not be terminated. He was the Eternal Cowdaddy of this town, Javier told me with a laugh, the same way Kim Il-sung was the Eternal President of North Korea.

We lay on a bed beneath a window looking towards the Zaldos Mesa. On top of a mildewed blanket, I curled into

Javier's side, a little sister holding onto a big brother surrogate. We were drunk, a bottle of half-consumed sotol resting on the marble floor, the inconsolable conclusion to our two-day long conversation about Jakob. After hours of exchanging memories about my brother, we had come here to mourn, to dissolve the edges of perception. The Hotel Jaspeado—an icon abandoned over a decade ago by insolvent owners—still had most of its décor preserved within its legendary suites. Situated on one side of the agave plaza, looters had spurned its treasures due to proximity to the sheriff's office. Thrill-seekers, however, were not dissuaded. When Jakob still had a material presence in Rosadero, he and Javier would quietly break into the landmark, slipping through its slim front door as though they were its new owners. Inside, they discovered a lightless lobby and lounge space, a century-old watering hole favored by movie stars during the town's heyday as a backdrop for Westerns. Buckskins and leather furniture and mounted longhorns remained across the unoccupied chamber, cobwebbed and coated in dust. A grand fireplace whistled with wind. Despite the mausoleum quality of the hotel, the omnipresent pink marble evoked a quality of warmness, a fiction of heat.

My brother and Javier would sneak into the lobby with candles and blankets and—much like tonight—sotol. Sitting in armchairs furnished for Rosadero's former celebrity class, they would talk for hours about the borderlands, about art and the migration crisis and the Drug War; they would kiss, touch, fuck; they would dream about the future.

Some nights, they would fall asleep on a blanket laid out in the middle of the lobby like children camping in a house. Then they would awaken with a start, sitting bolt upright, looking around at the pass-through connecting the kitchen with the bar with the feeling that they were being observed. An inside joke developed between them that John Rodger Hollis had come back as a voyeur, aroused from the afterlife by their homoeroticism.

On other nights, Jakob and Javier would creep up the spiral staircase to the wrought-iron balcony on the second floor. Five exclusive suites—one in honor of each of the Families—awaited behind five mesquite doors, still somehow polished after all these years. Tonight, my brother's lover led me to the John Rodger Hollis Suite.

Upon entering the vast private room, we had stumbled over a buffalo hide rug onto the bed. At this point in getting shitfaced, we barely noticed the pronghorn heads on the wall, the rifle over the bathroom door, the elegant dresser and vanity mirror, the paintings of frontier landscapes. Good and drunk, we were here to grieve where nobody else could see or judge. The sunset poured in, liquifying the totems of the Old West into shadows.

It feels like we're in a cave painting, Javier said.

I raised my head, squinting at the dancing illusions. The sunset faded. Javier fell asleep first. I kept an eye on the shadows until they disappeared, hoping I would see my brother. Then I fell asleep, too, and it did not matter.

MARIAZUL'S BLACK BACKPACK sat by the door to the suite like a child waiting to be walked to school, the crucifix necklace glimmering around the handle. Javier and I awoke in the middle of the night as a moonbeam moved across our eyes, illuminating a pathway to the bag. Neither us could remember carrying it into the hotel. After looking at the inexplicable backpack for several seconds, Javier nudged me.

Why is that here? he asked.

I yawned.

It just needed to be seen, I guess.

What's inside it?

I can't look inside it.

Why?

Because it doesn't belong to me.

Who does it belong to?

Someone who disappeared. A woman I picked up in New Mexico. Even though she had asylum, a legal right to be here, she was…arrested.

Arrested?

Yeah. It was scary. We got pulled over by the Border Patrol in this ghost town.

Border Patrol? Didn't you just say she had asylum?

Yeah, but…I don't know…I didn't ask questions. I didn't want to be detained with her.

Why would you be detained?

I don't know. Why was she?

My brother's lover sat up. Swinging his legs over the bed, he staggered over the buffalo hide rug. He brought the backpack to the antique trunk at the foot of the bed and began unzipping.

Please, don't, I said. That's not ours. That's not ours, Javier.

He ignored me, unpacking the bag item by item: energy bars, a small box of tampons, prayer cards, a water bottle, gloves, pepper spray, birth control pills, her wallet. Javier opened the wallet. He took out each piece of documentation, perusing through her information like a one-man checkpoint. As he lingered over the green card, I could see contempt in his eyes.

She wasn't arrested, he said. That was a kidnapping, Anna. But you knew that already, didn't you?

I did, I said.

You allowed that woman to be abducted by the state. And you've looked away ever since. Haven't you?

She's not that woman, I said.

What?

She's not that woman. Her name is Mariazul Lluvia Cenote Bautista. Look. It's also written on a patch stitched near the top of the zipper.

Javier inverted the inner fabric of the backpack, reading the patch, apparently forgetting the name he had just read on the green card.

So it is, he said.

He set down the pack with disinterest, toddling back to bed as though immediately forgetting about everything. He fell back asleep. I stayed up, crying, my mind an incoherent splice of Jakob and the young woman I picked up in Lordsburg. Eventually, I forced myself to my feet. After relieving myself in the bathroom—the toilet still worked—I stood over the trunk where Javier had unpacked Mariazul's remains. Taken altogether, the only physical evidence of her looked like litter.

I tried repacking. I couldn't do it. I returned to bed. While Javier slept without any covers, I rolled under the blanket, whimpering into the musk of the pillow.

WE WOKE UP during the night's penultimate hour. A high-pitched wail ascended from the bowels of the hotel. Coyote-like at first, the shriek took the form of a young man's voice, increasing in octaves of pain. Suddenly, a series of clatters and booms reverberated throughout what sounded like the kitchen: metal on metal, metal on tiles. Then more shrieking, more yipping, more banging. Fists against stovetops. Pots and pans against refrigerator doors.

Eventually, the racket died down. Javier and I were left with impermeable silence. Not knowing what to do, I shook him by the shoulder. He grunted in anger, rolling away from me.

I'm sorry, I said.

Javier did not respond. I settled down, deciding the noise had been a hallucination. I drifted in and out of a dream about the Pacific Ocean, the commotion downstairs reattributed to a warship under duress from a great storm. When daylight filled the suite, Javier and I stirred without acknowledging one another. I collected Mariazul's possessions, strapping the backpack to my shoulders, slipping the crucifix into the pocket of my skirt.

We descended the spiral staircase, seeing nothing in the lobby to explain the apparent poltergeist. Opening the front door, we did not bother with covertness as we stepped onto the sidewalk. In the cold gray morning, we did not say goodbye. The memory of my brother was no longer able to tether us together.

On Juan Sabeata Street, I walked by the adobe studios for Rosadero Public Radio. I paused, listening to what sounded like Benicio Washington's voice on the outdoor speakers. The special agent appeared to be in the middle of a live interview. As I lit up a cigarette and listened, a tumbleweed rolled into the asphalt of the road. The tumbleweed rolled backwards and forwards for several minutes before exploding beneath the tires of a pickup truck.

· Ten ·

Nec Terra Nullius

YOU'RE LISTENING TO *Talk of the Plateau* on Rosadero Public Radio. I'm your host, Olivé Bouchard. *Talk of the Plateau* is our daily interview show broadcasted from our studio here in downtown Rosadero, Texas. All week, we've been talking with members of your community about the one thing that perhaps defines how we spend our day-to-day lives more than anything else. That's right, we're talking about jobs. If you're just now joining us for the final episode of our mini-series, today's guest is Rosadero native and twenty-four-year veteran of the Border Patrol, Special Agent Benicio Washington.

Buenos días.

Special Agent Washington, right before we went back on the air, my producer told me to ask about your work as a local historian. Apparently, you're a bit of a familiar face in the archives at Sul Ross State. What sparked this interest in local history?

Growing up in this town, you live with a sense of mystery. I don't care if you're a child or an adult, there's something hard to explain about this place. Even without all the art stuff and celebrity visits, Rosadero has always had an otherworldliness to it. I figure most of that comes from the story of the Zaldos.

For listeners unfamiliar with the Zaldos, would you mind explaining who they were?

Well, since time immemorial—about one millennium, give or take—the Zaldos People occupied the Narváez Plateau region. The centerpiece of their culture seems to have been the massive pueblo built into the western edge of the Zaldos Mesa, which is still standing today. Like the mesa itself, the pueblo is on private ranchland owned by the Hollis family, inaccessible to the public. As a result, it has been very difficult for archaeologists to conduct field research into who these people were, or more importantly, why they seemed to disappear so suddenly.

Now, when you say disappear—

I mean that the available evidence shows that for about a thousand years, right up until John Rodger Hollis—the so-called Father of Rosadero—arrived here in 1880 with the first ranching families, a thriving culture existed here. There's evidence that the Zaldos survived Spanish conquistadors, Apaches, Comanches, you name it. But sometime around the founding of Rosadero, they vanished. The handful of artifacts researchers have been able to date via radiocarbon attest to this timeline.

And nobody knows what happened?

Nobody living. No existing tribes lay claim to the ruins. And like I said, the Zaldos Pueblo and the Zaldos Mesa were quickly incorporated into the Hollis family's ranching enterprise. It's been private land for more than four generations.

Fascinating.

Have you ever flown over Rosadero in an airplane? Like, one of those little propeller planes?

I have not. Why?

Well, from the air you can see that the Zaldos Pueblo appears to be the converging point of two ancient roads. These roads lead to other important archaeological sites, the first being the Paquimé complex near Nuevos Casas Grandes in Mexico, the second being the Pueblo Bonito in Chaco Canyon, up in the Four Corners region. Centuries of neglect and private development have made it difficult to see these ancient highways. But the road between Paquimé and the Zaldos Pueblo is still used by border crossers, so the Border Patrol has to survey it pretty regularly.

Wow. I had no idea.

The road works both ways, too.

How do you mean?

You got border-crossers coming in one way, weapons traffickers going the other.

Really?

Well, in the case of weapons traffickers, that's more of a figurative description than a literal one. Let me qualify that.

Most of the cartels use American guns, most of which come through Texas. Speaking of which, in case any of your listeners come into contact with a gun whose origin can't be explained, law enforcement would like to have a word with you, especially if the gun's got its serial number filed off.

There is so much more I'd like to ask you. But unfortunately, we're almost out of time.

Well, dang. I was enjoying this.

Anything else you'd like to say either about the Border Patrol or your work as a historian?

Sure. The Zaldos Mesa is more of a butte. Look at the way it towers into the sky, just like something out of Monument Valley. It's clearly a butte. John Rodger Hollis apparently did not know that when he went around naming everything. Bless his soul.

And with that, we are out of time. Benicio Washington is a Special Operations Supervisor based out of El Paso, formerly of the Narváez Plateau Border Patrol Sector. Thank you for stopping by, Special Agent Washington.

My pleasure.

This has been *Talk of the Plateau* on Rosadero Public Radio. I'm Olivé Bouchard. Tune in tomorrow. Same time, same station. Have a great day, everybody.

CAPTAIN WINSTON BRYCE Jr. left a brief message on my voicemail, telling me that my brother's abductors had ceased cooperating with the FBI's negotiators. The line had gone dead. Jakob's fate was unknown, and, pending new developments, the case was cold. The Rangers planned to put up billboards around Texas with Jakob's picture and the number to a missing persons tip-line. To prevent antagonizing the kidnappers or exciting the media, the Rangers would continue referring to Jakob's disappearance without criminal context.

On my bed in the Celenia Inn, I called my father. He was keeping himself together, though he had not slept. Despite his relentless petitioning, the FBI had recalled its negotiators. Because Jakob had spent the last few weeks before his abduction living in Rosadero, the crime was considered a Texan matter. My father was now thinking about hiring a private investigator, though doing so would be prohibitively expensive.

I just don't understand, my father said. We were prepared to pay. We were prepared to pay anything.

I nodded. We began to talk about arranging a memorial service at our synagogue—not quite a funeral, but an intimate gathering of mourners. To set the schedule, I would need to decide when I was departing Rosadero, and how long it would take to drive back to Portland.

I'll leave the day after tomorrow, I said.

Dad nodded. Unprompted, he told me my mother was taking a bath. She'd been in the tub for about two hours. Every fifteen minutes, my father was checking on her, much to her irritation.

This would all be so much easier if Jakob had died suddenly, I said. Like in a car crash or a shooting. The shock would be over, and we could heal. Instead, it's like he's dying again every single day, over and over.

The conversation did not last much longer after that.

The call ended. I rang up Sabana. After updating her and accepting her condolences, we made plans for a final adventure while I was still in Rosadero. She was working a morning shift at the coffeeshop today and would return to pick me up from the motel in the early afternoon.

SABANA PARKED HER jeep along the ancient highway, faded but still visible in the high desert soil. As we stepped out, I looked at the immense crack running through the Mesa, almost biblical in scope. Between soaring red walls, an Edenic canyon thrived: juniper and piñon and mesquite trees creating a shelter of branch and pine. The handful of times covert archaeologists penetrated the canyon, Sabana told me, they found evidence of advanced agriculture. In open areas, where shafts of sunlight fell unimpeded onto the floor, nameless farmers cultivated squash and beans and maize. Of all the nations to inhabit the Chihuahuan Desert before the arrival of Europeans, only the Zaldos had been able to sustain a permanent settlement. Their Rain Goddess blessed the top of the Mesa with clouds, creating a microclimate of moisture. During monsoon season, a dozen waterfalls poured forth from the rock, nourishing the earth. Deep beneath the Mesa lay a subterranean lake that had been collecting water in micro-installments for hundreds of thousands of years.

Up close, the pueblo conjured the impression of a fishing vessel stranded in the drought-stricken remains of an ecological disaster. The structure of the pueblo was a gigantic one-story semicircle, fanning out along the entrance to the canyon. Every few feet, trapezoidal windows provided even breaks in the red stone. As a consequence of the canyon's east-west orientation, a blade of light pierced through Mesa at sunrise and sunset, a golden saber along the roads that led to other pueblos hundreds of miles away.

Despite the antiquity and grace of the Zaldos ruins, my attention had fallen on a beat-up mauve pickup truck on a small hill a few hundred yards away. A disheveled white man with long hair was surveying us with binoculars.

Who is that? I asked.

Sabana squinted. The binoculars flashed in the daylight.

Some yahoo, Sabana said. I can't imagine he's connected to any of the ranches around here. Maybe he's some wannabe rustler a couple generations too late. I can call my uncle, if you want.

Let's hold off, I said. I don't want this to escalate.

Sabana nodded. She and I stood together, waiting. The long-haired man lowered his binoculars and slipped into his pickup truck. He tore away across the terrain.

Sabana shook her head.

I can guarantee that idiot will set off some ground sensors, she said. The Border Patrol hates dealing with that. Thanks to Benicio, I know all the places to avoid.

Sabana walked to the far side of the pueblo, reaching the very end before gesturing at me to follow. I set off across the outer wall of the ruins. With every window I passed, a sharp crosswind flowed by, resonating in different notes, the pueblo's architecture filtering the wind into music, geometry converging into a thousand-year-old song.

I arrived at the square entryway.

Do you think we'll find anyone in there? I asked. Like…the sort of people who make their way to your family's motel?

Always, Sabana said. You never know.

She walked inside.

A few seconds later, I went in after her.

The interior of the Zaldos Pueblo felt like a mausoleum. Great horizontal rectangles in the upper backwall mediated the flow of light and air. A large stone entrance opened into a subterranean series of passages, some of which led to the canyon, others to ceremonial chambers or storage cells. In one corner of the pueblo, stone pens held the memories of exotic animals, cawing and snorting as their handlers bartered for water and shelter. Informal digs had recovered seashells from the California coast, residue of ceremonial Aztec cacao, Tarahumara running shoes, Navajo mohair, mummified macaws from Mesoamerica. The Zaldos Pueblo represented the most isolated node in a continental trade network, an American Timbuktu. Hunters from nomadic nations, mostly bands of Apache and Comanche, brought the meat of buffalo and antelope in exchange for refuge. With its arable soil, the canyon could support a year-round population of up to five hundred residents. Due to the defensive position of the pueblo, potential raiders never mounted a successful attack.

Sabana and I stood with reverence. I had brought Mariazul's backpack with me, wearing it on my front like she had. Presuming the pack's presence to be pragmatic and ordinary, Sabana had not commented on it. I slowly crept towards the center of the pueblo, as though being pulled.

When I collapsed to the floor, Sabana rushed to my side.

Before she could get a handle on my crisis, I unzipped the pack, showing her Mariazul's name, suddenly confessing everything about the abduction.

Sabana listened, her expression hardening. When I was done, she helped me to my feet. She had to make a phone call, and we had to return to the Celenia Inn immediately. Keeping our arms interlocked, she walked me back to the high desert, exiting a thousand years of enigma as quickly as we had entered.

SPECIAL AGENT BENICIO Washington knocked on my door in the early evening, escorted by Angelica and Arturo Ybarra. I sat on the edge of the bed like a misbehaving teenager awaiting punishment. Angelica Ybarra lingered in the doorway before stepping out in disappointment and grief. Deputy Ybarra stepped inside and closed the door, standing by the peephole.

Mariazul's backpack and crucifix sat at my side.

Special Agent Washington crouched in front of me. Taking a small notebook out of his jacket, he told me I was not under suspicion of any crime, and though I had the legal right to an attorney, he did not believe the situation warranted it. I decided I agreed. I would cooperate with his questions to the best of my ability. With that, we launched into a reconstruction of everything that had happened since Lordsburg. Special Agent Washington pressed me to describe every detail about our stop at the Sierra Blanca Border Patrol Checkpoint, whether I noticed I was being tailed. Above all, he asked me to corroborate a physical description of Agent Taylor.

Her name was already well known to Special Agent Washington. He did not provide any more information about her, nor did he seem interested in talking about her partner at the checkpoint, Agent Gallegos. Instead, we picked apart the abduction in Beauvoir, moment by moment. He told me a little about Mariazul's circumstances: how she was traveling from Tucson to El Paso for help paying her kidnapped brother's ransom, how her first ride—a foreman at the factory where she worked—abandoned her in Lordsburg after she refused his sexual advances, how she was terrified of waiting alone in New Mexico to be picked up, how she believed it would better for her safety to meet the Ybarras at the Celenia Inn rather than their church in El Paso.

This is where I came in, and where I left her.

Special Agent Washington suggested my actions had probably kept me safe from harm. He did not speak to how they had affected Mariazul.

Satisfied he understood what transpired, the Special Agent turned to my time in Rosadero.

Did you discuss the presence of Babajide Canul or Cadmael Canul with anybody outside the Celenia Inn? he asked.

No, I said.

Special Agent Washington wrote on his notepad.

When are you leaving? he asked.

The day after…tomorrow. No, actually. Tomorrow. I'm leaving tomorrow.

You sure?

Yes sir. This is my last day in Rosadero. Unless you need me to stay.

Benicio put away his notepad.

Your departure is for the best. I'll be in contact in the event I need further statements. Sorry, again, for your loss, Ms. Tatevyan. Deputy Ybarra updated me on the latest. Your brother was a remarkable person. A true joy to know.

He told me he would like to confiscate the backpack and necklace for evidence. I told him I had no say in the matter. Special Agent Washington took the evidence, passing it to Deputy Ybarra before raising his cowboy hat in goodbye. Before they stepped out, I thanked Deputy Ybarra for everything he and his sister and niece had done for me.

He wished me safe travels.

Alone in my room, the fate of the disappeared seemed as opaque as ever. Bolting and locking the door, I took out my smartphone and called Sabana. We talked for a few minutes, exchanging fondness and regret, promising to stay in touch. We did not discuss my conversation with Benicio.

When I was done speaking with Sabana, I tried calling Javier Galvenez to tell him the news about Jakob. He rejected my call after three rings. Trying again, Javier rejected me after two rings. Taking a long shower, I did not attempt a third call.

For a few hours, I tried to sleep.

THE ROSADERO FIREBALLS erupted and splashed over the twinkling frost of the prairielands. Behind the Celenia Inn, I shivered in the early winter chill, smoking my last cigarette. As I studied the Fireballs, a ghostlike fog crept the landscape, drifting from Paisano Pass to suffocate countryside.

I finished my cigarette. Touching the hem of the Virgen's robe, I apologized one last time. Then I returned to my room to pack.

Two hours later, I was driving on Highway 90 towards Van Horn. Freezing mist engulfed the ranchlands, occluding the grass and mountains. Slowing down through Beauvoir, I peered at the uninhabited casita where Agent Taylor pulled me over and where Mariazul exhaled her last free breaths. Somebody had restored the casita's door to its rusted hinges.

Passing through the length of town, the fog devolved into rain. Fourteen hundred miles away from the Pacific Northwest, the wet monotony of an Oregon winter was preemptively asserting itself.

When I got home, we would hold Jakob's memorial service, unable to divulge the true details of his absence. Most would probably assume he had committed suicide.

ONE MONTH LATER, I would return to Narváez County. Once again, I would come alone.

Jakob, I would believe, was still alive.

MIDNIGHT IN ROSADERO, a day after my departure—

A young man burst out of the backdoor of the Hotel Jaspeado's kitchen in nothing but torn jeans and handcuffs. Careening into dumpsters, the man raced through the town's alleyways until reaching the Bluebonnet Food & Gas. Under fluorescent outdoor lighting, he hurtled towards Deputy Arturo

Ybarra, who was fueling his SUV for the sheriff's office. Drawing his service weapon, Deputy Ybarra ordered the man to his knees. Unable to halt his momentum—and unable to balance himself due to his handcuffed wrists—the man fell facedown onto the concrete. Pistol still in hand, Deputy Ybarra approached with caution, noting the bruises and cigarette burns on the man's bare back, arms, and feet. Crouching by his bleeding face, Deputy Ybarra asked where he had come from. In Spanish, the man explained he was being held captive in the kitchen of the Hotel Jaspeado, but tonight, his abductors had left him alone and he had been able to escape. Though he was a legal resident of the United States, the man's kidnappers had stolen his green card. He begged Deputy Ybarra not to turn him in to the Border Patrol.

Deputy Ybarra helped the battered stranger stand up, leading him quickly into the back of his SUV. Taking his position in the driver's seat, Deputy Ybarra phoned Sheriff Alire, relaying the situation, suggesting the county judge be called to approve a search warrant for the Hotel Jaspeado. Sheriff Alire concurred.

Before taking him to the sheriff's office, Deputy Ybarra drove the escapee to the Celenia Inn, where he would be provided with a fresh shirt, socks, and sneakers. Over and over, Deputy Ybarra assured him he would not be turned in to the Border Patrol. Right now, the goal was to establish who had abducted the man, and where the fugitive party might be. To open an investigation, the sheriff's office would need to take a full statement, beginning with the young man's name and point of origin.

The young man—at twenty years old, not much more than a boy—said he hailed from a small village in Veracruz, born and

raised near the Río Coatzacoalcos. His name was Alejandro
Bartolo Cenote Bautista.

Part II

Rather than be driven out of this country, I will leave my bones to blanch on the plains of Texas.

—Private G.A. Giddings, March 16th, 1836

· Eleven ·

Another Arrest

THUNDERCLOUDS TIGHTEN BEHIND *the mountains over Lordsburg, New Mexico. Special Agent Washington and I are sitting in an undercover vehicle in the parking lot of an abandoned diner. From our unmarked brown sedan, we have a full view of the adjoining truck stop, as well as the cumulonimbus building itself across the summer sky. From the Mojave to the Chihuahuan, monsoon season is rumbling towards its apex.*

Without divulging specifics, Special Agent Washington—he insists I call him Benicio—has brought me here to participate in a stakeout. All he tells me is that he is acting on a tip from a confidential informant. Benicio won't even tell me from which country his informant hails. And still, I have agreed to come here.

Lordsburg is roughly equidistant to both Tucson and El Paso. After meeting up at the Border Patrol station south of town and driving a mile and a half to the truck stop, we've been seated here for over three hours. Aside from listening to the public radio out of Silver City, talking is the only way to pass the time.

Following a prolonged lull in our conversation, I turn my audio recorder back on.

Do you still believe in the mission? I ask.

Which mission? Benicio asks.

The one stated on the Customs and Border Patrol's official government website. Do you still believe in it?

Refresh my memory, if you would.

On my phone, I pull up the webpage containing the mission statement.

To detect and prevent the illegal entry of aliens into the United States, I read.

Special Agent Washington nods.

Well, Mr. Tatevyan, he says, you know I am dutybound to enforce all immigration laws of the United States of America.

We both laugh. But I persist.

It's just…you've spoken so much about the continuity between the United States and Mexico, how the border represents a distortion of the two nations. Yet, your entire career is premised on policing the border. How do you reconcile this?

Benicio thinks about it.

I don't perceive a contradiction in what I do, he says, at least not in the Constabulary Division. My role is to keep the agency accountable to itself, morally and legally. You have to understand something, Jakob. Those words you recited are elastic. The definition of alien, the definition of prevention, the definition of legal versus illegal: it's all subject to intention. An institution is a body, not a mind.

How do you mean?

I'll put it this way: at the end of the day, the only real authority conferred to members of the law enforcement is our gear. Handcuffs, batons, radios, cruisers. Our guns above all. That's the only measure of power. Morals are not a necessary component.

Benicio's eyes burn with intensity, the same intensity I remember from our first meeting at the hotel bar in El Paso. He tells me a story.

Down in Mexico, he says, in the state of Michoacán, there's an Indigenous mountain village called Cherán. The village is surrounded by a pine forest sacred to the Purépecha people who live there. At some point, the cartel in Michoacán organized an illegal logging operation in the forest, devastating the community. One day, the Purépechas took up arms against the loggers and their cartel protectors, driving them all out of town. But they didn't stop there. The citizens of Cherán also made sure to drive out the local police. Do you know why, Jakob?

I can guess.

Every single officer in the police department was on the cartel payroll. Like the rest of Mexico, civil corruption was the primary reason the cartel could operate with impunity. Since driving out the police, the people of Cherán have not had any more problems with the cartels or illegal logging. They govern themselves, and they do it well.

He looks out the windshield again. Lightning flashes out of the purple thunderhead. Nobody in the truck stop seems to notice.

Corruption destroys society, Benicio says, from the inside out.

I write down this sentence on my notepad. Special Agent Washington's mind is alive with a current of his own generation. Hours of monotonous surveillance have worn down the barriers between us

¿Qué sabes de Jerónimo? he asks.

Sorry? I say.

Benicio laughs.

My apologies. What do you know about Geronimo? The Mescalero Apache chief?

Not a thing.

That's okay. Let's begin with the fact that the United States settled westwards and Mexico settled northwards. The Apache's ancestral lands exist in the nexus of two colonial frontiers. As most of the bands were semi-nomadic…

Benicio begins a new lecture. I position my audio recorder as he deconstructs the interminable conflict between America and its Indigenous populations, jotting down key phrases. Like all his thoughts, Special Agent Washington traces his insights back to historical sources.

…the Founding Fathers, first and foremost, were land speculators, as the historian Greg Grandin reminds us. King George III had forbidden land acquisition west of the Ohio River with his Royal Proclamation of 1763. Abolishing the proclamation line was the original motivation for the Revolutionary War. And when the slaveholding class—hold on.

What is it?

I peer over the dashboard, heart racing. A beat-up mauve pickup truck with Arizona license plates has pulled into the fueling station. Out steps a white man with long brown hair. He is dressed in black boots, a bomber jacket, and torn up jeans. He turns away from us, staring into the thunderhead before walking to the diesel pump.

Benicio holds up a pair of binoculars. In slow, careful words, he begins reciting a series of letters and numbers, as well as the make and model of the truck. In haste, I write down what he's saying. As he continues his recitation, I realize this is an act of memorization, perhaps to avoid leaving a paper-trail. I was not meant to write anything down.

I turn my notebook over in my lap.

Benicio keeps his eyes on the long-haired stranger. Returning the diesel pump into the fuel station, the man looks over at us. With an unmistakable smirk, he returns inside his pickup. Refueled, he leaves the truck stop and drives along the rutted road back to the interstate, another motorist among the countless many. After almost three and a half hours of sitting here, our anticlimax has come and gone.

That's it, Benicio says.

What's it?

Today's operation. Hoped we'd get something more. But, sometimes, this is how these things go. Assembling discrete pieces of data. This will not be my last encounter with this gentleman, I assure you. Thanks for coming out, Jakob. Hope it wasn't too boring for you. Sometimes, this is the job.

Benicio turns his key in the ignition to drive us back to the station. Due to the nature of his work, he will not share the information he has culled with anyone else in the Border Patrol, unless compelled to by the top commanders in the agency. This is the shadow realm of anti-corruption work.

We drive through a rundown community of shacks and motels.

Who was that? I ask.

Jace Tarrant, Benicio says. He used to run with a citizen militia in Southern Arizona that patrolled the wilderness between Tucson and Yuma. Before their disbandment, they were known as the Ditat Deus Reconnaissance Team. I led an investigation into their organization which determined Ditat Deus to be a criminal enterprise, though I could never prove it in a court of law. Before I was done, they self-imploded, and the case went nowhere.

Criminal enterprise? Who was in this group? What sort of people?

Most of these guys were ex-cops, unemployed veterans, a few ex-Border Patrol agents. Then there was our friend here. Tarrant has an extensive criminal record in Texas. He's done two bids at the state penitentiary. In the Ditat Deus case, I had reason to believe he was serving as a liaison between the militia and bajadores. You know what those are?

Professional abductors, right?

Something like that. Most are based out of Phoenix. Bajadores target migrants in remote smuggling routes, kidnapping them and blackmailing their families for money. I guess the boys at Ditat Deus discovered there was more money turning over migrants to bajadores rather than the Border Patrol. In fact, I was on the verge of cracking a network of border agents who were assisting in Ditat Deus' criminal operations, not just in Arizona, but several states.

What became of Ditat Deus following its disbandment?

Some are dead, some are in prison. But some have gone legitimate.

What do you mean?

The senior recon guys all got hired by a private security firm out of Laredo. Texaulipas Security Solutions. They've been around for a little over a decade. Recently, they've expanded to a second headquarters across the river in Nuevo Laredo, Mexico. What's troubling is that a sitting congressman happens to be on the board and owns a significant stake in the company.

A sitting congressman? In Texas?

With these words, Benicio gives me a serious look.

I need you to promise me something, he says. I trust you, but you need to keep yourself safe. I know this is for your writing, but you are a civilian. Speak to no one about this, especially on the phone. Do not contact anybody implicated in what I've told you. Do you hear me?

I hear you, I say.

He asks me to turn off my audio recorder. He wants to believe I am worth his trust. I want him to believe it too.

But two weeks later, I will return to the truck stop to interview Jace Tarrant.

OUR SYNAGOGUE GLOWED with candles to honor the life of Jakob Levon Tatevyan. My premonition proved correct: his absence was treated like a suicide.

Whispers fluttered throughout our temple. My brother's inferred self-destruction led to a series of speeches about suicide and self-harm rates among young people. A donation box was placed at the front of the synagogue for a nonprofit working with queer, at-risk youths, along with pamphlets detailing the warning signs of suicidality, and how to address the topic. Conversations, we were advised, should open with the unreserved question—Are you thinking about killing yourself?—before pivoting to more pragmatic considerations: Have you thought about how your death would affect your loved ones? This, I supposed, was how my absenteeism at the memorial service was interpreted by my well-intentioned neighbors.

I was affected.

While my mother and father sat and wept at the service, I hiked through the dark canyons on the edge of the city. Deep in the muddy trails of Forest Park, I found solitude among mushrooms and streams, stepping over the rain-slicked roots of old growth conifers, observing waterfalls bursting out of volcanic rock. Since returning to Portland from the borderlands, my time was devoted to days-on-end internet binges—videos on videos, thinkpieces on thinkpieces, playlists on playlists, insomnia on insomnia—or hiking. Because my academic schedule had cleared up, my sojourns could take place on weekdays, and because it was November, I would find myself alone on popular trials, guided only by a desperate connection to my brother.

On a drizzling afternoon on the Pacific Crest Trail, I encountered a shard of mahogany obsidian amid a grove of ferns. Picking it up and wiping away the raindrops, I felt as though I were holding a talisman containing my brother's last known essence: fiery and black, a solidified mixture of his drive and intellect.

Confiscating the obsidian, I drove myself home. The next morning, I told my mother and my father I would take another semester off from college, delaying my degree in neuroacoustic studies even further. Over her morning coffee, my mother screamed, and my father said nothing. Then they both left the apartment for work.

Alone with the mahogany obsidian, I renewed my dedication to the truth: my brother could still be alive.

SABANA AND I stayed in touch, talking on the phone every few days. Rosadero felt like the only place where I could understand the man Jakob was becoming, more so than Tucson, and certainly more than the Pearl District. In a careful tone, Sabana told me I could count on seeing her if I chose to return to Rosadero. But her family would no longer be able to host me at the Celenia Inn.

I understood.

When I tried to inquire into the investigation into Mariazul, Sabana cleared her throat, acting as though she had not heard me. When I read about the young man who ran out of the Hotel Jaspeado in handcuffs, I tried to inquire after his fate as well. For a second time, Sabana cleared her throat. Long distance, we could not say anything about the subject.

We talked about things like dating, college, and employment. The tourist off-season was taking its usual toll on Sabana's winter earnings, though her workload at Move Bricks Coffee had doubled due to a co-worker's abrupt resignation. I asked Sabana how much the job paid per hour, and whether Move Bricks' management would be willing to hire someone without any prior service experience.

Sabana laughed, telling me to stay in school. She was determined not to remain in her hometown much longer. Broader, more urban horizons still held her attention: El Paso, Los Angeles, Tucson. Her pitches to the *Texas Observer* may have fallen short so far, but she refused to settle into an adulthood characterized by part-time hours and calibrating an espresso machine.

Still, I held onto the idea of relocation.

Sabana was not the only Rosaderan with whom I stayed in touch. Professor Juanita Ochoa reached out soon after my return to the Pearl District. After a brief but intense conversation about the nature of grief, Professor Ochoa asked what I wanted to do with Jakob's shrine. Holding the mahogany obsidian, I considered the incompleteness of the situation. Anything I said could be wrong.

I may come to pick it up, I said. Would you be all right with that?

Professor Ochoa told me I could visit her home anytime, and stay with her and her granddaughter, Kiki, as long as I wanted. The hospitality she extended my brother would be conferred onto me as well.

I thanked her and told her I would be in touch. At night, I searched the internet to determine what it would take to work as a barista, and what sorts of complications would come with relocating to the West Texas desert.

With his death seemingly preordained, the FBI was unwilling to send their negotiators to try again. The Texas Rangers, while maintaining that the case was still open, also maintained that the trail was still cold. Captain Bryce encouraged my family to pray.

I was becoming more desperate.

When I tried to reach Javier Galvenez, his phone sent me straight to voicemail. He texted back that he had decamped to Mexico City for the month. He did not respond to my other messages.

EVENTUALLY, MY MOTHER told me that I would have to get a job if I wanted to remain in the apartment without continuing my college education. I told her I was planning to move to Rosadero, that I had a promising line of employment down there. She called me an unserious brat and reiterated how she and my father continued working despite their heartbreak.

My father said nothing. He stayed later and later at the office. My mother spent more and more hours on campus.

Amid my internet surfing and day trips, the magnetism Rosadero held over me grew stronger. Even once my mother rescinded her ultimatum, I could not leave alone the idea of moving into Juanita Ochoa's guestroom, living and working in town to feel closer to Jakob. My parents, disbelieving everything I said, would not indulge such a conversation.

Nonplussed, Sabana told me she would put in a good word to the manager at Move Bricks Coffee on my behalf.

Reconfirming with Professor Ochoa that I could stay with her, a plan to return to the borderlands began to cohere, the same way a dream cohered. All I needed was an accelerant.

I would learn his name soon.

DEPUTY ARTURO YBARRA spent the last hour of his shifts staking out the Hotel Jaspeado from across Rosadero's central plaza. Since receiving the search warrant from the Narváez County judiciary—and after conducting several surprise raids to no avail—the Deputy made it his self-assigned mission to watch the place where Alejandro Bartolo Cenote Bautista had been held captive. On the first of these lonely nights, he speculated whether this was what it would be like to work for a police department in San Antonio, Dallas, or Houston.

Rosadero was no longer Rosadero.

Two weeks into his stakeouts, a beat-up mauve pickup truck with Arizona license plates pulled up to the alleyway behind the hotel. The time was around midnight. Deputy Ybarra sat up straight. Out of the pickup stepped a pale white man with long brown hair, dressed in workman boots, a bomber jacket, and wrinkled jeans. The long-haired man strode down the alleyway, purposeful yet oblivious. He entered the building from the door through which Alejandro had escaped.

Deputy Ybarra radioed for backup. His nearest counterparts were in Fort Davis and Alpine, both twenty-five minutes away. In Presidio, his peers were more than an hour away. Biding his time, Deputy Ybarra sat in his SUV, hand on his service weapon, sweat trickling down his cheek.

Twenty minutes later, the long-haired stranger reemerged through the hotel's front door. He stood with his hands on his hips, looking up at the pink marble façade with irritation. He cursed at no one in particular, spitting tobacco onto the wide sidewalk.

Cruisers for Jeff Davis County and Brewster County roared into Rosadero from two different directions. As their red-and-blue lights filled up the empty town, Deputy Ybarra jumped out of his SUV, pistol aimed. Ordering the stranger to his knees and to place his hands on the back of his head, the Deputy charged like the linebacker he used to be in high school.

Without any resistance, the stranger complied. Deputy Ybarra cuffed his wrists just as colleagues from other sheriff's offices joined him. The stranger wore an expression of amusement.

What is your name? Deputy Ybarra asked. ¿Cuál es tu nombre?

The long-haired man grinned, saying nothing. Deputy Ybarra reached into his bomber jacket. He withdrew and safely emptied a small silver pistol. Taking out a wallet, he identified the man by his out-of-state driver's license: Jace Tarrant.

Hauling him to his feet, Deputy Ybarra and a deputy for Jeff Davis County brought Jace into his SUV. He was driven to the back of the Narváez County Courthouse and walked into the county jail. After a brief and pointless interrogation, along with a review of Jace Tarrant's criminal history and running his license plate through an interstate database, the prosecutor's office was called. By the end of the night, a series of charges would be issued against Jace Tarrant, corroborated by Alejandro's statements and other investigative material: racketeering; illegal possession of a firearm by a felon; human trafficking; false imprisonment; slavery. After a few hours, another charge was added: criminal conspiracy.

NEWS OF JACE Tarrant's arrest made regional headlines. Immediately, I called the Narváez County Sheriff's Office, asking for Deputy Ybarra. When he got on the line, I asked whether he believed his new long-haired inmate knew what happened to my brother.

Deputy Ybarra did not deny the possibility. But Mr. Tarrant was refusing to talk. Whatever he knew, he was adept at maintaining his silence. I thanked Deputy Ybarra for his time and wished his family well. Then he hung up on me.

BY THE END of the week, I returned to Rosadero, living in the home of Juanita Ochoa, and working alongside Sabana at Move Bricks Coffee. Upon arriving, my first act was to place the mahogany obsidian with the rest of my brother's shrine.

· Twelve ·

Come and Take It

REPRESENTATIVE AUGUSTUS PRESCOTT Horne stepped out of a bulletproof SUV onto the football field of Fort Davis High Senior School. Clutching a framed portrait against his chest of the late border agent, Denton Pierce, the Congressman acknowledged his audience with an expression of sorrow. A heavyset, blue-eyed, Anglo-Texan man in his late sixties, the Representative was dressed in his preferred attire: a brown cowboy hat with a turquoise-studded band; caiman-skin, steel-toed cowboy boots; and a three-piece, pinstriped, dark gray suit with a yellow tie and yellow pocket handkerchief. An enameled six-shooter revolver pin decorated his left lapel. His right lapel bore an imitation Texas Ranger badge, which he had worn since his days running the Department of Public Safety.

Striding away from the caravan of black SUVs that brought him here—three in total, each reinforced with layers of armor, each branded by Texaulipas Security Solutions—Representative Horne commanded the attention of the memorial service. As he approached the podium at the fifty-yard line, Texaulipas personnel stepped out of the other SUVs, carrying automatic rifles and dressed in black uniforms, several with Arizona flag patches sewn into the shoulders. They were all men, bearded and wearing wraparound sunglasses, some bald and some with crew cuts. Despite only standing a few feet away from each other, they communicated via walkie-talkie, generating a storm of static as they flanked the vehicles.

Supervising the personnel was a square-jawed individual named Matthias Littlejohn, board member and Chief Operating Officer for Texaulipas, as well as tonight's acting head of security. Fortifying the perimeter of the football field in coordination with the Jeff Davis County Sheriff's Office, Matthias Littlejohn sauntered over to Sheriff Edward Lee Horne, son of the Congressman. With his athletic build and boyish smile, Edward Lee Horne was a prodigy of his profession compared to his peers. Satisfied that the memorial service was secure, the sheriff and head of security leaned against a pickup truck, watching Representative Horne take the stand. Beneath the floodlights, the audience on the bleachers was barely visible, a scattering of dots against the twilight sky. Rising behind the football field, a ridge of stone framed the event on an epochal scale.

Congressman Horne placed the portrait on the podium.

Good evening, he said. Thank you for joining me tonight to commemorate the life of Denton Pierce, son of this great county. His murder in the line of duty is an affront to all we hold sacred. Though we are still searching for his killers, his sacrifice will never be forgotten. Let us hold a moment of silence in Agent Pierce's honor.

The Representative raised his head to the sky. The audience—staff and students from the high school, retired and active members of the Border Patrol, a few others—did the same. As the moment of silence came to an end, Congressman Horne began to weep. Wiping a tear from his eye, he continued.

I would like to speak to you tonight about sovereignty. When a nation takes the final shape God intends, there is no greater duty than the preservation of borders. Agent Denton Pierce served in a tradition familiar to all Texans: from the Old Three Hundred to the Texas Rangers to Thin Green Line, there have always been guardians of our land who guarantee liberty for the rest of us. The mission of these men is so much greater than justice.

Representative Horne looked at the framed portrait.

We all know what justice looks like, he said. Give me a rope and a tree and I'll bring justice to whoever wants it. But the work of Denton Pierce was far nobler. He stood watch on the edges of our civilization—yes, our civilization—holding back the invading tide from our small towns. We must never forget that Lady Liberty is a maiden, and that it is the duty of all strong men to defend her maidenly virtue. Denton Pierce was one such defender.

Wiping his face again, he turned to his audience with sudden rage.

And let me tell you something else, folks. If it is a choice between illegals prospering or American families prospering, I choose American families every time. Every. Single. Time. Some might take offense to the term illegals. Those folks need to read their Bible. Like it says in Exodus 23:1, Thou shalt not spread false reports. An illegal is an illegal. A hero is a hero. I've done my share of ride-alongs with the Border Patrol. Hardest working men you'll ever spend a night with. These are the people you want safeguarding America's scrimmage line. That line is an unfriendly place, as Agent Pierce first learned on this very field.

As the night sky descended over Fort Davis, Congressman Horne continued talking about football. Before too long, he took a Biblical turn again, comparing the Border Patrol to God's celestial hierarchy and elevating Denton Pierce to the Archangel Gabriel. By the time his address was over, he had also called for ten-thousand Americans to patrol both sides of the Rio Grande on horseback, just like the old days. He would be co-sponsoring a horseback security bill the moment he returned to Washington, D.C.

Then, concluding his remarks, the Congressman suddenly pulled out an automatic pistol from a holster beneath his jacket.

This was Agent Pierce's service weapon, he said. If he had seen his assailants coming, this is the tool he would have used to defend himself. In commemoration of Agent Pierce's end-of-watch, I am going to demonstrate its power one last time against one of my own vehicles. Stay clear, folks.

On cue, the security personnel trotted away from the caravan of SUVs. Stepping away from the podium and marching to the thirty-yard line, Representative A.P. Horne took the pistol and fired multiple rounds into the side-door to his vehicle. After puncturing the first layer of armor, the Congressman re-holstered the handgun and opened the door. The bullets had failed to enter the interior of the vehicle. The protection offered by Texaulipas Security Solution's custom-made SUVs, the Congressman told his audience, was the best on the market.

The audience was silent.

Signaling to his head of security and his sheriff son, the Congressman bid the mourners farewell and boarded into his shot-up SUV. With the caravan reassembled, sheriff's deputies provided an escort out onto the street for the highway towards Rosadero. Gunsmoke from Denton Pierce's service weapon dissipated over the empty podium.

SABANA AND I stood at the counter of Move Bricks Coffee, watching a video of A.P. Horne's speech on the *Texas Observer*'s newsfeed. A cold, dreary Saturday afternoon in December, we were at the end of the second of my three training shifts, serving about seven customers since opening up that morning. Once I demonstrated I could calibrate and clean the espresso-maker, Sabana decided to share with me the most recent outrages committed by the man in whom my brother had taken so much interest.

Congressman Horne sits on the board of Texaulipas Security Solutions, Sabana said.

Are you serious? I asked.

Sabana nodded.

Keep in mind, this clown is one of the most powerful politicians in a state with a population of about thirty million people. He's been saying and doing shit like this for years, and his constituents love him for it. They love how much the rest of us despise him.

Isn't Fort Davis just up the highway?

They're good people up there, for the most part. If I had to guess, only a few of the folks in the bleachers were actually there for A.P. Horne. I mean, they were probably entertained by the spectacle, as most of us are on some level. But Fort Davis is a tightknit community. When somebody like Denton Pierce gets killed, you can bet everyone will pay their respects, no matter what bullshit they have to sit through first.

Sabana pointed at the square-jawed man in the corner of the video.

This guy over here is much scarier.

Who's that?

Lieutenant Colonel Matthias Littlejohn of the Marines— retired now—better known by his nickname, Tomahawk. Before joining the private sector, he was a commander in the Iraq War, where he ordered the massacre of seventy-three unarmed civilians.

Holy shit. What?

Holy shit is right. During his court martial, Tomahawk Littlejohn insisted he was acting on intelligence suggesting the village where the massacre took place was a terrorist training camp. One of his men had been killed by an IED in the area a few days prior. He was exonerated, of course. Since his retirement, Tomahawk's become a hero to certain political talking heads. I wouldn't be surprised if he ran for governor someday. And won.

I looked at the video's thumbnail, studying the portrait of the deceased agent.

I've seen him before, I said.

Seen who?

Denton Pierce. The woman who kidnapped Mariazul…at the highway checkpoint, she was looking at that exact same portrait.

Before I could say anything more, the door to the coffeeshop opened. Arturo Ybarra walked inside, bundled up in a thick jacket over his uniform, smiling at his niece. Raising a stainless-steel thermos, he ordered a sixteen-ounce Americano with three shots. Sabana took his thermos and passed it to me, her trainee. Returning to the espresso-maker, I got to work on the high-powered drink while Sabana and her uncle chatted. Pouring the steaming mixture into the thermos, I handed the beverage to the deputy in silence, unable to make eye contact.

Arturo paid his niece in cash, gave me a polite nod, and stepped outside.

Sabana looked back at me. Excusing myself for a moment, I went around the counter after her uncle. Bursting into the cold of the converted lumberyard, the deputy and I were alone for the first time since my return to Rosadero.

Arturo, I called out. Wait.

The deputy halted. He turned around, waiting for me to speak.

I want to meet him, I said.

Arturo raised his eyebrows.

Meet who?

The man you arrested. Jace Tarrant. I want to visit him in jail. Is there a waiting list I can get on or something?

Are you out of your mind? Do you have any idea what that man has been charged with?

He knows where my brother is, I said. He knows whether Jakob is still alive. I'm sure of it. He may be the only person I can talk to. The Texas Rangers say the case is cold, Arturo. The FBI isn't touching it. Everybody else is looking for Denton Pierce's killers.

Anna, I can't help you. I would encourage you to reach out to Sheriff Alire. You should try contacting him through his secretary.

I've already done that. She says his schedule is full.

It probably is. He's the top law enforcement official in one of the largest counties in the country. Sorry, Anna. Rules are rules.

I looked at Deputy Ybarra's thermos.

Does he ever go out for coffee? I asked.

I'm sorry?

Unless Sheriff Alire works one hundred sixty-eight hours a week, he has some free time, yeah? Time he spends in the community? I can at least get a ten-minute conversation over coffee, can't I?

Deputy Ybarra shook his head. As he turned to leave, I took him by the shoulder.

Arturo, I'm sorry. I'm sorry I didn't come to you about Mariazul sooner. I didn't know how serious the situation was. Please. Help me out here. I didn't come back to Rosadero for nothing.

The deputy glared at my hand. I withdrew it.

Taking a deep breath, he looked away from me.

On Sunday mornings after church, Deadeye likes to have breakfast at the Chisholm Drugstore & Diner up in Fort Davis, he said. He used to go there with his wife, but ever since she passed, he's been going by himself. He's usually there around ten-thirty. At the very least, he may enjoy having some company. Don't tell him I sent you. Pretty sure he'll figure it out anyway, though.

Thank you, I said.

Arturo shrugged.

How's her brother? I asked. Alejandro? How is he?

He misses his sister, he said. She's all he thinks about.

Deputy Ybarra turned away, continuing back to his service vehicle on the graveled the sidewalk. I stood alone in the lumberyard, my eyes stinging against the wind.

SLEEPING ON THE guest bed in Juanita Ochoa's house, I woke up around midnight. Lying on my side on the college dorm-style mattress, I looked at the electric typewriter on the desk beneath the window. Yellow moonlight bathed the desert, a horizontal crescent radiating over the high plains. My brother's shrine glittered in the darkness. The mahogany obsidian's unpolished surface appeared to be burning. To the side of the obsidian, Mariazul's crucifix—somehow returned from Benicio's custody—had come returned to me, lit up like a shard of sunlight. Covering my eyes, I fell back into a dreamstate. My mind conjured the silhouette of a woman sitting on the edge of a bed somewhere, her skin sweating, red light coming through the blinds, a family on the other side of the bedroom door, listening to the evening news out of Phoenix, Arizona.

When I woke up again in the morning, the crucifix necklace was hanging on a nail over the bed. Then it was gone.

DEADEYE ALIRE'S LAUGHTER filled the Chisholm Drugstore & Diner with late morning mirth. Seated at a booth in the middle of the restaurant, he thanked the waitress as she set down a plate of chicken-fried steak with a side of biscuits and white gravy. Taking a sip out of his coffee mug, the sheriff—today dressed in a tasteful suit for church service—waited for his breakfast to cool off. He opened the newspaper, licked his thumb and forefinger, and turned to the weather forecasts. With his good eye, he scanned the wind and temperature projections across the Narváez Plateau for the upcoming week.

Gonna be chilly, he declared.

The front door opened. Deadeye Alire looked up as I entered. A genuine smile erupted on his face. Before walking over to him, I took a moment to survey the interior of the eatery. Half of it appeared to be a gift shop, comprising trivia books, belt buckles, pecan candies, and hiking guides for the nearby Davis Mountains State Park. The restaurant half was arranged along a decommissioned soda fountain counter and several booths. Photographs of cowboys and cavalrymen decorated the walls. A taxidermized wildcat swung its paws at a taxidermized javelina near the cash register.

On a support beam in the middle of the room, a photograph of Denton Pierce as a high school quarterback stared at me. Several cards of grief and prayer were pinned beneath it.

I walked over to the booth and slid into the seat across from the sheriff. He regarded me with grandfatherly interest.

May I buy you a cup of coffee, Ms. Tatevyan? he asked.

I don't want to take too much of your time, I said.

Arturo told me you want ten minutes, Sheriff Alire said. He also told me to pass along his regret for tattling. Anna, I want you to know that you can talk with me as long as you need. I'm sorry Marlene has been stonewalling you. That's my secretary. She can be overly protective.

The waitress—an elderly Anglo woman—came over and placed an automatic cup of black coffee in front of me with a small saucer of cream and sugar packets. She told me she'd be back with a menu if I felt like ordering anything. She gave Deadeye a wink and headed over to the cash register.

So, Anna, the sheriff said. What is it you wanted to discuss? My deputy left that part out.

I want to visit Jace Tarrant, I said.

Sheriff Alire sipped his coffee.

Why would you want to do that? he asked.

Because he knows where my brother is. When can I see him?

We've already tried questioning him about your brother. Talking to that boy is like pissing up a rope. Ain't no point to it. Anna, if there were a break in the case, you would have heard about it. The Rangers would have gotten in touch.

Have the Rangers interviewed him? I asked.

Sheriff Alire wiped his brushy silver mustache.

Strictly speaking, no. They have not.

Do the Rangers know he's in your custody?

My office left them a couple messages. They haven't gotten back. They're still in the midst of a statewide manhunt over Agent Pierce. They ain't gonna relent on that. They only got so much attention to spare. There's nothing much to do with a case that's gone cold.

Who's his lawyer? I asked.

Jace Tarrant's?

Yeah.

He ain't got a personal lawyer, the sheriff said. He's asserting his constitutional right to public representation. Unfortunately for him, we only got a part-time public defender for Narváez County. She's in Odessa and only comes down once or twice a month.

Can you give me the public defender's number?

Sheriff Alire shook his head.

Listen here, he said. You have my deepest condolences over this mess, but I cannot allow you to converse one-on-one with dangerous criminals. This Tarrant boy is as nasty as they come. You ain't doing yourself any favors getting fixated on him. You wouldn't be doing your brother any favors neither.

Sheriff, I said, as far as I can tell, I'm the only person trying to do favors for my brother right now. It's been over a month. Over a month. We don't know he's dead. And, in case your deputy didn't tell you, I'm not just visiting Rosadero again. I moved here. Even got a job down here. I'm not leaving Texas until I find out what went down, and if you don't feel like doing your job and helping me, so be it. But I will not leave.

A look of mild shock came over Deadeye Alire's face.

You moved to Rosadero? he asked.

I did. Even got a job. So, can I meet Jace Tarrant or what?

The sheriff drummed his thick fingers against the tabletop. He picked up his newspaper and folded it up.

I'd like to have my breakfast first, he said. You're welcome to stay and order something on my tab. After this, we'll drive back. We ain't need to contact the fella's attorney. He's just gotta approve your visitation himself. There ain't much I can do if he declines. Sound all right with you?

I nodded. Sheriff Alire tucked his napkin into his collar and began to carve out pieces of his steak. I sat with my coffee, an unnamable feeling rising in my chest.

· Thirteen ·

Visiting Hours

I PULL INTO *the lot of the abandoned restaurant, taking the same shaded spot where Special Agent Washington and I did our stakeout two weeks earlier. Above the truck stop, the sky is banded with hues of early morning orange. Just like last time, this is an exercise in patience. This time, I am alone. The only people who know I am here are Carlos, who is programming all day, and Javier, who is in the middle of line-editing his manuscript. My intention in Lordsburg is difficult to articulate, even to myself. But I do know this: the story I aspire to tell needs Jace Tarrant.*

Time passes. The sun rises. Eighteen-wheelers and passenger vehicles come into the truck stop, fuel, and depart. Jace Tarrant's pickup truck is nowhere. Waiting with neither companionship nor a clear goal, the monotony is almost unbearable, even with the radio. My mind drifts into ever more esoteric places. I notice that the abandoned restaurant next to me is named after the Anasazi, the logo a faded kachina doing a millennia-old ceremonial dance. The faded kachina is striped and feathered with the head of a buffalo, holding a spear. My mind connects the kachina to the abandoned mining town by the Arizona border, a collection of decaying hovels also lost to a consciousness that no longer exists.

My internal elaborations circle back to my body: four hours into my stakeout, I need to piss. Unbuckling my seatbelt, I leave my audio recorder and notepad on the front passenger seat. Crossing into the truck stop lot, I walk quickly into the store, cutting a direct path to the men's room. When I'm done, I float over to the coffee machine, allowing myself an over-sweetened indulgence. I set a cardboard cup beneath the nozzle for a peanut-butter cappuccino, trying not to think about the nutritional impact.

As I press the button, a man approaches me. He has long, greasy brown hair. He is without his jacket today, dressed only in a white undershirt, baggy jeans, and boots. His skin is grayish with small, inexplicable scars on his shoulders and arms.

Jace Tarrant's appearance is so nonchalant, I'm almost in shock. We are mere inches from one another. He grins with stained yellow teeth.

All alone, huh? he says. Benicio couldn't get away from El Paso? Does he even know you're here right now?

I say nothing.

Jace laughs.

The Gila Gulch, he says. Tomorrow at seven. We'll talk in Tucson.

With that, he takes the energy drink in his hand and walks out the automatic doors; either he's already paid, or he has just shoplifted. With trembling fingers, I finish filling my sixteen-ounce container, lidding it and paying quickly.

As I leave the store, there is no sign of Jace anywhere, or his truck. But on the way to my station wagon, I stop. A green and white cruiser for the Border Patrol has parked by my car. The agent in the driver's seat is a woman with frizzy brown hair tied back in a ponytail, wearing reflector sunglasses, a toothpick sticking out of her mouth. She is staring at my front license plate.

She looks at me. Acting casual, I continue to my vehicle, giving her the fastest of nods. The agent turns the key in the ignition and begins to drive away. I stand by my sideview mirror, lingering for a moment. The agent notices. Her vehicle slows down. I clamber back into my station wagon, locking the doors and turning on the engine. I take out my phone and dial Javier, though I do not know how he could help me.

The agent picks up speed, her cruiser rolling out of the truck stop. When Javier answers, all I can tell him is that I'd like him to accompany me to the Gila Gulch bar on Fourth Avenue tomorrow night.

He says I sound frightened. He asks if everything is okay.

I tell him I love him.

DEPUTY YBARRA ESCORTED me down the basement hallway of the Narváez County Courthouse. Despite the small facility's modernization several years ago, there were only three cells, each with antiquated iron bars. The suspect I had come to see was the jail's sole occupant, housed in the middle cell.

Before descending from upstairs, we had gone over the rules of conduct: not getting to close, not passing anything to or accepting anything from the inmate. For the duration of the visit, Deputy Ybarra would stand at the desk at the end of the hallway, monitoring our communications.

I arrived at the cell, keeping a distance of at least five feet. Jace Tarrant was sitting in his bed, leaning into his knuckles. With his hunched posture, he had a slight potbelly. He was older than I expected—somewhere in his late-thirties—rough and unshaven, still in the clothing he was arrested in.

He glanced at me.

You look just like your brother, he said. Just like Jakob. Same eyes, same cheekbones. Same nose, same chin. Same girlish figure.

Taking a step forward, I looked at Deputy Ybarra. He shook his head.

The man in the cell studied my every microexpression.

Tell me my brother is alive, I said.

Jace stood up. He walked over to the stainless-steel sink, spitting a brown mass into the drain. He returned to his bed, picked up a copy of the Bible, lay on his back, and began to read. The soles of his black boots were all he would show me.

I sat down on the floor, crossing my legs and folding my hands in my lap. We would not speak. But he would not tell me to leave.

This was the closest I had come to my brother since arriving in Texas.

JAVIER IS UNEQUIVOCAL: this meeting will endanger us. Nothing I say can dissuade him.

He and I have been arguing for almost a day and a half. To wear down his resistance, I list the risks he took covering the migrant trails in Mexico. His face reddens. He reminds me of his time training with the Zapatistas, the personal mentoring he received from the Subcomandante, the powerful protections his family enjoys. Moreover, his mission was different from mine: journalism. I am only an MFA student, honing the craft of fiction. I have no good reason to imperil myself.

Sitting next to me on the sofa, he takes my hands. The air conditioner is the only noise in the casita. The high temperature for the day has broken, rolling back into the lesser heat of evening. But we are both sweating, wearing nothing but boxers and t-shirts.

Let's look ahead to better things, Javier says. I want to buy a house in Rosadero. Juanita's guest bed is cozy, but I want a place where we can spread out and be ourselves. Somewhere tasteful. I'm more than happy to take care of the down payment.

I shake my head.

My work is serious, I say. And I'm serious. I want to craft a credible story. I'm meeting this guy at the bar. I'm not stupid. I recognize that this guy is trouble. That's why I want backup. But I will be fine going on my own. This may be my only opportunity to get straight answers on questions I can't bring to Benicio.

Like what? Javier asks.

A knock at the door interrupts us. Quickly, I slip on a pair of jeans and cross the length of the room. Javier leans into the couch, aggrieved.

I open the door. Carlos is standing before me. He's pale.

Hey, I say. What's up?

You have a visitor, he says. He's on my front porch. He won't leave. I told him to go down the driveway to speak with you, but he refuses. He wants me to bring you to him. Please make him go away.

Javier sits up.

Hey, Carlos. Is he a long-haired white boy? Do you get criminal vibes off him?

Carlos nods. I roll my eyes.

Let me put on my shoes, I say. We're getting a drink tonight.

How did he know to come here? Javier asks. You didn't give this guy your address, did you?

No, I say. Relax.

I thought you said this meetup was happening at seven, Javier says. It's not even six-thirty.

I'll take care of this.

Javier's eyes burn as I close the door. Without another word, Carlos retreats up the backstairs into the main house, bolting the kitchen door. I stride up the driveway. Jace Tarrant is waiting for me on the porch, highly amused. Despite the summer temperature, he's wearing his bomber jacket.

For a moment, my mind catalogues all the surprises his jacket could be concealing.

What are you doing here? I ask.

He laughs.

I got in town early. Thought I'd come by and offer you a ride.

His pickup truck is parked on the curb, a rundown eyesore against the adobe-colored palette of the neighborhood. The glee in his eyes increases. Jace knows the effect of his unannounced arrival.

How did you find me? I ask.

Your license plate, he says.

He doesn't need to say more.

He looks over my shoulder. I turn to see Javier, now fully clothed and apparently having had enough time to brush and ponytail his hair. He is carrying my backpack and keys.

Caballeros, he says. I hear we're going out for a night of drinking. Mind if I come with?

Not at all, Jace says.

Jakob and I are walking there, Javier says. You all right if we meet you in fifteen minutes? You can find us a table.

The long-haired stranger glares. Eventually, he nods. Descending from the front porch to the sidewalk, he climbs into his pickup truck. The vehicle roars, the tailpipe erupting with black smoke. He peels away from the curb. The sound of his engine tears through the tranquility of Dunbar/Spring.

Javier passes me a black, cylindrical object.

Pepper spray, he says.

He takes off down the sidewalk. Pocketing the little canister, I follow him from several feet behind. We keep this estranged pace until reaching Fourth Avenue, where he takes my hand. For the last block to the Gila Gulch—a dive bar in a nondescript blue building—we feel like a couple again.

We enter the Gulch.

Jace Tarrant is sitting by the jukebox in the corner of the bar. Three beer bottles are in front of him, one for each of us, glass sweating with condensation, his most of the way consumed. Javier and I take our seats. Immediately, Javier opens my backpack and produces my audio recorder. He presses the on-button.

Jace smirks. Both he and Javier look at me. That's when I remember that I'm the reason we're all sitting here.

I take the recorder, directing it at the stranger. Boisterous cowpunk is blasting out of the speakers around us. Still, I resolve to document every millisecond of this encounter.

Could you please state the date and your name? I ask.

Jace drinks his beer.

It's September, he says. My name is Jace Silver Tarrant. Silver because my birth mom had silver in her teeth, Tarrant because that's the county I was born in. Your name is Jakob Tatevyan—which is the dumbest shit I've ever heard, by the way—and you are from Portland, Oregon. Last year, your name came up in a police report. Something about a scuffle with a naked woman. That's some dirty business, Jakob. Dirty business.

Javier shoots me a look. I ignore him.

You used to be a member of the Ditat Deus militia, I say. A group that was being investigated for racketeering. You yourself are a two-time convicted felon in the state of Texas.

Convictions ain't shit, Jace says. It's easy to read a file, Jakob. Harder to know the truth, ain't it?

That's why I'm here, I say. To know the truth. I'm writing a novel about—

Wait, wait, wait. You're writing—a what? A novel? That's what this fruity business is about? You're tagging along with that Benicio Washington asshole and stalking me because you're writing a fucking novel? What is it, some gay cowboy shit? That's what's going on between you two, ain't it? Maricónes. Putos. I know what you are.

He makes grotesque kissing noises. Javier takes his beer and walks over to the bar, sitting on a stool near a pair of tanned bikers, pretending he came in alone. Aside from his glances towards our table, his act is convincing.

I lean in towards Jace. He leans in towards me, mimicking my seriousness.

I'm writing about power, I say. How it distributes itself on the border. This is a story that touches all of us. But you're closer than most. I don't want to write about you. I want to write about who you take orders from. You can remain anonymous, if you like. In fact, it'll be better that way. All I ask is you tell me who you answer to.

Jace finishes his beer.

You want to know about Texaulipas, he says. That's why we're here, ain't it?

Yes. And A.P. Horne.

He raises his eyebrows.

No kidding, he says. That's interesting.

Have you met the Congressman? I ask.

Nah. Not me. But I got buddies down in Laredo who see our man once or twice a month. Buddies who work in that security company of his.

The same buddies who were part of Ditat Deus?

Jace smiles.

You don't know what you think you know.

Tell me what I need to do. What is the Congressman's connection to Ditat Deus?

You tried calling Representative Horne's office? You've been spending so much time in Rosadero lately, you're practically a constituent.

How do you know I spend time in Rosadero?

Jace shrugs.

Never mind, I say. Look. Even if I get in touch with him, he's not going to say anything to me. Not about this.

No shit, vaquero. But you need to think about who you're pursuing. A.P. Horne is, above all, a man about business. His company has two headquarters, right? One in Laredo, one in Nuevo Laredo. I can guarantee you don't know too much about his counterparts on the other side of the river. One in particular will interest you.

Jace reaches into his jacket. He pulls out a white envelope, dropping it onto the table. I pick it up. By instinct, I hold the envelope up to the light, as though I were working retail again, checking for counterfeit bills. I can tell that the envelope is filled with photographs, the type taken by a disposable camera. When I turn it over, three letters appear on the front:

D.Á.V.

What do these letters stand for? I ask.

A warning, Jace says. You'd be a brave man to open it.

Why are you giving this to me?

Because now you are part of this thing. Because now the story is about you, too.

Jace takes my beer. He cracks it open, drinking half of it before lurching to his feet. He sweeps the dim bar with his eyes before settling on Javier.

Your friend over there is a liar, he says. I know all about the Nogales Twenty-One. He was there when they got arrested, but he wasn't part of them. He didn't get himself dirty. And he sure as hell never traveled no trails in Mexico or rode on top of La Bestia. The only thing he did was stir up some shit and write about it. Any pendejo can do that. He ain't hard. Just some rich kid in the desert.

Without explanation, he snatches the envelope back off the table. He takes out a black marker from inside his jacket, writes something on the back, then tosses the envelope back down.

Text me at this number, he says. See you soon, vaquero.

Rolling his neck around his shoulders, Jace heads out of the dive bar as though we had never met. I turn off my recorder, stashing it in my backpack with my notepad and the forbidden envelope.

I approach Javier. His breathing is heavy, irregular. Placing a hand on his shoulder, I want to comfort him, to take him back to when I was only a grad student and he was only an activist, and all we had in Tucson was romance. But it's impossible.

Do you know what D.Á.V. stands for? I ask.

Javier raises his head. He leaps off his stool and runs into the bathroom by the pool table. Leaving the door to the restroom and the stall open, he collapses onto his knees, puking into the toilet to cheers and groans. The two bikers are in hysterics. They would probably be more hysterical if they knew about Javier's familial and artistic pedigrees, savoring his downfall in a sweltering Tucson dive.

I wait outside. He comes out twenty minutes later with nothing to say.

AFTER FORTY SILENT minutes in front of Jace Tarrant's cell, Deputy Ybarra terminated the visit. As I stood up and walked away, I heard something heavy and flat—presumably the Bible—fall against the concrete floor.

I asked Deputy Ybarra when I could come back. He told me to check-in during the week. Sheriff Alire would have to sign off, and, once again, so would Jace. Returning to the courthouse lobby, I shook Deputy Ybarra's hand, and made for the front door. On my way out, I passed Benicio Washington, who had just come in. Out of uniform and wearing a fur-lined denim jacket, I almost failed to recognize him. Under one arm, he was carrying a thick case folder, labeled Confidential. On the tab of the folder were five words I was sure I was not meant to see.

Mia Jo Taylor, TX DFPS.

Benicio caught my eye, and with refined quickness, hid the folder behind his back. I stopped, nodding in his direction. We had not encountered one another since the dinner with the Canul twins.

Hey, I said.

Afternoon, Anna, he said. I'd heard you came back to Rosadero.

Yes sir, I did. Moved here, in fact.

Benicio smiled.

It's a special town, isn't it?

Yeah, definitely. Jakob certainly thought so.

Benicio sighed.

I'm glad I caught up with you, actually, he said. Do you have a minute?

Is it about Agent Taylor?

You're perceptive, Anna. Just like Jakob. Unfortunately, that is not your business.

I'd say it is very much my business, Benicio. What do you have on Agent Taylor?

Nothing I can share with you. Look, Anna…I want to apologize to you, personally, and to your family. I let your brother come too close to dangerous elements. He's a strong-willed young man—I'm sure you know that—but I should have enforced certain boundaries between him and his subject matter. I should have told him no. The least I can do is keep you from making the same mistakes.

You're too late, I said.

Benicio frowned.

I just spent the last hour with Jace Tarrant, I said. He's the key to all this. He knows the truth. Assuming the sheriff clears it, I'm coming back later this week. You have no authority over what I do, Special Agent Washington.

You're right, he said. You're right. But I can advocate.

You can, I said. In fact, you're the only person to take any responsibility so far. Thank you, I guess.

We all deserve better, Benicio said.

He checked the time on his watch. Excusing himself, he continued past me towards the underground jail. On the stairwell, he ran into Deputy Ybarra. With the courthouse silent in its Sunday emptiness, I could hear almost every word exchanged between the two men.

Special Agent Washington had been suspended from the Border Patrol. He was the subject of a very serious disciplinary hearing. Babajide Canul and Cadmael Canul never made it to Sabana's grandparents in El Paso.

And Agent Taylor had been missing for several weeks.

· Fourteen ·

Veracruzanos Por Vida

LESS THAN THREE miles from his former place of captivity, Alejandro Bartolo Cenote Bautista enjoyed the most generous motel room he had experienced on either side of the Rio Grande. Lounging on a king-sized bed in the Celenia Inn, his sheets were changed and cleaned by Angelica Ybarra once every two days. Three times a day, he was invited to the apartment behind the motel office to share in a homecooked meal. On Sunday mornings, he was driven into town by Arturo to participate in mass. He was outfitted with new clothing purchased at an outlet mall in Alpine, and though he had not been allowed to come on the shopping trip, his selections from the catalogue were all honored. Toiletries were purchased on his behalf, all expenses at the Celenia Inn waived.

He would soon be transported to the home of Lucia Ybarra and Rafael Ybarra in El Paso, where he would begin his apprenticeship in the Ybarra family bakery. On top of the monthly stipend from the bakery, Alejandro could count on free room and board with the Ybarras while his legal status was fought for by a pro bono attorney. His fulfillment of his apprenticeship duties would be the keystone argument to the reacquisition of a green card, a provision the young Veracruzano did not understand.

He had already been a legal resident in the United States for over a year.

Alejandro had tried to explain his status to Deputy Ybarra and Special Agent Washington. Arriving in Juárez, he and Mariazul applied for asylum, waiting several months in detention in El Paso before completing and passing their credible fear interviews, approved by an immigration judge to settle as refugees. Fewer than a dozen Mexicans each year were allowed into the United States on such a basis. With the help of a pro bono attorney, a process that could take a decade took under a year—an attorney associated, it turned out, with Madre Lucia Ybarra's church and labor center.

The good fortune of the Bautistas was due to the holocaust of their home village near the Río Coatzacoalcos. Named La Lancha due to the area's traditional role as a ferry landing, the adjoining town had aroused the pecuniary interests of not one but two competing cartels. First came the Bizantinos, who arrived with pamphlets quoting the New Testament to justify their arrival. Identifying themselves as the foot-soldiers of a new religious order, the Bizantinos specialized in smuggling and extortion. Their reign over the riverport manifested in the collection of tithes from local businesses and schools, money which would be delivered to the new local boss, known as El Patriarca, who reported directly to the cartel's papacy in Nuevo Laredo. Placing a massive ceramic bust of their kingpin—a businessman known as Don Gregorio— at the northern entrance to town, their control over La Lancha proved to be a period of peace, lasting about a decade, though the tithes exacerbated the poverty of the already desperate river village.

Then came the Cóndores.

They struck at four-thirty in the morning, boiling into the village like pestilence. Out of the jungle, scores of anonymous men in black fatigues and ski-masks rolled out of SUVs bearing the insignia of the Cóndores del Norte. Sealing off the town at both ends, the marauders secured the riverport immediately.

They set everything on fire.

Storefront after storefront burned along the commercial strip, igniting apartments and thatched-palm shacks. With their automatic rifles, the men shot down survivors as they raced out of the inferno, laughing as their victims twisted in heat and fear.

Somehow, Mariazul and Alejandro escaped into the river, swimming across the current to its southern side. Their parents ran to the family tienda, never to be seen again; never to be buried. From the opposite bank of the Coatzacoalcos, the new orphans felt hypnotized by the orange flames, intoxicated by the billowing smoke. In their earliest childhood memories, they had heard warnings from elders about what would happen if the Pico de Orizaba erupted, the stratovolcano whose preeminence in Indigenous lore had carried into government evacuation plans. The burning of La Lancha looked like something out of myth: violent magma imposing its will upon the innocent.

The Cóndores seized the village as an infrastructural asset for petroleum-trafficking. Cleared of its inhabitants, the charred remains operated as an import-export site, the former town minimized into a hideous parody of efficiency.

With no money and no family, Mariazul and Alejandro set out for El Norte, hoping their story could save them. In the Mexican media, official information on the destruction of their hometown was hard to corroborate. Rumors on narcoblogs claimed over a hundred were killed. One journalist from Oaxaca traveled to neighboring towns, questioning survivors. After conducting three interviews, the journalist was picked up by a black SUV, his decapitated head later rolled into a local church during mass. In the new totalitarianism of the Cóndores, gossip resulted in capital punishment.

Still, the firestorm of La Lancha had been confirmed by the Drug Enforcement Agency. The unique horror of the event granted special consideration to those who had survived. But even with this privileged status, almost eight months passed before the Bautista siblings could depart their temporary home in the Anapra colonia on the western outskirts of Juárez. Processed and approved at last by the U.S. Department of Health and Human Resources, the Office of Refugee Resettlement moved Mariazul and Alejandro into a two-bedroom apartment in South Tucson. They worked at a furniture factory on the outermost edge of the metropolitan area, taking city buses to and from work six days a week. While assembling footstools, Mariazul sometimes practiced English with her co-workers, and tried to avoid the leers of her male supervisors. In the upholstery department, Alejandro put himself in competition to outwork every man on his team. More often than not, he won. But because his English was not improving, neither was his place in the factory's hierarchy. For the time being, he did not mind.

As their first year in the United States passed, the Bautistas achieved a material status unthinkable in La Lancha. Despite the long rides on public transit, their unreliable air conditioning, the necessity for security bars on their windows—despite the police and neighborhood dramas that sometimes roiled through their street—their lives were steady. Sometimes, they wept, reflecting on the annihilation of home that had resulted in their comfort. The siblings carried this contradiction of grief in their hearts every night, right up until Alejandro's abduction.

Leaving the factory by himself at the end of a twelve-hour shift, Alejandro was approached by Jace Tarrant, who pulled out his silver pistol and led him into an alleyway. Handcuffing him from behind, the long-haired man informed Alejandro that he was with Immigration and Customs, that he knew that Alejandro was in the country illegally, and that Alejandro's family would have to pay for his release. Tying a bag over his head and shoving him into the back of his pickup truck, Jace Tarrant conveyed the young Veracruzano hundreds of miles away. Alejandro would not be allowed to see anything again until he arrived in the abandoned kitchen of the Hotel Jaspeado.

Handcuffed to an industrial-scale stove, the bag was removed at last. The long-haired man was standing with a female Border Patrol agent. With the kitchen illuminated only by electric lamps, the two Americans appeared demonic. In broken Spanish, Jace explained to Alejandro that bail was no longer an option. As punishment for his illegal status, he would work. Jace detailed how Alejandro would now be kept in custody via a special guardianship program in which unauthorized migrants would be paroled to employers, their paychecks diverted to paying off civil penalties.

Then came the interrogation.

On his first night in the kitchen, the border agent—a white, frizzy-haired woman wearing mirrored sunglasses—burned him with cigarettes and kicked him in the diaphragm, demanding he tell her whether he had any other family members in the country. When he let slip the name of his sister, the agent beat him harder, seemingly in retaliation for the very betrayal she had just induced.

As more days and nights—and more beatings—passed in the kitchen, Alejandro prayed. He took the beatings as they came, and in the back of his mind, began to understand that his abductors did not know what to do with him. After Jace relieved Alejandro of his shirt, shoes, and socks to discourage running away, his foremost antagonist became the cold seeping into the marble building. The last few days in the hotel felt hallucinatory, a blur of random assaults. He saw faces and had conversations he did not recall.

He could not remember, for example, how he came to his moment of escape. As though locating himself within a lucid dream, he found himself standing alone in the kitchen, the door to the alleyway open. He was still handcuffed, but not to the stove. Out of this nightmare, he ran towards the gas station where Deputy Ybarra intercepted him.

For the duration of his imprisonment, two certainties forged Alejandro's resolve to survive: that he had legal documentation, and that he would reconnect with his sister again.

In the Celenia Inn, he could not believe he had lost both.

Regarding his legal status, Special Agent Washington had checked the databases: there were no records of either Mariazul or Alejandro receiving green cards. Though he had strong reason to believe that a malicious actor had deleted such information, he could produce no evidence. For all intents and purposes, the Bautistas had lost asylum. While his situation was sorted out, Alejandro would need to remain in the shadows.

What about my sister? he asked in Spanish. Where is she?

Deputy Ybarra got on one knee. Alejandro was sitting on the edge of the bed. The deputy passed along what I had told him about Mariazul's abduction, confirming that the border agent who appeared in the Hotel Jaspeado matched the description of the woman who had taken Mariazul. He and Benicio were doing everything they could to locate her. Mariazul, they believed, had been taken back to Arizona, the Phoenix metropolitan area the most likely destination. They would update Alejandro as they could. But their resources were limited, especially the resource of time.

Alejandro took his sister's backpack from Deputy Ybarra. Her bag, torn and dusty, was the only evidence he had of the trials they had endured together. He did not look at her necklace. Unable to leave the motel, he spent his days consuming television: black-and-white Westerns, where heroic Anglos shot down Mexican bandits and Apache and Comanche warriors; cable news programs where celebrities debated with politicians; commercials for prescription drugs, for-profit colleges, bullion investment services for gold and silver. With his cursory English, all he had were flashing images, interchangeable and fleeting. His room, with its bland comforts and isolation, felt like a set-piece, an extension of the lightshow before him.

For now, Alejandro inhabited an America of the senses.

JUANITA OCHOA WAS sitting at her kitchen table in her red bathrobe with a mug of coffee, perusing a wide book of high-resolution photographs. She looked up at me with surprise, which quickly shifted into concern. It was five-thirty in the morning.

Did Kiki wake you? she asked.

No, I said. I'm opening Move Bricks today. It's my first non-training shift. Guess I'm a little nervous, so I got up early.

Juanita nodded.

Well, I'm glad my granddaughter did not disturb you. Some nights, she'll wake up screaming. She has night terrors, mostly about Nuevo Laredo. One of the last things she saw was a parade of naked, blindfolded men being led down the street at gunpoint.

The professor returned to her book as though she had said nothing. I poured myself a cup of coffee and prepared a bowl of instant oatmeal before settling down at the table's other end. As I waited for breakfast to cool, I looked at the upside-down photographs.

What's that? I asked

Justin Lehenwesen's untitled outdoor pieces, Juanita said. Do you know his work?

Not really. I suppose I should, now that I'm living here. The Lehenwesen Foundation is just down the road, yeah?

Right across the highway. I still remember the first time I saw it. I was home from my doctoral studies for Easter. Some random Anglo had purchased the abandoned army base and converted into the strangest garden of installations. You have to remember, Anna, this town didn't have an art scene until Justin Lehenwesen. Most of us old-timers still don't know what to make of it. Took me a long time to appreciate his work. That only happened once someone explained to me that they weren't sculptures, but objects.

What's the difference?

Juanita reoriented her book towards my perspective, allowing me to see the untitled pieces for myself. Hollow prisms of concrete and stainless-steel sat in clusters across the desert grasslands. Photographed at different times of day and under different weather conditions—including an impending thunderhead—the pieces appeared to expand, elongate, widen, reduce, hover, or bury themselves into the soil. The horizon transformed in every photograph, as well as the colors of the land and sky, contrasting and creating new forms despite remaining in permanent positions.

Think of them as visual anchors, Juanita told me, guiding your attention as though the landscape were a three-dimensional matrix. Your movement and the movement of light are the actual artworks. If you really immerse yourself in Lehenwesen's ideas, you develop insight into everything from architecture to how poetry assembles itself on the page. Please borrow this book, if you'd like.

I nodded. Despite my tired eyes, I tried to pay close attention to the triumphs of Justin Lehenwesen's vision. Juanita sipped her coffee.

Not that it's my business, she said. But what were you hoping would come from visiting this man in jail?

I don't know, I said.

Juanita looked out the window, contemplating the blue-black darkness.

The presumption of innocence is necessary, she said, even with this Jace Tarrant fellow. We cannot know his true story. I often think about my grandfather, one of the first men ever arrested by the Border Patrol. Ignacio Velázquez. It was the late 1920s. The Patrol was only a few years old, a rag-tag group of random hires. All but a few were Anglo. My grandfather worked as a sheepherder, but with the Prohibition era in full swing, he thought he'd make some extra money. He had a connection in Ojinaga. Tejanos were poorer back then—the poverty a century ago was another kind altogether. Anyway, two border agents stopped him on the highway between Rosadero and Van Horn, arresting him after finding a barrel of bootlegged mezcal in the back of his Model T. He was guilty as a sinner on the sabbath, but he fought the case. He grabbed the nearest attorney he could find and accused the agents of racial profiling. As a citizen, the agents had no standing to pull him over.

Juanita sighed.

He lost, she said. Quickly. The case didn't make it to a jury. The judge ruled that, because we are so close to Mexico, it was reasonable for the Border Patrol to pull him. Driving while Mexican was codified into case law early. It did not matter that the agents had no real probable cause. A scholar named Kelly Lytle Hernández wrote an excellent book about all this. I can lend that to you, too.

I listened in silence, eating my oatmeal, checking the time on my phone. Juanita waited for me to look up at her.

Institutions don't think, Anna, she said. They obey the power that already exists. I pray for your brother. But without mercy from the people who took him, I'm afraid we must brace ourselves. He will not be rescued by justice.

I nodded.

I pray for my brother too, I said.

I gulped down the remainder of my coffee and took my half-eaten oatmeal to the kitchen sink. Before leaving for Move Bricks Coffee, I took the Justin Lehenwesen book from the kitchen table. Juanita wished me luck as I strode out the door past the makeshift restaurant portion of her home. In front of Adelitas Burrito, ice glittered on the highway to Mexico.

HIS NAME IS Dionisio Ángel Verrado.

I spread the photographs across the kitchen counter, a dozen in total. The subject of each picture is a broad-shouldered man who looks to be in his late thirties, cleanshaven with spiky gelled hair. This is D.Á.V. He looks vapid and self-impressed, adhering to the latest trends in designer jeans, designer sunglasses, and designer cowboy boots, wearing a rotating ensemble of bright guayabera shirts: gold, red, lime-green. White is his favorite. Taken together, the photographs depict a man in perpetual celebration: kicking back with a martini on a beach outside Corpus Christi; playing blackjack at a casino on the Kickapoo Reservation near Eagle Pass; ordering falafels from an artisan food truck in Rosadero; laughing and smoking his cigar behind the Lehenwesen Foundation; attending a rodeo in Fort Worth. Dates and locations are written on the back of each image.

The most compelling photographs—the ones pertinent to why Jace and I met—come from the same place: a private hunting ranch belonging to A.P. Horne. On a sprawling estate outside the South Texas town of Falfurrias, Dionisio hunts and poses with nilgai. Imported from India, the exotic antelopes lurk with primitive blue faces under sprawling live oaks. In the winter mating season, males spar by locking horns and bashing skulls, thrashing their thick bodies in storms of dust. Dionisio Ángel Verrado and a man identified as Tomahawk Littlejohn watch the animals spar in the scrublands. The two men appear to form something of a hunting partnership. They pose next to their trophies with pride, displaying the high-powered rifles that dropped the half-ton beasts.

From a cursory internet search, I learn the Falfurrias Border Patrol Sector is home to the highest death rate of undocumented migrants in the country. Thousands of dried and scattered corpses have been recovered from the landscape. In the mesquite thickets surrounding D.Á.V.'s hunting parties, secluded eyes were watching, waiting for darkness to fall.

I learn all about Tomahawk Littlejohn's war crimes in Iraq. His records are not difficult to find.

When I type Dionisio Ángel Verrado into my phone's browser, I am referred to the Anglicization of his title: The Prince of Nuevo Laredo. At first, concrete details about the Prince are scarce. But after some prowling, I uncover a narcoblog based in the Mexican state of Tamaulipas. In translated English, post after anonymous post asserts the Prince's alleged centrality to a paramilitary syndicate called the Cóndores del Norte, who appear to control territory from Nuevo Laredo to as far away as Michoacán and the Mexican Gulf Coast.

While I research, Javier simmers on the sofa. When I tell him about the narcoblog, he explodes.

194

Don't you know how dangerous this is? he yells. In Mexico, journalists get killed every day for looking into people like Dionisio Ángel Verrado. You're putting so much on the line, and for what? A grad school project? What's the point of this, Jakob?

Javier rocks back and forth, clutching a pillow close to his chest. He looks like a small boy.

I'm trying to write a true story, I say, about the society we live in.

You want the truth? Javier yells. Look at my family. Look at my father, Enrique Galvenez. Do you know why my family has so much money? Because my father's job at the bank is to launder cartel profits into the global economy. He cleans blood money, turning it into equity and asset portfolios. He enables terrorists and gangsters so that he can take home commissions, so that my mother and sisters can live in a gated community and enjoy the high life.

Javier, I say. I'm sorry. I never—

And you know what else? That blood money has funded my art. It has enabled everything I cherish about who I am. I've tried so hard to get away from all that. And here you are, some dilettante whiteboy with no idea who you're chasing, pulling me into all the shit I tried to leave behind.

He tosses the pillow onto the floor, stands up, and walks to the rolling closet, where he takes out his duffel-bag of clothing. He stares at me, as though daring me to ask him to calm down.

I'm sorry, I say.

Javier walks out, slamming the door behind him. A few hours later, he texts me to say he's in Rosadero. He will be there for the rest of the month to supervise the installation of his exhibit at the Naranjoven Gallery.

A WEEK INTO Alejandro's stay at the Celenia Inn, Immigration and Customs Enforcement executed a dawn raid in the suburban foothills of the Superstition Mountains, acting on a tip by wintering retirees. For the last few nights, a man and woman from Idaho woke up to expensive cars and suspicious men ushering women in and out of the faux-mission domicile across the street. On the morning of the raid, they watched as an ICE battering ram cracked open the front door, murmuring in awe as armored agents cuffed menacing bajadores and as well as almost a dozen women. The raid would be reported in the metro section in Phoenix's daily newspaper, as well as the *East Valley Tribune.* The safehouse appeared to be linked to a broader criminal conspiracy, though no further arrests were immediately expected. The women held in the house were all undocumented, and were all taken to a private detention center in Pinal County, where they would await deportation to their countries of origin.

Only one was bound for Mexico, scheduled by a judge to be sent to Veracruz.

· Fifteen ·

Locked Rooms

SHERIFF DEADEYE ALIRE called my phone twice in the night before I picked up. Vibrating across the wooden surface of Jakob's writing desk, I thought Kiki Ochoa was screaming. Instead, I found myself hearing the only news I had cared about for almost seven weeks.

Ms. Tatevyan, we've had a major break in the search for your brother. Sorry to call at this late hour. Is this a good time?

A good time would have been a month and a half ago, I said.

Sheriff Alire cleared his throat.

We believe your brother is being held in a house in the Panhandle. That's a few hundred miles north of here. Deputies for the Erastus County Sheriff's Office are sweeping through the vicinity. Coming up with a specific address has proven difficult. The area is mostly farm country. Still, we believe him to be alive. We don't know if his kidnappers are still at the site. As a result, Erastus County is taking every precaution. But I thought you should know. If we're going to get to Jakob, it could be a matter of hours.

Jace knew all along, didn't he? I asked.

We're acting on intelligence culled from several sources, Sheriff Alire said. But the Texas Rangers did sit Mr. Tarrant down for an interview yesterday evening. Not only did he provide this tip about your brother, but he admitted to a slew of other crimes. Mr. Tarrant is taking sole responsibility for charges related to that boy imprisoned in the Hotel Jaspeado. Now, here's the part you won't believe. Are you ready?

I'm listening.

I don't know what the old boys had over him, but the Rangers got him talking about the murder of Denton Pierce. When Captain Bryce and Ranger Flores emerged, they had a signed confession. Mr. Tarrant will never breathe free air again, but at least this way, he's spared himself lethal injection. Can you believe it, Ms. Tatevyan?

No, I said. I can't.

The Texas Rangers always get results. But now, I must draw your attention to something of a peculiar matter.

What's that?

Mr. Tarrant has requested to see you.

What? Why?

I'd wager emotions are running high. He's just avoided death row but landed himself in the penitentiary for the rest of his natural life. He wants to say his piece to whoever'll listen. I'd advise you against giving the man an audience, but you can expect my office to accommodate any decision. Due to the gravity of his confessions, Mr. Tarrant will soon be transferred to a more secure facility ahead of his hearing. Opportunities to visit will be severely restricted from here on out.

When can I come by?

We can be ready for you at eight-thirty sharp. Do you have any other questions at this time, Ms. Tatevyan?

I thought I could see Mariazul's crucifix glinting in the corner of my eye.

It's the border agent, isn't it? I said. Mia Jo Taylor? She's the one who has my brother, isn't she?

Appears so.

She kidnapped someone else, too. I saw it happen. Mariazul Lluvia—

Arturo told me all about that. Rest assured, you aren't in any sort of trouble. But that case is out of our hands. Now, Ms. Tatevyan, it is very late. I'll see you in the morning.

Thanks for everything, Sheriff, I said.

The call ended. I would not sleep for the rest of the night. Turning on the lamp on the bedside table, I collected the mahogany obsidian from the shrine, along with Juanita's book on Justin Lehenwesen. Setting the volcanic shard by my pillow, I opened to the series of untitled outdoor works.

THEY WERE IN love once, and for many years. That was Jace's telling, anyway. From his cell in the Narváez County jail, Jace told me he had thought about Mia Jo Taylor every day since she disappeared from their home in the Panhandle nine years ago. Two stints in prison later, he caught up with her after tracking down her name on a list of Border Patrol agents in West Texas. Why the two-time convicted felon had such a list, Jace would not tell me. He would not tell Mia Jo, either.

But he had her attention. Six months before my brother's disappearance—before the captivity of Alejandro, before the abduction of Mariazul—Jace persuaded her to see him for the first time since she was a teenager.

This, Jace told me from his cell, was where everything went wrong.

Ahead of their reconnection, he waited for Mia Jo at a diner on a farm-to-market road between Odessa and Midland, arriving almost an hour early. He took a seat by the window so he had a clear view of the who came and went. Oil derricks bobbed on the horizon. At the height of the fracking boom, trucks carrying colossal equipment—drills, jacks, pumps— rumbled up and down the road every few minutes. Jace told me he had never seen anything like it. Sitting alone in the diner drinking coffee, he felt as though he had dropped into the far-distant future, infiltrating an advanced civilization.

It was the closest he'd ever felt to being humbled.

By Jace's third cup of coffee, Mia Jo Taylor arrived, pulling into the parking lot in her cruiser. Dressed in full uniform with mirrored sunglasses, Agent Taylor ignored the elderly white couple who tried to shake her hand as she stepped through the front door. She sat down in the booth.

Jace said he sat there with an idiotic grin. Agent Taylor's expression was unreadable. After a few seconds, she extracted a white envelope from inside one of her pockets. She slid it across the table. His grin fading, Jace picked up the envelope, squeezing the paper sides with his rough fingers.

Where's the ring? he asked.

Pawnshop outside El Paso, Mia Jo said. Just off Highway Sixty-Two. You can take that money and buy it back, if you want. Course, there's no guarantee the shop ain't sold it already.

I wanted the ring, he said.

Well, boohoo. You got twelve-hundred dollars.

Twelve-hundred?

Count it yourself.

I asked you to bring the ring because I wanted to know whether you'd kept it. I wanted to know whether it still meant something to you.

Honestly, I forgot I had the damn thing until you came calling for it, Mia Jo said. I'm married now anyway. To a real man.

How come your last name is still Taylor?

Made my husband take my name. I refuse to hide who I am. Now, look. You got your money and you got my attention. Could you please tell me why we're here?

Jace ran his hand through his hair. As he took a deep breath, a waitress approached the booth, a middle-aged woman with an apron over her light blue uniform. She set two menus on the table with a big smile.

Just wanted to let y'all know, you're eating for free today, the waitress said. Order anything you like.

Mia Jo removed her sunglasses.

Free? What for?

We don't get Border Patrol up here that often. We wanted to show our appreciation. Do y'all know what y'all want?

Mia Jo looked through the menu. Jace could not take his eyes off her.

Eggs and toast, she said. Sunnyside. Hot sauce and salt with that. Coffee, too.

You got it. Sir, do you know what you'd like?

Wait a minute, Mia Jo said. Does my hero discount extend to my friend here?

Sure, if you'd like, the waitress said.

Well, this man ain't no hero. Matter of fact, this good-for-nothin has never done an honest day's work in his life. But I'll leave the decision up to y'all.

The waitress turned to Jace.

Eggs and toast, he said. Scrambled. More coffee too, please.

The waitress took the menus and returned with a pot of coffee and a mug for Mia Jo. She poured a fresh round and asked whether they wanted cream or sugar. Neither spoke.

The waitress left them alone.

Mia Jo picked up her mug. She looked at the austere countryside, her face bathed in whiteness.

You look so good, Jace said.

Mia Jo glanced at him.

You look like shit, she said. Hell of a gut you put on.

Been nine years, Jace said. People change. Their bodies in particular tend to change.

I would've expected the opposite, seeing as how you've been in and out of Huntsville. Ain't prison time supposed to teach a man some discipline?

How'd you find out I been in Huntsville? Jace asked.

I'm law enforcement, dumbass. I got access to every criminal database in Texas. A few federal ones too. There ain't much on your record that surprises me. Weapons charges, possession with intent to distribute. That's run of the mill for you. Only thing that really stuck out was your involvement in a human trafficking case. You want to tell me about that?

Jace looked around the diner. Two old men sat at the counter, one reading a newspaper, the other watching a World War Two documentary on an old television.

Those charges got dropped, he whispered.

You took a plea deal. That ain't the same as a jury finding you innocent.

This ain't what I wanted to talk about.

You trafficking girls, Jace?

No. I never trafficked no girls.

You sure? I hear there's good money to be made selling girls outside truck stops. Young girls especially. You find yourself a good lookin girl who ran away from home, set up shop outside of Amarillo or Lubbock. Bet you could pull in a few hundred dollars in a few hours. Maybe a thousand a night. Ain't that how it goes?

I never got involved in nothin like that. I swear to you, Mia Jo.

How'd you get charged?

It was a round-up. One of those RICO deals. I got caught doing business with some bad men. I had nothin to do with it.

You were just there for the guns?

That's all.

So you were just selling guns to the bad men who were selling girls?

The waitress arrived with two plates of eggs and toast. The border agent dug into her food without hesitation. After a minute or so of waiting, Jace picked up a piece of toast. He began to spread a chunk of scrambled eggs over its crisped surface.

I want you to know I'm doing good these days, he said. I'm living in Arizona. Used to be part of one of those citizen's militias. Ditat Deus, we called ourselves. We helped keep the border around Ajo clear of illegals until the team dissolved. We were good at it, too.

Mia Jo glared.

I heard about Ditat Deus. Y'all weren't anything like you thought. Bunch of wannabe gunslingers roving around, interfering with operations. What would have happened if you'd been mistaken for drug smugglers? What would have happened if y'all got yourselves stuck in the middle of a firefight?

I could ask the same of you, Jace said. What's gonna happen when somebody takes out that pretty boy who ranks you at the Sierra Blanca Checkpoint? The football player, Denton Pierce. What about that, Mia Jo?

Agent Taylor stared.

What in the hell are you bringing up Denton for?

He's dirty, Jace said. He picked a side in a game he shouldn't be playing. Some loads from Mexico get through that checkpoint. Others don't. But you already knew about that, didn't you?

Her faced reddened.

I don't know anything, she said.

Well, the people whose loads don't get through are onto the pattern, Jace said. What's more, they're in the market for someone to solve the problem. They're putting out feelers for the right contractor. That's how I came to know all this. I'm here as a courtesy. You tell Agent Pierce to un-dirty himself. I'd be happy to pass along the number of the man he needs to talk to.

You're so full of shit, Mia Jo said. Your mind's full of fantasies. Get yourself a job, Jace. A real job. These oil companies in the Basin will hire out anybody. Maybe even you.

You ever been down to Laredo, Mia Jo? he asked. Nuevo Laredo? That's where there is money to be made. You ain't gotta be living on scraps with that husband of yours out in Hudspeth County. And you wouldn't have to get involved with anyone you ain't want to. Me and you could be like contractors. Self-employed. Working on our own terms with a roster of clients. The Border Patrol ain't pay so much these days, does it? They ain't too good on overtime either, are they?

Agent Taylor slid out of the booth. She placed her mirrored sunglasses back on her face and looked down at Jace one last time. In the throes of heartache, he tried to finish his sales pitch.

You remember what you said when I took you into our house? he asked. You said I saved your life. That's all I'm trying to do now.

I never want to hear anything about this ever again, she said.

Mia Jo. Please.

I was a girl.

We could be like we were. We could go back.

I never want to see you again. I never want to hear no more conspiracy theories about Agent Pierce. I never want to think about that house again. Goodbye.

She walked out of the diner, returned to her cruiser, and drove away.

Jace looked out at the white-and-brown horizon before returning his attention to the money. He counted the bills three times before he was convinced of the twelve-hundred-dollar amount. He resumed his breakfast, then moved on to Mia-Jo's unfinished plate. As he devoured the second dish, the waitress approached, her arms crossed.

Jace spat amber-colored saliva into his mug.

These meals still paid for? he asked.

THE INTERVIEW WITH the Texas Rangers had yielded a blackeye and two chipped teeth. When I first sat down in the hallway for our visit, Jace, unprompted, told me how he had banged his face against his bed. He was thinking about bringing a lawsuit against the sheriff's office for failing to meet safety standards. Then he started talking about Agent Taylor. From his fast and relentless manner of speech, I could tell I had not been invited for a conversation, but a monologue.

By the time Jace was finished unspooling his story, I was curled up on the floor, trying to stay awake.

Why are you telling me all this? I asked.

Because Agent Taylor ain't got anyone to speak for her, he said. Thought I'd set the record straight, at least for you. Fact is, she probably ain't ever gonna have a chance to speak with the authorities. She's gone.

Gone where?

We used to talk about Mexico. She scoped out a few places to cross.

At the end of the hallway, Deputy Ybarra tapped on his wristwatch. I stood up. Jace turned towards me one last time.

Your brother seemed like a good kid, he said. We didn't know what to make of him when he got caught up in our world.

If the cops find him, I'll be sure to tell him that, I said.

We didn't know what to make of it when you got caught up in our world either, Jace said. Very generous of you, providing a ride for that girl all the way from Lordsburg. Pretty cowardly, though, leaving her to get taken like that. All you would have had to do is tail Agent Taylor. Tell someone it wasn't right. Heck, you probably could have gotten Agent Gallegos on your side. He never trusted Mia Jo. You'd probably like an update on Mariazul while you're here, huh? Wouldn't you?

I waited. He stared at the wall of white painted cinderblock. In profile, the swelling and discoloration in his face were more visible.

She's in Eloy, Arizona he said. Out in some shithole in Pinal County off Highway Eighty-Seven.

Who has her? I asked.

The United States government. Unless she got swept up in some expedited processing, she's in a detention center. I don't know for sure. Things are hectic these days. The system is overloaded. Children are getting lost, sent who knows where for who knows why. I ain't gotta tell you that, now do I?

He smirked at me. I walked over to Deputy Ybarra to tell him where to find Mariazul. He wrote everything down. When our conversation was done, Arturo had nothing to say about Jace Tarrant's injuries. He would hardly confirm that the Texas Rangers had even visited him.

ON HIS LAST night in Rosadero, I was introduced to Alejandro Bautista. After finding out about his sister's location, he had asked for me. We only had a couple minutes.

As we met, he held Mariazul's crucifix. Deputy Ybarra stood in the doorway with Sabana. Time went by in silence.

The young man from Veracruz looked at me.

How far? he asked.

Sabana walked across the room, crouching at our side, prepared to serve as translator.

What do you mean? I asked through Sabana.

How far is Eloy from El Paso? Alejandro asked.

Deputy Ybarra came into the room. Sabana stood up, gesturing for me to do the same. Our meeting was already up. We said our goodbyes, leaving him to rest and gather his feelings before the early morning transition. My last sight of Mariazul's brother was of a lonely, quiet boy staring at a cheap piece of jewelry. Deputy Ybarra closed the door behind us.

Arturo told me he would call the moment the deputies in Erastus County recovered Jakob.

WE WAITED ALL day for word that my brother was alive. No assurances came.

At sunset, Sabana and I sat on the grass behind the Celenia Inn. An embered sky lowered itself behind the Zaldos Mesa. Pink Fireballs formed, streaking across the prairielands, extinguishing before our eyes.

The mahogany obsidian lay on the ground between us. Pink radiance danced on its surface.

IN TOWN, BENICIO Washington sat on the porch of his mother's bungalow, reading a historical account of the early cowboy days in Narváez County. Sipping espresso from a demitasse, he, too was waiting for word on the fate of my brother.

When the coyotes began howling, Benicio's concentration did not break.

· Sixteen ·

The Entrepreneur's Ball

E CRADLE EACH other on our picnic blanket in the abandoned Hotel Jaspeado, naked and reconciled. This is the first cold evening Javier and I have spent together. We clasp each other's bodies for warmth.

It is October in Rosadero, a time and place far-removed from summertime Tucson. Our reunion has come in slow, then sudden releases. Spending the last few weekends in the home of Juanita Ochoa, I have kept myself in Javier's proximity while he oversees the construction of his inaugural exhibit at the Naranjoven Gallery. From text messages to phone calls to a sit-down lunch date in Juanita's burrito restaurant, our love has reconvened, though with new taboos. I do not ask Javier about the true—or fictionalized— extent of his involvement with the Nogales 21, or anything about his father's money. In turn, Javier does not ask me about my manuscript. I do not tell him how many times I have emailed and called Congressman A.P. Horne's office.

We are in love again, but with limits.

So far, our overnight adventure in Rosadero's premier ruins has featured candlelight, Ultracedar *playing from Javier's phone, a picnic on the pink marble floor, and the exhaustion of every intimate exercise two men can do alone. Between the leather sofas where movie stars and cattle barons once lounged, we lie in post-coital comfort. Javier is already asleep. I stroke his hair, nuzzling his shoulder as his ribcage rises and falls with snoring.*

Past midnight, the story I've been chasing tracks me down a second time.

Though I have not seen Jace since our encounter at the Gila Gulch, he is never far from my mind. Now, I am certain it is he who flashes truck headlights through the hotel's slim glass door. After the second flash, he guns his motor, the sound of his engine reverberating. My love sleeps through this event.

I stand up, slowly and gently. I tiptoe across the lobby, looking over my shoulder at the wrought-iron staircase to the second story. Approaching the door, I see an envelope addressed to me—Mr. Jakob Levon Tatevyan. The backside is embroidered with a design of bluebonnets and cattle skulls.

I tear open the envelope and take out a golden card. Inside is an invitation for myself and a plus-one to a fundraising dinner for Representative Augustus Prescott Horne. The event will take place a few days from now in the Empresario Ballroom at the legendary Mirabeau Hotel in downtown Austin. The most powerful Republicans and Republican donors in the Lone Star State will be in attendance. Tomahawk Littlejohn—proud son of Uvalde, Texas—will deliver a keynote address.

My heart pounds.

Before returning to our nest, I stash the invitation inside my jeans. Javier stirs but does not wake up as I collect him in my arms. I spend another hour awake, stranded with knowledge of the inevitable.

AT DAWN, I rouse him by proposing a spontaneous trip to Austin. We already conquered Tucson, I tell him. Why not conquer Austin, the most youthful city in Texas?

Javier jumps to his feet, joyful and full-frontal.

Now that's what I'm talking about! he yells. Austin! ¡Sí, Se Puede!

Three days later, we're on the road, Lakeith Mercy on the stereo, a room with a balcony booked at the Mirabeau Hotel. But our love would not endure.

WE ARRIVE IN Austin in the late morning. Seven hours of driving through the desert and the Hill Country have left us exhausted. The day is humid, seventy degrees, yet also cloudy and autumnal. We lounge on an outdoor patio a block off Guadalupe, a house converted into a tranquil coffee shop by day, a rowdy honkytonk by night, with a warehouse-sized music annex and a parking lot of vegan food trucks. Stringed lights lead from the café to the patio, where picnic benches and mismatched furniture sprawl between fences overgrown with kudzu. After a late lunch of vegan chili burgers and horchatas spiked with espresso, I lie my head in Javier's lap. We are both wearing t-shirts advertising the Naranjoven Gallery, mine orange and Javier's white, the gallery's name printed in cerulean-blue. Combined with our basketball shorts and flip-flops, we look like undergraduates lazing between studies.

Javier sighs.

Why don't we move here? he asks.

I laugh.

I'm serious, he says. We're strung between Tucson and Rosadero. You're doing a low-residency phase this semester. You won't be in school forever. Why don't we do some apartment hunting around here? Or downtown? We could get ourselves a condo overlooking Lady Bird Lake, set you up with a writing studio over the Colorado River.

I could never afford a place like that, I say.

I could, Javier says.

I raise myself off his body, yawning and stretching. He ruffles my hair.

Come on, I say. Let's see Austin. Check-in at the Mirabeau isn't for three more hours.

And our tuxedos won't be ready for two, Javier says.

I nod. Tonight, we plan to dine at the Mirabeau's steakhouse—I plan on salad—where we intend to look as though we belong to the Texan elite. Javier does not yet know why we are in Austin. He does not know that the Mirabeau is hosting A.P. Horne's fundraising event. He is here for vacation, to dress-up, to dream.

But the countdown has begun.

We stand up and meander out of the garden down to the street. My station wagon is parked in front of the café, packed with luggage suitable for a three-day stay, the golden invitation hidden under one of the seats. Hand in hand, Javier and I stroll along Guadalupe, *past murals and holes-in-the-wall, past bar after bar with live music in the evenings, making our way towards the University of Texas campus and beyond. We'll wander all the way to the Colorado, past the Texas State Capitol, looking up at skyscrapers of glass and digital ambition, believing we have accomplished something by coming here.*

THE MIRABEAU HOTEL luxuriates across an entire city block, its grand entrance opening to the corner of Brazos and Old Pecan Street. Since 1886, the hotel has been the crown jewel of Texas' high society aspirations: Romanesque on the outside, Art Deco on the inside. Conceived by its original owner to be the most magnificent hotel between the Pacific and the Atlantic, the hotel's exterior shimmers with brown marble columns. Facing Old Pecan Street— known to less perceptive revelers as Sixth Street—numerous balconies jut out of the glossed façade. One in particular looms broadly over the sidewalk, a viewing platform for guests for whom the three-thousand dollar a night rate is no object. Two flags pop along poles jutting out of the grand veranda, one for the Texas Republic and one for America. On the sidewalk, a horse and carriage are available for guests to rent. The Mirabeau, with its steakhouse, ballroom, cocktail lounge, and afternoon high tea, is a place of gathering, whose opulence dulls the rest of the city in comparison.

Checking in at the front desk—our rented tuxedos under our arms—Javier and I cut the least likely figures in the building: casual, queer, Mexican and pink-haired respectively. Underneath the chandeliers, we ignore the stares of old patrons on lobby couches. We take our key cards and ascend the grand staircase.

We sleep for two hours, then don our formal attire, helping one another adapt to the standards of our environment. When it comes time for dinner, I present Javier with the invitation to the fundraiser. I confess the ruse and articulate my scheme of infiltration. Trying to ease my love's shock, I attempt to weave the fundraiser into the story of our holiday, how this is just one more adventure, a vignette of our boyish escapades.

But Javier is too devastated.

His lips tremble. His eyes fill with tears. He slaps away my hand as I try touch his shoulder. He stands up and makes for the door.

Where are you going? I yell.

The South Congress Bridge, he says. To see the bats.

Javier closes the door behind him. I picture him in the streets of Austin, elegant and alone, looking like a jilted groom.

I lie down on the bed, checking the charge on my phone and audio recorder, preparing for the most singular stumble I will ever make.

TOMAHAWK LITTLEJOHN STANDS at the podium on the stage of the Empresario Ballroom, his medals pinned to his tuxedo. I arrive late so that I may enter inconspicuously. I stand at the ballroom entrance, waiting for my invitation to be accepted by men dressed in black Texaulipas uniforms. Every guard is young, ex-military, and visibly armed, with wraparound sunglasses, short hair, and thick goatees. Most of them are white and tall. While they check my information, I peer inside. The former Lieutenant Colonel stands beneath a spotlight, his audience glittering around their dinner tables. Sharing the stage with Tomahawk, A.P. Horne sits at a table with a set of elderly men and women.

While the guards confer, I listen to the keynote address.

Thank you, thank you, Tomahawk says. Tonight, I want to speak about our right to free enterprise. Every day in this country, outdated legal notions are holding back our prosperity, notions that the honorable A.P. Horne has worked hard to repeal, both in Congress and on the board of Texaulipas Security Solutions. When President Rutherford B. Hayes signed the Posse Comitatus Act into law in 1878, the country was barely over one hundred years old. The West was still wild. Out in Washington, D.C.—

Here, the audience jeers. Tomahawk waits, barely suppressing a smile.

Out in Washington, D.C., where politicians had no idea what life was like on the border, they set themselves the task to soften the criminal justice system. By taking away the military's right to enforce our domestic laws, our pioneers struggled to tame and settle the frontier. But with the market success of Texaulipas—founded here in Texas, with our primary training facility down in Brooks County—our civilization may at last achieve parity with the enemies pouring over the Rio Grande. Our warriors are the best in the world, alumni of every branch of the military and special forces units. Because they are actors of private enterprise, they can enforce the law with the full might of American military power, without being constrained by some out-of-touch D.C. bureaucrats. With Texaulipas, the Posse Comitatus Act has at last been defeated.

Tomahawk's proclamations are met with applause. In the shadows of the stage, Congressman Horne grins, leaning into the old tuxedoed man at his side, whispering something to make the old man laugh. I lean forward, trying to hear what comes next. Tomahawk Littlejohn launches into a description about his time in Iraq and his first encounters with private contractors.

Just as I reach for my audio recorder, two guards seize me. Forcing my arms behind my back, they bind my wrists together in plastic zip-ties. Before I can protest, they march me away from the ballroom down a short flight of stairs to a subterranean corridor. A golden door waits for us. A brass key is required to unlock it, a key that one of the guards produces immediately.

They take me up a private elevator to the Lyndon Baines Johnson Presidential Suite.

THE THIRTY-SIXTH PRESIDENT of the United States studies me with a stern expression from a portrait hanging on a wall. At his side is a similar portrait of his wife, Lady Bird Johnson. Between the auspicious paintings, a plaque explains how on Tuesday, November 3rd, 1964, LBJ and his campaign staff watched the results of his historic landslide victory from a television set in this very room.

Past the foyer, the suite opens into a chamber of polished wooden furniture, sleek leather couches, an elegant dining room set, a golden chandelier, and stained-glass windows depicting bluebonnets. The living room is filled with armed men dressed in black: more thick white guards for Texaulipas, but also a dozen much younger, Latin-looking boys with prepubescent mustaches, as well as a few short, squat men with Indigenous faces. These latter two groups are also dressed in black, and also have firearms visibly tucked into their uniforms, though their clothing does not bear the Texaulipas brand. These seem to be informal guns, compensated perhaps on a shadow payroll.

Everybody stands with the same deadness in their eyes.

On a massive flat-screen built into a bocote cabinet, a soccer game commands the armed men's attention. Around the suite, oil paintings of cavalrymen and pioneers provide a different kind of spectacle, a fine arts ode to the era preceding the Mirabeau's opening. In one corner, a large desk has been converted into an ad hoc surveillance center: three computer monitors displaying a dozen live feeds from cameras throughout the Empresario Ballroom, the lobby, and the hotel's street entrances.

That's when I see him: The Prince of Nuevo Laredo. Broad-shouldered with gelled hair, the Prince is leaning against the open doorway to the balcony, smoking a cigar. Unlike his peons, he is dressed in a white guayabera, white steel-toed boots, and bright, acid-washed jeans. He glances my way with vague interest.

Before I know it, I am standing in front of one of the most fearsome men in North America. The two guards who have brought me here are searching the pockets of my tuxedo. They remove my phone and audio recorder, passing them to their boss. In silence, they undo my zip-ties, unbinding my wrists.

El Principe looks at me expectantly. Somehow, his words come out of my mouth.

What are you doing here? I ask.

The Prince does not answer. He takes out a smartphone from the pocket of his jeans. He shows me the screen, on which he has set a timer for ten minutes. He activates the time, then turns on my audio recorder and passes it back to me. I look at him, stunned.

El Principe nods.

I am granting you an interview, he says. Now ask your questions.

I tremble. He stays still.

Shouldn't you ask for my name? he asks at last.

Okay, I say. What's your name?

My name is Dionisio Ángel Verrado. Do you still want me to tell you what I'm doing here?

Yes, I say. I do.

Protecting the principals. Do you know what that means?

I think so.

Good. Tonight, the principals are the most powerful men and women in Texas. That man on Representative Horne's left, for example, is the chairman for the Texas Railroad Commission. My men pulled you because they received a tip that a pink-haired boy with a forged invitation would try to infiltrate tonight's event, putting the principals at risk. I know all about you, Jakob Levon Tatevyan. Perhaps I should be asking questions of my own, hmm? For example, what is your interest in Representative Horne? You've been on his trail for a few weeks now, no?

Dionisio waits.

I'm just…trying to piece together the big picture, I say.

The big picture of what?

I'm trying to…to write the story of…I'm trying to illuminate the ligaments of power.

And how does Congressman Horne fit into these ligaments?

He's connected to you.

Of course he is. We're both on the board of Texaulipas. We attend quarterly meetings together in Laredo. So what?

You're more than that, I say. You're…you're the heir apparent.

He raises an eyebrow.

Yeah? To what dynasty am I alleged to be the heir?

To the…you're…you're the Prince of Nuevo Laredo.

Am I now?

Dionisio puffs on his cigar. He looks over at the monitors on the suite's desk before returning his attention to me. He looks bored.

You want my story? he says. Will you leave Congressman Horne alone if I tell you?

I nod.

Alright, he says. I am a dual citizen of Guatemala and the United States. I was raised in Nuevo Laredo. When I was young, I returned to Guatemala to serve in the Kaibiles. During that service, I trained at the School of the Americas at Fort Benning. From there, I was recruited by Texaulipas to be a security contractor in Iraq. The pay was outstanding. That was in March 2004. My unit participated in the First Battle of Fallujah, directing a platoon of Marines cut off from their commanders. Though the siege was a failure, word of our professionalism went up the chain-of-command. Tomahawk Littlejohn was impressed—so impressed that when he joined Texaulipas a few years later, he insisted I be put on the board. And here I am.

No, I say.

He tilts his head.

No? he says. Why not?

That's not your story.

Dionisio Ángel Verrado sighs with impatience, as though we're in a play and I've forgotten my lines.

Okay, he says. You want a hot tip? You want to know about the bad boys? I'll be your source, kiddo. At our training facility in South Texas, we employ Chilean commandos as instructors, commandos who cut their teeth under Augusto Pinochet. That's right. Our recruits are now integrating the Pinochet Method into their work protecting celebrities and CEOs. Our men are aggressive, dangerous even. There have been injuries, lawsuits. Now you have something else to occupy yourself with.

Tell me, I say, about your cartel.

He ashes his cigar onto the balcony.

There are no cartels, the Prince says. That is a fairytale made up to keep good American boys like you off drugs. I would hope you'd be smarter than that.

The Cóndores del Norte used to serve as the enforcement wing of the Bizantinos, I say, before they went out on their own. Nothing existed like them before.

Is that so? Sounds exciting. Tell me more.

The Cóndores are a paramilitary, almost. Professionals of violence. When you worked for the Bizantinos, you lured away soldiers from the special forces and applied their tactics to the drug trade. The Cóndores kept the Sinaloa and Gulf cartels from claiming Nuevo Laredo. You succeeded in protecting Don Gregorio. But something went wrong.

¿Qué onda, güey? What went wrong?

I don't know. The Cóndores declared war on the Bizantinos. Nuevo Laredo has been under siege ever since.

Under siege, Dionisio says. How would you know?

I've done research, I say.

Yeah? Where?

The narcoblogs. The war is terrorizing Mexico. And war is what it is. Massacres in the street, beheadings, corpses dangling from bridges, bombed police stations…every day, citizen journalists publish stories about the war. They put themselves at great risk to do so.

Risk? What risk? I know these sources. They are all anonymous.

They're not wrong.

You believe in the power of anonymity? ¿Verdad? In this moment, Jakob, do you believe your anonymity is keeping you safe? Hmm?

Dionisio turns off the timer. We had three minutes left. He reaches over and shuts off my recorder. He can do anything he wants.

He points his cigar at me.

You have no idea what you're talking about, he says. The problem you do not see, Jakob, is that the government—your government—has lost its monopoly on legitimate violence.

What?

You feel it, don't you? Mmm?

I'm sorry—I don't know what you're talking about.

The dread. The decay. I know you feel it. The state has absolved itself of its obligation to protect you. Same as Mexico. You see it every day. Mass killings—in schools, at music festivals, in churches. They are unstoppable. Your rickety country is coming undone. The only certainty left for America is the dollar. The dollar is why Texaulipas exists. The dollar is why I am a rich man. God has lost His respect for the United States. But not for the dollar. Not yet.

From somewhere outside the Mirabeau Hotel, hoots and cheers erupt. We are still on Sixth Street, I remember, a corridor of live music, plastic beads, drinking, and fighting. Passing beneath the balcony, a group of young men is whooping at nothing in particular. Simultaneously, the computer monitors on the desk show the end of Tomahawk Littlejohn's keynote speech. His audience rises from their tables in applause. Representative Horne stands up and joins Tomahawk at his side, as though they are running mates.

Dionisio Ángel Verrado looks at me again.

Our interview is done, he says. Write whatever you like about me or my company. Publish with whomever will take it. The problem is not that the truth is hidden. The problem is that nobody can do anything about it. Now, I have one more suggestion for you.

What's that?

Leave Representative Horne alone. Leave this hotel at once. Tell your lover to do the same. This is your only warning. I do not want you near the Congressman anymore. I cannot protect you from what you do next.

I am in real danger now. But around the LBJ Suite, nobody appears to be paying any attention to me. Despite the aggressive manner in which I was brought here, I have been forgotten.

This is my last chance.

Slowly, I walk back to the foyer with the portraits of the thirty-sixth President and the former First Lady. Closing the door behind me, I feel as though I have just returned from an alternate dimension most will never be allowed to see. As I cross the hallway, the golden doors open to the private elevator. Two Texas Rangers step out, one an old Anglo, the other a middle-aged Chicano. They nod as they walk towards the suite. Quickly, I slip into the suspended Art Deco container, pressing the button back to the real world.

My last glimpse of this gilded blacksite is of the two Texas Rangers, stepping inside as though they belong.

MY BROTHER WAS still drunk when sheriff deputies for Erastus County found him sprawled behind the farmhouse. Overnight, an ice storm had coated the Panhandle in a pitiless glaze of white. Shirtless and barefoot, my brother had made it through the backdoor of the house before slipping and falling down the steps to the tundra. He was wrapped in a frayed blanket. At his side, the fire-iron he had used to keep balance pierced the soil. He lay in a crooked heap, his skin freezing in the subzero temperature.

When the first two deputies arrived, they checked his vital signs and called an ambulance, applying emergency treatments to prevent hypothermia and frostbite. One deputy stayed behind while the other walked around the property, weapon drawn. Jakob raised his head.

Take me home, he said.

More deputies arrived. Some stood guard while others descended onto the isolated property and conducted a search of the house—a warrant was forthcoming, they were assured— searching for a culprit and coming up with nothing.

An ambulance appeared out of the featureless landscape. The deputies assisted the paramedics in strapping my brother to a gurney and loading him into the vehicle. Staying behind to canvass the scene, they watched as the ambulance transported Jakob to the intensive care unit in Amarillo, the nearest city. For the second time in as many months, my brother was conveyed across Texas by strangers.

Seventeen

Operation Cleanup

MIST SHROUDED THE ranch country outside Alpine as I barreled towards Amarillo. Four hundred miles north, my brother was in serious but stable condition. Back in the Pacific Northwest, our parents were driving to Portland International Airport, hoping to purchase last minute tickets to anywhere near the Texas Panhandle. Though we had received good news, until we could see Jakob in person, we would not feel relief.

Red and blue lights emerged in the fog behind me. I pulled over, quickly taking out my driver's license and insurance card. A silver pickup truck slowed down, passing my side, drifting long enough for me to see the insignia of the Texas Rangers before shooting off into the darkness.

I returned to the highway and drove for six straight hours to the hospital in Amarillo.

HE WAS LUCID when I arrived, set up with a rare private room for his safety. The medical staff were tight-lipped about how long his stay would be, any estimation contingent on insurance. Under fluorescent lights and bland lavender walls, my brother had been speaking all day from his hospital bed, calling our mom and dad and giving statements to sheriff deputies, corroborating Jace Tarrant's confession. The Texas Rangers had dispatched two members from C Company to interview him, and though they had nothing to do with Captain Bryce or Ranger Flores, my brother refused to speak. They left him alone.

When I arrived at last, he was tired again, but happy to see me. Alone together, I told him to sleep if he needed to. He closed his eyes. I closed my eyes, too. For a few minutes, he appeared to be snoring.

Then:

Did they find the boy in the kitchen? he asked.

I sat up.

What?

Alejandro Bautista, my brother said. He's from Veracruz. He was being held captive at the abandoned hotel in Rosadero. The Hotel Jaspeado.

I sat in silence

Yes, I said. He's safe now. On his way to El Paso.

Thank god, Jakob said. Thank god.

I moved to the bed.

How do you know about Alejandro? I asked.

My brother looked at me.

One night, I was feeling lonely, he said. Before our breakup, Javier and I used to camp in the Hotel Jaspeado. It was so romantic. So I went in for a visit. I heard a noise from a kitchen, like an animal, so I went in. That's how I met Alejandro. He was handcuffed to the stove and in pretty bad shape. He told me he'd been kidnapped, that his captors were trying to sell him to the highest bidder since his family hadn't paid his ransom. He told me not to call 911, that they were still in the hotel. And they were.

Jakob sighed.

The plan was for me to walk to the sheriff's office and get help. But they heard me. They came running down the stairs. I ran to my car, got in and…I was so scared. I wasn't thinking. I just raced down the highway towards Alpine. Didn't occur to me to call 911. A few miles outside of Rosadero, this pickup truck caught up with me, ran me off the road. It felt professional.

Jakob reached towards me. I took his hand.

They'd been planning to take me for some time. That's why Jace led me to Dionisio: to convince him I was a problem. Dionisio wasn't interested, and he would not give a greenlight for my kidnapping. But I wasn't supposed to find Alejandro. So they took me anyway, thought they could get a good payout in the process. Everything fell apart so quickly.

He shook his head.

I'll never forget the Fireballs, he said. My station wagon got run off by the Zaldos Mesa. This woman…this Border Patrol agent…took me at gunpoint, handcuffed me, tossed me in the back of a pickup truck. But all the while, pink Fireballs burst across the ranchlands like stars. I never stopped thinking about them.

My brother began to cry.

Do you know if Alejandro's sister ever got to her brother? Jakob asked. Her name is Mariazul. Have you heard anything?

That was when I broke down. Despite his weakness and confusion, Jakob tried to comfort me. He told me his question did not matter, that the only thing that mattered was that we were both safe and alive, waiting for our mother and father, for the perpetually-fissured Tatevyans to find our ways back to one another.

But I told him everything.

MY BROTHER LET me speak. He did not judge, and I did not understand. I could have saved Mariazul, but I also could not. He could have saved Alejandro, and he could have done nothing. He carried his own terrible knowledge.

We are all in the wrong, he tried to tell me.

He should have heeded the warnings.

On his last night in Tucson before his low-residency semester, Jakob had dinner with his adviser at El Charro. Professor Erickson listened as my brother described his conversations with Benicio Washington, his encounters with Jace Tarrant, the conversation with Dionisio Ángel Verrado. Milos Erickson sipped his red wine, deep concern in his eyes.

All this for your novel? he asked.

I want authenticity, he said.

Sure, Professor Erickson said. Unfortunately, I must agree with the sociopath you interviewed. The problem is not that the truth is unknown, but that the truth cannot be met by action. Not yet. Take a few steps back, Jakob. This is not worth your safety.

Jakob ate his enchilada. Professor Erickson asked whether he had any plans for further travels. Yes, my brother answered. He planned to visit Laredo and possibly the Texaulipas training facility near the Falfurrias checkpoint in South Texas. He understood the dangers. But he had an idea in his mind, an idea that could not be extinguished. He would crisscross the entirety of the borderlands to shape his manuscript.

Professor Erickson advised Jakob to stay out of Mexico unless he had someone to travel with him, someone he could trust. Jakob agreed.

As they hugged and departed the restaurant, Professor Erickson told my brother to give his love to Professor Ochoa.

My brother sat in the driver's seat of his packed station wagon, leaving the Sonoran Desert for the Chihuahuan Desert, beckoned to the horizon like so many young men before him.

WHAT DID HE expect from Laredo?

Or Nuevo Laredo?

He still could not say.

His first impressions came in the form of an ink drawing by Juanita Ochoa's granddaughter. On a poster-sized sketchpad, Kiki laid out the border crossing between Nuevo Laredo and Laredo: on the Mexican side, the vast center of the page comprised a dozen empty vehicle lanes. The inspection stations were unmanned and uncanny. On the left end of the page, Kiki drew a large bleeding Cross; the necrotic residue of the Savior, with the Savior's body snatched away. Surrounding the Cross, piled skulls filled the negative space to the edges of the sketchpad. On the opposite end of the page, Kiki's pen had created a multi-textual wall of fire and black smoke, representing the other half of Nuevo Laredo.

Presumably, one end of the city—the one with the Cross—belonged to Los Bizantinos. The other belonged to Los Cóndores del Norte.

Across the middle was a depopulated trade-zone. Beneath the empty lanes were the memories of her parents, her school, her home, her church, all drawn with minimal detail.

Juanita showed the sketchpad to Jakob as he collected dinner plates. Kiki was in the kitchen, cleaning out pots and pans and wiping down counters. Before assisting, my brother stood over his host's shoulder, looking over Kiki's artwork.

This is her trauma, Juanita said. A psychologist friend of mine taught her to process her experiences into art. She has an entire sketchbook of these. She writes poetry, too. My granddaughter has a very bright future, if only she would do her homework.

Juanita looked at my brother.

Remember the trembling hand, she said.

My brother nodded. He took the dishes to the kitchen. Stepping aside, Juanita's granddaughter could not look at him.

ALL HE HAD in those last days before his abduction was what he read on the narcoblogs, the work of unnamed citizen-journalists putting more on the line than he ever could. Anyone could access these stories. Few did.

From his hospital bed, Jakob insisted he share with me, so that I could believe him. So that I could believe what our country had created.

THE RISE OF Dionisio Ángel Verrado and the destruction of Don Gregorio displaced history itself. This was what violence did.

This was what my brother wanted me to know.

In an era of massacres, extortion, corruption, and rape, the year was inconsequential. A date could tell nothing. The founding of the city never happened. The business cycles fueling the maquiladoras had no beginning. There were no corporate charters. There was no Catholic Church. The mayor's office and the police department and the governor's palace were all vacant. Laredo, Texas had no continuity with its Mexican counterpart.

Only one truth prevailed.

Before there was the Prince, there was the Patriarch.

Don Gregorio's fortunes began in the trucking industry. In the decades before globalization, he served as an apparatchik for the Partido Revolucionario Institucional, a successful bureaucrat working under the various Secretariats of Communications and Transportation. Cultivating a loyal network of appointees in his hometown of Nuevo Laredo, the Don set the terms of the city's trafficking plaza for a generation.

In the 1980s, he purchased a fleet of refrigerated trucks to ship agricultural goods to El Norte.

In the 1980s, Don Gregorio also found Christ.

Born again in the Rio Grande, he had seen the halo encircling the United States, where God and Business were merging. The prophecy of a common North American trading bloc was on the lips of every American leader. Anticipating the destabilization of Mexico's internal economic hierarchies, Don Gregorio assembled an army of Christian warriors—officially, security personnel—to guard his many enterprises, training them on a rancho in the hinterlands of Coahuila. Once the neo-crusaders were combat-ready, they fanned out across Nuevo Laredo: protecting business owners from harassment, arresting and prosecuting thieves and robbers, maintaining order in the Zona de Tolerancia. By the moment of NAFTA, Don Gregorio's men—the Order of the Byzantines—had superseded the authority of Nuevo Laredo's traditional institutions. They were righteous, tucking the Don's written sermons into the doors of tiendas late on protection fees, killing those who refused to pay for their own safety. They killed coyotes and contrabandistas who broke the rules. Chivalry provided a set of ethics, the specifics of which would wave from narco-banners posted on streetlamps.

Don Gregorio himself was a shadowy figure. In newspapers, he appeared as a slight, light-skinned gentlemen with a penchant for sunglasses and pinstriped suits, and, from the 1980s onwards, with rosaries tucked between his fingers. His public appearances were limited to attending Christmas mass in the city's largest archdiocese in a section of pews cordoned off by a dozen heavily armed Bizantinos.

He was a man of divine right.

He was a man of patronage, too.

As prophesied, the economy collapsed in the 1990s. The Patriarch grew his trucking business into a nationwide empire. Soon, the monopolistic authority of the Partido Revolucionario Institucional began to reach its limits. Mexico was on the cusp of remaking itself after being unmade, as it always was, by foreign money and foreign coercion. The congregational ranks of the Bizantinos would soon have an unparalleled opportunity for upward mobility.

Out in the slums, a Guatemalan-Mexican teenager—a barrel-chested, fifth-grade dropout with an appetite for street fights, who regularly crossed into Texas to practice his aim at gun ranges—was recruited to help load Don Gregorio's eighteen-wheelers. Dionisio Ángel Verrado was an unreserved hustler, whose athleticism and efficiency with cargo quickly ranked him above his peers. Put into a supervisory role, D.Á.V. commanded his own unit of box-throwers, empowered to hand down discipline or terminate contracts at his discretion.

Eight months into working in Don Gregorio's export business, the teenage Dionisio shot employee to death whom he had caught stealing a kilo of black tar off one of the trucks

An anonymous witness tipped city police about the murder, who arrived to take the prodigious supervisor away for questioning. The police drove the teenager to Don Gregorio's palace on a rancho outside town, taking him to the horse stables in the vast, unlit chaparral. Handcuffed and silent, D.Á.V. waited. When the Don arrived, he made unbreaking eye contact, and did not speak. After examining his employee and his substantial pistol, he ordered the police to free him. Don Gregorio patted him on the cheek.

God has blessed you, he said.

From there, the two discussed Dionisio's future, beginning with his citizenship and his eligibility for military conscription in Guatemala. The teenager would honor his obligation to the nation his parents left behind, and by the grace of God, leverage his duty into something greater.

For the remainder of the '90s, as Don Gregorio tightened his grip on the marketplace, his protégé trained across the Americas in the art of war. His debut in Nuevo Laredo would come not come for almost a decade.

MY BROTHER HAD a cursory handle on the cartels and their corridors. He knew about the Sinaloans and the Gulf Cartels, knew about their ambitious designs for Nuevo Laredo, knew that by the time President Felipe Calderone had taken office, the Bizantinos were already a decrepit institution with no clear order of succession. Nuevo Laredo was for the taking.

With advance knowledge that the new President would declare total war on the narcos on December 1st, 2006, rival cartels descended upon Nuevo Laredo in the last days of November, holing up in the Zona de Tolerancia as they planned their seizure of Don Gregorio's assets.

But the old cartels did not know what was coming.

The Cóndores.

Their first operation would be remembered as the Battle of Boystown.

THE FIRST PINK rays of daylight broke across Nuevo Laredo at exactly 7:14 a.m. Two massive semi-trucks pulled in front of the military barracks on the edge of the city, sealing the entrance shut. As trapped soldiers for the Mexican Armed Forces scrambled to their armory, a third semi-truck pulled across the westbound lanes of the nearby highway, bringing traffic to a standstill. Thousands of tense commuters watched as a caravan of school buses shut down the eastbound lanes next. Scores of young men in black tactical gear poured out of the buses, dressed in bulletproof armor and carrying assault rifles, securing the choked roadways.

This, in the words of their commanders, was a containment strategy.

They did things the American Way.

From their stalled vehicles, commuters documented the scene on their cellphones, footage that would begin circulating on narcoblogs within minutes, generating the propaganda demanded by the spectacle before their eyes.

Then came terrorism.

At 7:15 a.m., a dump-truck pulled in front of the news station in the city's core, exploding in a crowded intersection. A fireball swallowed up the radius of damage. Hundreds of pedestrians and shopkeepers fled into surrounding side-streets. Flaming debris struck a gas station. A plume of black smoke erupted into the sky, towering with such height that it was visible from office buildings in Laredo's suburbs.

At 7:16 a.m., a helicopter gunship entered airspace over the city—the American Way—surveilling the federal highways from the sky. At 7:16:30 a.m., a second helicopter rose from a covert asphalt pad in the countryside—also in the American Way—making its way to the city.

At 7:17 a.m., less than a mile and a half from the international bridge to the United States, an armored truck with a battering ram roared into the front entrance to the Zona de Tolerancia. To keep customers in the red-light district at ease—especially American customers—gun confiscation checkpoints operated at the entrances to the concrete-walled enclave. Inside, none of the men conspiring against Don Gregorio were armed.

As the front checkpoint descended into chaos, a dozen SUVs screeched out of neighboring streets, pursuing the armored truck into the Zona. Armed men fanned out into the cantinas and bordellos, screaming at the women in tight clothing to drop to the sidewalk. The women complied, covering their ears. Seeking only to survive, they had come from across the hemisphere, some from as far away as Brazil. Most were teenagers, some in their twenties.

In the more sequestered corners of the Zona were girls as young as eleven.

As the raiders surged through the walled district, vehicles bearing the insignia for city and state police rolled to the emergency exits, securing the alleyways, vigilant for any vehicles that had not been authorized to participate in the mission.

For seven and a half minutes, the raiders searched through every room—the American Way—kicking in door after door, shooting anyone who could not provide information leading to their targets. Blood seeped into mattresses, staining the clandestine venues for years. Many of the commandos brandished machetes. In moments of frustration, they beheaded several stammering customers, dragging their decapitated bodies to the windows and dumping them into the street.

After breaking into four out of every five establishments in the red-light district, the raiders reached their targets in a second-story suite of the most expensive pleasure palace in Nuevo Laredo.

They executed every last man.

They executed them the American Way.

The pleasure palaces began to rattle. While the first gunship hovered in the sky, the second one landed in the unpaved intersection in front of Boystown at 7:26 a.m., its propeller blades rocking the makeshift shacks of the neighborhood. By 7:30 a.m., the commanding officers of the operation boarded into the gunship, which took off immediately. At 7:31 a.m., the occupying platoon of SUVs and pickup trucks raced through the destroyed checkpoint one last time, disappearing onto the highway. The city and state police returned to their cruisers.

By 7:32 a.m., the Zona de Tolerancia was a place of post-traumatic silence, interrupted only by the wails of survivors.

Twenty-eight collateral lives were terminated, along with the assassination of Sinaloa and Gulf conspirators.

At 7:34 a.m., the invaders on the other side of the city retreated from the military barracks, running back into their semi-trucks and school buses. By 7:36 a.m., the vehicles were racing beyond Nuevo Laredo's outskirts along the eastbound lanes of the highway.

At 7:37 a.m., the gunships swooped over the city one last time, dropping a payload containing thousands of pamphlets and fliers, taking credit for their counterinsurgency maneuvers against the Sinaloan and Gulf syndicates.

The Cóndores del Norte completed their first operation in twenty-three minutes. The lifecycle of their psychological operations would last a generation or more, seeded in the nightmares of children. Knowledge itself was a manmade pathology, a cannibalistic fungus transmitted from host to host, a plague of awareness.

This is how the hegemony of American violence communicates itself, over and over and over.

Co-opting, neutralizing, reproducing.

Over and over and over.

What could be done? Jakob asked. What could be done?

FIVE YEARS AFTER the Battle of Boystown, a scout reporting to the Prince shared a cache of photographs of Don Gregorio outside the Drug Enforcement Agency office in Laredo, laughing with a group of agents.

The DEA was why the Cóndores broke away from the Bizantinos.

The narcoblogs were the closest my brother would ever come to the reality of mass violence: lives looted from bodies; peace looted from the facsimile of civilization. By most anonymous accounts, Dionisio Ángel Verrado had succeeded in his conquest, condemning the Bizantinos to flee and installing his paramilitary units into their territories. El Principe disappeared into his success, into the new, corporatized identity Jakob met at the Mirabeau Hotel, the one working alongside a sitting United States Congressman, and a decorated Lieutenant Colonel of the United States Marine Corps.

His predecessor, Don Gregorio, also disappeared.

Uncorroborated gossip told of the Don's final resting place: a remote canyon near the pueblo where Pablo Acosta Villareal took his last stand against the helicopters of the Mexican Federal Police, a place where the dehydrated carcass of the old man had been tortured and nailed, Christlike, against a wall of rock. Nothing would ever be confirmed.

JAKOB WOULD NEVER see Laredo, or Nuevo Laredo. But, unlike so many, he was still alive. Unlike so many, his fate would not be one of speculation.

But the same could not be said of the Bautistas.

· Eighteen ·

Peak Peak

THEY BOUGHT HIM a smartphone for his new life in El Paso. They helped pack all his new clothes for his transition to El Segundo Barrio and his apprenticeship at the Ybarra family bakery. They told him the family matriarch, Madre Lucia Ybarra, had secured a pro bono immigration attorney through her Coatlalopeuh Church and Labor Center, the same one who had helped Mariazul and Alejandro come into the country in the first place, who was dismayed but not shocked at the latest developments.

But after Deputy Ybarra told Alejandro about Jace's tip, Alejandro no longer cared about El Paso, his apprenticeship, or his right to be in the United States.

So Sabana told me.

He had developed a singular obsession with the private detention center in Eloy, Arizona. He was fixated on visiting his sister, regardless of his exposure to Immigration and Customs. Although Angelica and Arturo emphasized the risk of traveling through the borderlands without papers, he believed his physical presence essential to securing Mariazul's freedom. On the long, early morning ride from Rosadero to El Paso in the back of Arturo Ybarra's official SUV, Alejandro played with the map on his phone, waiting with patience as the signal dropped and picked up again. Scrolling through the highways around Pinal County, he paused over a picture of a bizarre monolith named Picacho Peak. Sculpted like a menacing tsunami of rock, the undulating swells of the mountain did not look real. He entered the name of the mountain into a translator, which turned out to be a linguistic redundancy: Picacho Peak in English was Peak Picacho in Spanish. The translator then reduced the name to Pico Pico, babytalk for the most intimidating structure Alejandro had ever seen.

On his first night in El Segundo Barrio, the young man from Veracruz set down his phone and turned away from the window looking into Mexico. A few blocks away, a sudden gust rushed out of Juárez, howling through the chainlike fence on the international border. A metallic wail rose and fell.

ON HIS SECOND day in the hospital, my brother fell into melancholy.

I was still his only visitor. Our parents were struggling to find a flight to Amarillo. After much haggling at Portland International Airport, they had put together an itinerary that would route them to Dallas-Fort Worth, after which they would drive seven hours across Texas to the Panhandle. But a series of winter storms had grounded flights and shut down airports across the country. Currently, our parents were trying to determine whether it would be more expedient to fly into Oklahoma City.

It may be a week before they reached Texas.

Jakob still did not know how long he could expect to be in the hospital. This final loss of control subdued his spirit. He did not want to talk anymore. My hours at his side alternated between napping and playing his favorite songs on my phone. Occasionally, I caught my brother lost in thought, staring at the ceiling.

We had not yet discussed Mia Jo Taylor, the person with whom he had spent the cruelest weeks of his life. Due to an interagency vow of silence, his case still had not made the news. The closest such story focused on Jace Tarrant's confession to the murder of Denton Pierce.

In the afternoon, Javier Galvenez video-called me from Mexico City. All he wanted was to see Jakob again.

The two boys gazed at one another with tears in their eyes, grateful and sorrowful, laughing at my brother's hair: the fading pink dye job intermingled with patches of natural dark brown. Javier planned to return to Rosadero at once. As soon as Jakob could be discharged, he wanted to honor his former love with a party at the Naranjoven Gallery.

When the call ended, my brother let out a long, pained sigh.

He did not know about the party. He had no opinion about finishing his manuscript or his MFA program, or moving back to Tucson or Portland. But he did know he wanted to see Rosadero one more time.

Discussing the prospect of moving back to the Pacific Northwest, I remembered the piece of mahogany obsidian from the forest. Taking the fiery black shard out of my backpack, I presented it to my brother in my palms.

He nodded.

We need to get some vinegar for that thing, he said.

Why? I asked.

To polish it. Vinegar is a weak acid. Soak it long enough and the carbonate will come right off. You'll have something worth looking at.

I said nothing. After a few minutes, I hid the obsidian in the front pocket of my backpack.

BENICIO WASHINGTON SURPRISED us with a visit towards the end of the day. He strode into the room in his off-work uniform of denim and boots, smiling broadly and removing his white cowboy hat. Jakob perked up more than he had at any point since my arrival. Benicio nodded at me and settled into the chair on the opposite side of my brother's bed.

Jakob's attention fell to something in Benicio's hands.

What's that? he asked.

Benicio held up a sealed plastic bag containing a slim antique book with a well-worn burgundy cover. The title had eroded to nearly indecipherable golden letters.

The Diary of Lewis Bitterroot, he said. Something you might want to read.

Why's that? my brother asked.

It's a piece of lost history, Benicio said. Miriam Hollis just had a massive estate sale. This was picked up by a private collector who wanted me to see it before it was donated to Sul Ross State. The collector is familiar with my research into the Zaldos People. He promised me this book is something like a Rosetta Stone. I've read it and I would agree. This seems to be the only copy ever printed. Anyway, I thought you'd like to see it. We could get some latex gloves so you can take a look inside.

That's kind of you, Jakob said. But my mind isn't quite up to such a task. Who's Lewis Bitterroot?

A young man who lost everything, Benicio said. Anonymous most of his life, until tragedy undid his world. His story is worth knowing.

My brother glanced at me.

What will happen to the Bautistas? he asked.

The same thing that always happens, if I had to guess, Benicio said. I'm sorry, Jakob.

The two men shook their heads. My cheeks burned.

It's funny, Jakob said.

What is? Benicio asked.

I got into more trouble for speaking to Alejandro, probably the most helpless man I've ever met, than I did the most dangerous man I ever met. Who would have thought…?

That's what power does, Benicio said.

Yeah, my brother said. I guess so. Speaking of which, what's life like for you these days? What's the Internal Constabulary Division up to? Care to share anything?

It's over, Benicio said.

My brother frowned.

Over? What do you mean? You quit?

Forced into retirement, pending a disciplinary summons. The Division has dissolved with me, like most of my peers always wanted.

What? What happened?

It was my mistake, Benicio said. I overreached. There were these refugees…there are always refugees. I thought I could play the role of shepherd. There were these twins—Anna met them—Babajide and Cadmael. They were from Guatemala. They're already back in Guatemala. Somebody was taking photographs of us outside the Celenia Inn and sent a tip.

Photographs? Who?

Probably Jace Tarrant, probably working with Agent Taylor. Not that we'll ever know for certain. I was caught abetting and harboring. I've tried to explain it away as a misunderstanding. We'll see what comes.

Benicio, too, was ensnared. He had always been ensnared.

His prosecutions into Texaulipas were dead.

ON THE THIRD day of my brother's hospital stay, Jace Silver Tarrant made an appearance before a judge in the Narváez County Courthouse. He pled guilty to every charge against him. Shackled and standing in an orange jumpsuit, he affirmed to the white-haired magistrate that he had murdered Denton Pierce, that he had trafficked and held captive a Mexican national under false pretense, that he had trespassed on private property, that he had violated his terms of parole, that he had been carrying an illegal firearm. But he would not admit to any collaborators.

His guilt was his alone.

He would spend the remainder of his life in the Huntsville Penitentiary, adjacent to the death row that his admission of guilt had allowed him to narrowly skirt. As the bailiffs led him to the armored bus awaiting him outside, Jace's face was flush and wet like a toddler's.

This was the price for defying orders, Jakob told me. This is what his bosses wanted for him.

If Mia Jo Taylor was ever found, it was unclear she would ever be charged.

THERE WERE CONPSIRACIES of morality and conspiracies of crime. Some would unravel, some would bind more tightly around the objects of their embrace. Benicio Washington and the Ybarras were a righteous conspiracy, forever on the verge of being torn.

The conspiracy that took my brother—the conspiracy of Mia Jo Taylor, the Texas Rangers, Representative A.P. Horne, Tomahawk Littlejohn, Dionisio Ángel Verrado, Texaulipas Security Solutions—should have unraveled.

But with the strategic self-sacrifice of Jace Tarrant, it would not.

Benicio was gone for the day. Out of guilt for endangering him, the former special agent had left behind *The Diary of Lewis Bitterroot* for my brother's free perusal. This, he was told, was a conspiracy of history.

For now, my brother was not interested. At last, he wanted to tell me about his weeks of captivity. With his signature compassion and attention to detail, he wanted to tell me about the woman who had taken him and let him free.

From the bedside chair, I listened.

· Nineteen ·

The Girl from Nowhere

S HE STRUCK JAKOB in the diaphragm and cuffed him while he struggled to breathe. On the night of his kidnapping, they were nearly invisible to one another, silhouetted by the streaking Fireballs. Banging his head against the mauve pickup truck, Agent Taylor shoved my brother onto the rough metal bed and yanked off his shoes and socks before locking him inside. She took her place behind the steering wheel, slammed her door shut, stashed the shoes and socks beneath the passenger seat, and turned the key in the ignition. The pickup peeled off the side of the highway and roared past the Zaldos Mesa towards the Brewster County line. Though the truck belonged to Jace Tarrant, Mia Jo Taylor was operating it alone. She was still dressed in her Border Patrol uniform.

248

My brother looked up. Waves of gentle pinkness splashed across the topper's ceiling. Slowly, the aurorae disappeared.

HE DID NOT recognize the route along which his abductor was transporting him. Crumpled and unsecured, his body was rolling back and forth. He had no concept of the towns and counties around him, except for Alpine, which came and went. In his fear, my brother's mind tried to sort his crisis into object-oriented terms, deconstructing how it felt for the human form to be commodified, for people to be hauled between terminals across the continent, reduced to x-variables chained to independent factors of distribution and capital. Notions about social stratification floated through his consciousness, almost connecting into a coherent idea. He felt solidarity with the Veracruzano being held prisoner in the Hotel Jaspeado, but his solidarity was useless.

Two hours passed.

My brother tried to speak with his captor. He raised his voice to penetrate the glass partition separating him from the truck's cab.

Where are we going?

A minute went by.

Are you taking me to Mexico? my brother yelled.

Taking one hand off the wheel, Mia Jo Taylor slid open the partition.

What? she yelled.

Can I tell you something? my brother asked.

You need to piss already?

Not yet. I wanted to tell you that I'm a grad student. That's it. I interviewed your friend Jace for a novel. That's all this is about.

Mia Jo looked in the rearview mirror.

You're writing a novel? she asked.

Yeah, my brother said. Maybe I could interview you, too.

What the hell for?

Background stuff. Are you from Texas?

What kinda dumbass question is that?

I read an essay that claimed the memory of frontier is still in the heart of every Texan, a memory not only of wilderness, but the possibilities to shape the future. Would you say this is true? The memory of the frontier?

You ain't know nothin about what you're talkin about, she said.

My brother stopped asking questions.

ON AN EMPTY highway outside the town of Tahoka, the pickup truck pulled into a gas station. Mia Jo Taylor rolled down her window to whistle at a pale, bone-skinny man standing on a concrete island. The man was dressed in a red trucker hat, denim overalls, a gray-and-white flannel shirt, and beige-colored boots. His skin was chalky, his hair thin and brown, his neck tattooed with the outline of a cow skull. He came up to the window, asking Mia Jo if she were a cop.

Thus began one of the rituals customary to illicit economies: the chalky farm-boy insisting he was only there to pump gas, Mia Jo pressing him for a case of whiskey, the farm-boy reminding her that Lynn County was a dry county, Mia Jo identifying herself as an off-duty Border Patrol agent who did not give a shit about illegal liquor sales. They were in the Permian Basin now, she said. The nearest city was thirty miles away, but the nearest oilfield was outside town. Where did those boys in the man-camps go to get a taste?

Finally, she withdrew a wad of cash. The farm-boy adjusted his hat and took the money. He crossed the parking lot into the convenience store, a low brick building with iron bars over the windows and doors. Thirty seconds later, he returned with a crate full of whiskey, which he loaded into the front passenger seat. Slamming the door shut, the courier strode around to the gas tank, unscrewing the cap, selecting the fuel, then setting in the nozzle. While the tank filled with diesel, my brother solved the riddle of why his abductor would avoid sanctioned liquor retailers in favor of the farm-boy: the sale put them in cahoots. If the farm-boy saw anything suspicious, he would never tell.

The farm-boy screwed the tank shut and returned to the open window, flashing a grin.

So, what's a Border Patrol agent doing all the way up here?

Nothing, she said.

A smile curled onto his thin lips. He took a step back as Mia Jo rolled up her window. She drove out of the parking lot and onto the highway, taking her cargo deeper and deeper across the Llano Estacado.

An hour passed. The lights of Lubbock came and went. Jakob lay on his back, his attention fixed to the ceiling. For a time, he forgot he was not alone.

Extraordinary rendition, he said to himself.

What? Mia Jo yelled.

Extraordinary rendition, he said. The CIA does it all the time. You're doing it to me now.

Hush up.

Hey, since we're talking again, what's the liquor for?

It's for you, boy, she said. It's for me and you.

She pulled the partition shut, sealing Jakob into isolation. The scent of whiskey leaked through the cab.

SHE KICKED IN the door to the empty house in Erastus County, destroying the foreclosure notice pinned above the handle. She hauled Jakob into the darkness with a thick aluminum flashlight, illuminating every corner of the compact, one-story bungalow. Dragging her abductee into the living room, she tossed Jakob onto a stained, torn-up gray sofa. Catpiss and the residue of tobacco and marijuana odorized the air. Orange shag-carpeting covered the floor, incubating a reservoir of dirt and ash and junk food and beer cans. Fist-sized holes punctured the wood-paneled walls.

Jakob lay prostrate on the couch, his wrists still behind his back. Mia Jo went back to the pickup truck for the whiskey, returning and setting the crate in front of a metal folding chair. She went to a closet and took out a set of electric lanterns, lighting them up and placing them around the room. The house's electricity had been cut for years.

But the heat had not. Mia Jo turned the thermostat dial to its maximum limit, countering the arctic night outside. As she settled into the chair, a shrieking wind rattled the doors and windows, evoking thunder. My brother eyed the border agent as she cracked open the crate with her pocket knife, unscrewed a bottle of whiskey, and took a long drink. For a while, Mia Jo was lost, gazing at the shadows of the fetid home. She looked morose.

Suddenly, she remembered Jakob. She jumped up and bounded across the carpet. Forcing her prisoner to sit, she jammed the whiskey bottle into his mouth, pinching his nostrils and pulling his head upwards by the scalp. He drank as much as he could before coughing. Mia Jo removed the bottle, spilling liquor across his button-down shirt. She reached beneath the couch, withdrawing a pair of rusted scissors she apparently knew had been stashed there. She took the scissors and sunk the blades into the fabric of my brother's shirt, cutting down and across his chest with jagged brutality, degrading his clothes into ugly tatters. The red blades sliced into Jakob's skin, peeling and irritating his epidermis.

Then she hit him: hard slaps across his mouth, a knuckled punch against the cheekbone.

She forced more liquor down his throat. She clutched his jaws in her hands, forcing his eyes to stare into hers.

I could do a lot to you, Mia Jo said. I could strip you naked, hog-tie you, and throw you into Palo Duro Canyon. You'd be all shriveled-up by the time search-and-rescue got to you. They'd say, look at this pretty boy we found. Shame he was so damn pretty. Probably the reason he's lying dead at the bottom of this canyon.

Agent Taylor released her grip, pushing Jakob into the couch. She stood up, sweating. The heat was rising, her hair curling and expanding in the manufactured humidity. She removed her hair-tie. For a moment, looked like a lioness, wearing the mane of a male she had killed.

Mia Jo removed the top layer of her uniform, revealing a white, drenched undershirt. She turned around, slow and deliberate, her skin shining with perspiration. On her left shoulder blade, scar tissue in the shape of the letter T appeared over and over, apparently scorched into her flesh by a branding iron. She pulled the band of her undershirt, providing Jakob with the fullest possible view.

My daddy did this, she said. You're the fourth boy to ever see it. Ain't you special?

That first night, the house on the plains burned like hellfire.

SHE WAS NOT always around. For the first two weeks, she reported to work in Sierra Blanca, coming back on her days off. My brother stayed on the sofa—except to relieve himself on the broken toilet in the nearby bathroom—exhausted and terrorized, his wrists still bound. The house remained hot and humid, ostensibly as a psychological tactic. He did not try to escape, believing the house to be under surveillance. The plains outside the living room window stretched beyond the horizon. He would not dare run across them.

Consigned to solitude, he would sleep.

Sometime after kidnapping—and selling—Mariazul, Agent Taylor returned to the house for good. She continued to drink, and she continued to reveal herself to him. By deserting the Border Patrol, my brother began to understand, Mia Jo Taylor had lost everything.

She was in mourning, and she was lonely.

She began to confide in my brother, whose pink hair, soft demeanor, and lack of sexual interest in women opened up her voice. Mia Jo's mind was splitting into pieces she was desperate to solder back together. She told Jakob about the summer when she was very young, living with her aunt near the blue shores of Lake Meredith. There was so much color in those memories: color and aroma. Evenings were defined by collard greens, biscuits and gravy, burgers. Fresh milk came in the mornings, sweet tea in the afternoon. On hot days—most days were hot—there was swimming in the lake. On weekends, Mia Jo went hunting with her aunt's neighbors. They took five deer that summer, ate as much as they could, and gave the rest to needy members of their church. On Sunday mornings, Mia Jo wore a clean blue dress and a shiny blue ribbon in her hair. She and her aunt sang Baptist hymns from their pews, loud and joyful. They ate lunch at picnic tables behind the chapel. On the Fourth of July that year, speedboats raced beneath fireworks in celebration of the greatest country in the world.

That was the last summer Mia Jo spent outside the foster care system. By autumn, she had been taken from her home permanently. Her aunt was deceased by winter.

Agent Taylor didn't tell my brother her whole story. Her biography came in confessional fragments, followed by a beating or cigarette burning. There were many aspects about Jakob's experience that still eluded him. He could not say who made the phone call to our parents or who engaged the FBI's negotiation team. Unknown sponsors delivered provisions to the driveway every few days: food, toiletries, magazines. Jakob knew better than to ask about Alejandro Bautista or how his predicament tied into Congressman A.P. Horne or Dionisio Ángel Verrado.

Sometimes, Mia Jo Taylor would curl up next to my brother like a teenager. She spoke about the night Denton

Pierce was murdered: how she held his head in her lap while he bled out. How she loved him.

Denton was a good man, she said. He would have taken me as his wife if I weren't already married. But he was dirty. I won't deny that. He took money from the Bizantinos and thought he'd be all right. He never figured the Cóndores were watching him. The bastards who did Denton ain't never gonna be caught. They're too good at what they do. They'll set someone else up to fall for them.

She drank more whiskey. Jakob drank more, too.

She talked about her husband in Hudspeth County: a former auto-mechanic named Leo Taylor, forced out of work by a series of tumors on his spine that had put him in a wheelchair. He was a civilian, clean and true. They met years ago when Mia Jo was a cadet at the Border Patrol academy outside Las Cruces. She was having a drink at the bar of a hotel when her future husband saddled up beside her and asked her to dance. Western swing was playing on the jukebox.

Mia Jo had jilted Leo in the aftermath of Denton's murder.

He would never know where she went.

Before walking off the job in Sierra Blanca, she began spending her nights in Rosadero, living with Jace Tarrant out of a suite in the abandoned Hotel Jaspeado, the same room where my brother sometimes stayed with Javier Galvenez. She and Jace's time in Rosadero was brief, the moments with her lover were dreamlike. They had sex and slept on the wide musty mattress. They looked out the window, Jace murmuring about cashing out and crossing over into Mexico, where they could live for cheap.

AS DAYS AND weeks accumulated, the scheme to reap money off my brother's disappearance collapsed. On the last night of Jakob's captivity, Agent Taylor told him a final story.

When she was a teenager, she and Jace lived together in the house where my brother was being held prisoner. Mia Jo had felt like a prisoner there too. That's why, one morning in the depths of winter, she found herself running across the ice of the Panhandle, insulated by a heavy parka, thermal underwear, two layers of sweatpants, and two layers of sweaters. Sweat stung the scars on her shoulder blade, chafing under her rapid movements. Gnarled trees cast shadows without dimension against the plains. Snowdrifts came in short bursts, forcing Mia Jo to hold her clothing tight to her body. On her teenage shoulders, she carried a backpack filled with canned meat and preserves.

She had left the pistol in the bedroom, where Jace still slept.

The keys to his pickup truck were under his pillow.

On that morning, Mia Jo told herself she only had to avoid the road for ten miles. Then she would have to risk the highway, hoping somebody would take her to Amarillo. Once in town, she would board a bus bound for California. Somewhere in Los Angeles—where, she believed, the sunshine would always radiate, and the temperature would never dip below seventy— she saw herself renting a room at a single-occupancy hotel. She would find a child welfare lawyer, who would work pro bono to complete her emancipation. Then she would earn her GED and one day enroll in a police academy. She would never need anyone else to protect her ever again.

But the winds and snow slowed her escape. Every few minutes, she ran out of breath. She put her gloved hands on her knees, panting, looking at the horizon.

Behind her, she heard the roar of Jace's pickup truck.

She turned around.

The mauve pickup rumbled across the landscape, its deep-tread tires following the trail of prints left by Mia Jo's boots. She looked over her shoulder, paralyzed.

Jace jumped out of the driver's side door, barefoot and shirtless, taut and muscular, wearing only a pair of blue jeans. He sprinted towards Mia Jo, his skin reddening. Before she could run, he threw his arms around her. She screamed. She twisted around and began beating him against the chest.

Let me go!

Jace pulled Mia Jo towards the pickup truck, her heels dragging against the frozen soil. She broke free. Jace grabbed the backpack, yanking it off her shoulders. He tore the pack open, dumping the cans and jars before scooping them up and hurling them into the white void. One by one, they burst open, processed chicken and pork, sugared berries and syrup exploding into the plain like viscera.

Mia Jo began to cry.

Jace took her in a tight hug.

Let's get you home, he said.

I'm gonna throw up, Mia Jo said.

Well, do it out here. Nasty girl.

Mia Jo stumbled away. She put her hands on her knees, heaving. A noise like a death rattle escaped her throat. Jace waited as she recovered. She walked with him to the truck and climbed into the passenger side. They did not bother buckling their seatbelts. Jace turned the vehicle in the direction of the house, a faint block in the distance.

Several white acres went by.

Why can't we be normal? Mia Jo asked.

Jace laughed.

Ain't nobody normal. Come on. You know better than that.

Plenty of people are normal, she said. Plenty of people got lives where they ain't gotta run from nothin. Not ever.

Jace did not know what to say to that. A year later, Mia Jo Taylor was gone for good.

So she thought.

ON THE MORNING my brother was found, the Panhandle looked crystalline. Jakob woke up with his wrists free. He was dehydrated, underweight, atrophied, and unhygienic. But Mia Jo had spared him the cruel humiliation of trying and failing to save himself. Unlike her, my brother would never have to run away from anything ever again.

THE HOSPITAL IN Amarillo discharged my brother after five days. Our parents were still nowhere near Texas. Humongous storm systems had conjoined across the Western United States, forming a blockade. The new plan was for Jakob and I to return to Rosadero for a few days before meeting up with our folks in El Paso. There, our mother reminded us, we could reclaim Jakob's impounded station wagon from the Rangers. Our father would take the opportunity to threaten Company E's major with litigation over gross incompetence.

All my brother and I wanted was to return to the tranquility of Juanita Ochoa's home.

On the long drive back down, my brother sat in the front passenger seat of my hybrid. Putting on a pair of latex gloves, he took out the rare manuscript Benicio had loaned him. An hour into reading *The Diary of Lewis Bitterroot*, his furrowed brow provoked my curiosity.

What are you learning? I asked.

That there was a massacre, he said. Outside Rosadero. More than one, actually. And the Hollis ranching family owned a slave. That's who Lewis Bitterroot was.

I said nothing.

He read on. I listened to the hum of our vehicle over the highway. From time to time, I searched the mirrors for anyone who may be tracking us, my paranoia expanding.

We were trailed only by memory.

· Twenty ·

American Quemadero

MANY YEARS BEFORE she was known as the First Lady of the Narváez Plateau, Katherine Hollis—née Katherine Wendell—was raised by a family of homesteaders in the easternmost fringes of the Washington Territory, two generations after the Corps of Discovery opened the Bitterroot Valley for white settlers. Katherine Hollis came of age at the onset of the Nez Perce War, only a teenager when Chief Joseph—Thunder Rolling Down the Mountain—led his displaced band into her family's ranch. Desiring only to take refuge near the river, Chief Joseph left Katherine's family alone. During the brief sojourn, Katherine and her parents marveled at the great leader and the Nimiipuu People, staring at their colorful striped blankets, their jewelry, and feathered headdresses. The Nez Percé stayed for three days, then vanished. For a moment, the resolve in Chief Joseph's eyes convinced the Americans that the cause of nationhood would be lost.

They heard nothing more of Chief Joseph for many months.

Then, a few hundred miles to the east, Lieutenant Colonel George Armstrong Custer perished at the Battle of Greasy Grass, along with most of the 7th Cavalry. With the Northern Cheyenne, Lakota, Dakota, and Arapaho victorious, the Great Sioux War would rage across the Black Hills for over a year, exploding in rifle-fire, galloping horse-hooves, and thundering war-cries, right until the moment an American soldier bayonetted Crazy Horse in September 1877. In October, Chief Joseph and the surviving Nimiipuu surrendered to the U.S. Cavalry at the Battle of Bear Paw. Now came the time of reservations and starvation, a cold that would not end.

From Canada to Mexico, the Great American Desert was open to Christendom.

In the spring of 1877, the Wendell family patriarch, Odysseus Wendell, brought his daughter with him to the Texas Panhandle. They rode in a stagecoach along the frontier, passing through the bleeding grasses of former Comancheria. On their way to Dodge City—where Odysseus hoped to purchase a head of cattle to drive to the Bitterroot Valley—they spent a few nights in Hidetown, Texas. When Odysseus left for Kansas, his daughter stayed behind, newly engaged to a brash young buffalo hunter named John Rodger Hollis.

Born to the Baltimore aristocracy in July 1842, Katherine's fiancé moved out West in 1862 to serve in the U.S. Cavalry in the Colorado Territory, where he was rumored to be at Colonel John Chivington's side during the Sand Creek Massacre. John

Rodger Hollis feared God and counted his blessings. He would fight or die for the right cause, and there was no greater cause than taming the frontier for the Kingdom of Heaven.

Katherine and John Rodger married in the summer, moving into a wooden shack on the edge of town. During the day, Katherine worked as a schoolteacher while her husband hunted, slaughtered, and sold the last of the bison to roam the Panhandle. With the termination of the buffalo trade in 1878, John Rodger turned to ranch work, participating in ever-greater empires of cattle ventures funded by industrialists from distant cities. He began sending telegrams to Maryland, imploring friends from his youth to join him out West to cultivate their fortunes. Over the next few months, his childhood friends made their way to the Panhandle, where they found the prosperity John Rodger had promised. Together, they plotted to expand into their own rangeland, forging a new universe of wealth in the process.

Five hundred miles north of their eventual destination, the Founding Fathers of Rosadero assembled themselves into a formidable cohort: John Rodger Hollis, Daniel Riggin, Percy Ogle, Jackson Peale, and William Matthew Bryce. In the spring of 1879, the cowboys from Maryland departed with their wives and infants down an old Spanish trail for the Narváez Plateau.

By the summer, the Anglos had settled twenty miles south of Fort Davis, forming an encampment near a gigantic agave. They arrived to find a company of surveyors for the Army Corps of Engineers, who tipped the cattlemen off that the southernmost route of the transcontinental railroad would soon be passing through these lands. The steam engine trains required water stops every thirty miles along the tracks. Beauvoir, Texas would be a water stop; so too would Alpine.

Between these settlements, a new town would be inevitable. With the new town, a new county could be pieced together out of the plains, the county government controlled by whosoever took the initiative to establish one.

On that first day camping by the agave, the cowboys contemplated the prospects of this last and wildest open place. Everything they saw, they believed to be theirs.

At sunset, a series of pink flames erupted along the road to the Zaldos Pueblo. Sentinels carried news of the Americans, not knowing these would be the last weeks of their millennium on the plateau.

THE CONFLICT ORIGINATED in an allegation of theft. In October 1879, seven breeding bulls went missing, according to a ledger kept by William Matthew Bryce. Rumors spread throughout the Anglo encampment that the Zaldos People sacrificed animals to their pagan idols, drinking their blood and discarding their wasted bodies, condemning prized beef to rot in the dust. While the ranchers tended to their herds and fought off rustlers, the Zaldos lay idle. Sloth and gluttony were their cardinal sins. With the alleged abduction and slaughter of the breeding bulls, the Zaldos were a proven threat to the dominion of the Anglos.

Those who were honest knew the dispute was over grazing pasture, and water.

With the passing of the monsoon season, the Anglos were desperate while the Zaldos enjoyed the bounty of their aquifer. The Rain Goddess was their right to life, pouring herself continuously onto the Mesa and trickling into their dreamworld.

One morning, the sunrise burst through the canyon. Carried on the light, the cattlemen rode towards the pueblo with cavalry troops stationed at Fort Davis, as well as a company of Texas Rangers. Their horses kicked up dust as though riding across the corona of the Sun, morphing in and out of the prairie like plasma. They approached the Zaldos with sabers and guns.

As the villagers watched the malicious spirits approach, somebody set fire to the canyon. Everything erupted in a singular burst: junipers and piñons, plots of beans and squash and maize, enclosures for mules and sheep. Somewhere in the firestorm, the flue used to signal messages across traditional routes ignited. The flames turned pink. The smoke turned magenta. In the madness, the Zaldos fled towards their attackers: screaming, burning, dying. Pistols and rifles fired into the villagers, targeting men and male children. Several Anglos leaped off their horses, bowie knives in hand, yanking survivors by the hair, slitting their throats, and sinking their blades into their hairlines.

A contingent of survivors—all women—passed through crevice hidden in the red rock.

They were free to leave and tell their story.

While the worst violence transpired, the women rejoined the ancient route to Paquimé. A second party of female survivors absconded along the highway to Chaco Canyon, a route not traveled for over six hundred years. Rumors suggested the second party had settled in a Hopi village in Northern Arizona, a tiny pueblo that would maintain its insularity from the United States well into the 21ˢᵗ Century. In Mexico and the United States, the Zaldos Widows, as they called themselves, grieved their lost world. In their legends, those who died in the firestorm inside the canyon would forever roam the Earth with those who were shot and slashed open. Incandescent spirits would streak across the plains as an eternal reminder. They would be known as the Pink Ones.

One hundred seventy-six died.

Scalped, charred, naked.

The counted kills were tallied in William Matthew Bryce's ledger with the disappeared bulls. The uncounted were Los Rosados.

BEFORE THE RAVENS and vultures could descend, John Rodger Hollis and his men swept the Mesa for survivors. The Texas Rangers found a teenage boy wedged in the porous red stone. The boy was squat and trembling, dressed in buckskin and moccasins. The Rangers dragged him to the gathering of patriarchs who led the assault.

John Rodger Hollis looked on with dispassion. William Matthew Bryce glanced at him through pince-nez glasses.

Looks strong, William Matthew said.

John Rodger nodded.

Could be the help Katherine needs, William Matthew said.

John Rodger spat into the ground. He directed his stallion towards the boy and dismounted, placing his gloved hands on his hips. The aroma of smoked bodies drifted through the air. The cattleman looked the boy up and down. He squeezed the boy's biceps and touched his chest.

You healthy? he asked.

The boy knew some English. Americans had traveled and traded through the area for decades. But he did not speak.

You wanna work? John Rodger Hollis asked.

The boy nodded.

John Rodger Hollis gestured at the cavalrymen. He passed them his bowie knife.

Cut his hair, he said. You find any others alive, do as you see fit. But this one is mine.

The cavalrymen readied the knife. The boy did not resist.

KATHERINE HOLLIS LOOKED up from the rolltop desk in her makeshift study. Blueprints and a provisional list of teaching materials for the town's first schoolhouse lay before her, covered in handwritten notes. Apart from the map of Montana pinned over her desk, the annex to her home was unadorned.

When her husband walked into the doorway with the Zaldos teenager, she did not know what to say.

This is our new boy, John Rodger Hollis said. You wanted help, so here's the help. Reckon I'll use him for cattle drives if he turns out to be trustworthy. We ain't gonna get no pushback from him. Trust me.

Katherine Hollis stood up. She wore a green prairie dress with long, sensible boots. She was raising three children, and the promise of a fourth child was already visible beneath her clothing. John Rodger Hollis gave the teenager a shove into the study. He left before there could be a discussion. Katherine Hollis and the teenager stared at one another, neither capable of articulating what had just taken place.

Do you have a Christian name? Katherine Hollis asked.

The boy said nothing.

Can you read? she asked.

The boy stayed silent. Katherine Hollis took a sheet of parchment paper from her desk. She took a fountain pen and dipped it in an inkwell. She stared at the map of Montana for nearly half a minute before writing out fifteen letters in immaculate penmanship. She stood up and crossed her study, passing the parchment paper to the teenager. He looked at the letters, uncomprehending.

L E W I S

B I T T E R R O O T

We'll begin here, Katherine Hollis said. This is your name now.

The boy nodded.

IN DECEMBER 1879, Brewster County and Jeff Davis County donated vast tracts of land to create Narváez County. The initial members of law enforcement and the municipal government all hailed from the Five Families. It would be this way for the next hundred years. Deep wells were dug across the new ranches, drawing from the aquifer beneath the Zaldos Mesa. In January 1880, the town of Rosadero, Texas applied for a post office. The application was accepted, the town incorporated later that year. Like Lewis Bitterroot, Katherine Hollis named both the county and town. The men had wanted to name the county Hollis County and name the town New Baltimore. But they did not contest the schoolteacher's selections.

The conspiracy of silence around the massacre would hold until the 1910s.

IN 1914, THOUSANDS of refugees from La Revolucíon trekked across the Chihuahuan Desert into the United States. Barefoot and possessing little more than burros and tattered clothing, the crowds crossed El Río Bravo del Norte, winding along dirt roads into the high country. The violent proximity of their homeland—torched pueblos, vigilante raids, generals who deified themselves as avenging angels—kept them from settling in Presidio. They were bound for an unfamiliar town, a crossroads of two American highways, a pit-stop for cross-continental freight trains. The refugees sang corridos as they marched, smiling for Anglo reporters who had come to take their photographs. Children winced as camera bulbs exploded into the dirt. Preachers and posses took special interest in the procession, as did coyotes and wolves. At night, the refugees slept under the stars. Around campfires, they told stories from the other side of the border. In particular, they passed along tales told by elderly women living in the caves of the Sierra Madre, women who had joined the enigmatic communities of the Tarahumaras and the Apaches. Tanned and wrinkled, they spoke in a dialect nobody recognized, hailing from a red rock in the grasslands of Tejas, a pueblo that had thrived for a thousand years. Sometimes, the ancient women would be seen begging in markets across Mexico, telling the story of Los Rosados to passersby.

As the new refugees settled in Rosadero, they formed a colonia out of the land south of the train-tracks, a makeshift neighborhood containing the original casitas of Rosadero, sharing meals and drink and community. In the daytime, the men drifted up and down Juan Sabeata Street, begging for work as ranch hands for Las Cinco Familias. Some of were lucky and were hired. Others found work at the feed mill. Some hitched rides to the mines. In the picking season, some worked the pecan orchard outside Van Horn. Those who found no employment drifted on wooden sidewalks, their aimless footsteps murmuring through the cowtown. In the heat of day, the unemployed shaded themselves against Anglo businesses where they were not allowed to shop. To pass the time, they recited tales of the pink Fireballs visible from their new homes, imbuing the lights with the souls of the dead. Their gossip revived the memory of those who came before.

Outside the general store one morning, Lewis Bitterroot was packing burlap sacks of flour and sugar onto a burro. Dressed in a brown three-piece suit, with a bolo tie, brown bowler hat, and black, polished shoes, Lewis Bitterroot was known around town as a servant, reliable and discrete. His black hair was cropped, hardly noticeable. He had a round face and a short body accustomed to labor in all seasons. As he tied his load to the burro, he listened to the three refugees exchange tales about the Pink Ones. His load secure, Lewis walked around the side of the store. Scraggly and unshaven, dressed in frayed ponchos without shoes, the three borrachos belonged to a contingent of refugees who crossed into Texas with no family, who drank heavily and had no place in La Revolucíon. They had broken teeth, glazed eyes, skin bitten by lice.

From participating in cattle drives over the decades, Lewis Bitterroot had absorbed some Spanish. He lowered himself, clearing his throat.

¿Qué saben sobre Los Rosados? he asked.

The men in the shade laughed. The tallest of them smiled.

Un dolár, he said. Each of us, un dolár.

Lewis Bitterroot took three one-dollar coins out of his pocket and distributed them.

Dime lo que ustedes saben, Lewis Bitterroot said. Por favor, señores.

The three men stood up, laughing. They walked along the wooden sidewalk, their rough feet catching splinters as they searched for a bar that would serve them. Lewis Bitterroot watched them disappear around the corner, absconding with the great taboo of his life. He returned to the burro, untying him from the post in front of the general store and walking him along Estevanico Avenue. Several gorgeous stallions were hitched to the wooden post in front of the Hotel Jaspeado. Inside, the sons of the Five Families lounged at the bar, boasting and drinking whiskey, paying women to spend afternoons with them on the second-floor suites.

Upon his return to the Hollis mansion, Lewis Bitterroot told Katherine Hollis about the borrachos. The mistress of the house listened with concern.

Thank you, she said. I'll tell John before supper. I'm sure he will resolve it.

Lewis nodded. He hauled the sacks of flour and sugar into the kitchen, where he began the preparations for dinner.

That night, John Rodger Hollis and his five sons rode into the colonia, each holding a fiery torch in one hand and a six-shooter pistol in the other. John Rodger Hollis II rode ahead of his father, yelling in Spanish, telling the residents to surrender the men who spent their days drinking and gossiping in the streets. The other Anglos circled the casitas, fumes from their kerosene-drenched torches wafting into the dirt-floor homes, filling the nostrils of mothers and children.

The fathers of the colonia took it upon themselves to placate the Anglos. They rounded up the borrachos, yanking them by the earlobe, spitting on them for disgracing their community. In total, the padres hauled out twelve young men before the cowboys. The Hollis clan kept their pistols drawn, their expressions stoic in the flickering firelight.

John Rodger Hollis II asked the padres whether there were any others spreading these vicious lies. The colonia fathers assured the cowboys that the rumors ended with these twelve drunks.

John Rodger Hollis II directed the colonia fathers to return inside their homes. Then the original John Rodger Hollis gestured at the sweeping darkness. Through his son's translations, he informed the borrachos that they would be returning to Mexico. Though the border was treacherous, to remain in Rosadero would be to insist upon death. Did the gossipers understand?

The young men nodded. John Rodger Hollis instructed his son to tell the men they had ten seconds to run. The countdown began.

Diez.

Nueve.

Ocho.

Siete.

Seis.

Cinco.

Quatro.

Tres.

Dos.

¡Uno!

¡Vamanos! ¡Corre, hijos de putas! ¡Corre! ¡Corre! ¡Vamanos!

The gossipers took off.

John Rodger Hollis fired the first shot. Then his progeny opened fire, laughing and howling under the desert moon.

Nine fell dead. Three more were wounded, hobbling in desperation. The Anglos fired their pistols into the air, their stallions galloping through the colonia, trampling anyone who stepped in their way. As they departed into the night, John Rodger Hollis II yelled that the community had an obligation to turn over any survivors who returned or endure collective punishment. The village fathers agreed.

Droves of refugees fled town the next morning, hopping trains for San Antonio or El Paso. Those who remained silenced themselves on the topic of the Fireballs. The stories told by the Zaldos women were forgotten once again. For the second time in history, knowledge of the Pink Ones disappeared from Rosadero, Texas.

· Twenty-One ·

Asylum Lost

ON THE EVENING of our return to Rosadero, a winter storm assaulted the electrical grid, putting most of Narváez County in the cold. Though Juanita Ochoa's home had a natural gas generator, electricity could only be siphoned for the kitchen, her bedroom, and her granddaughter's bedroom. The nook and living room where Jakob and I planned to sleep would be deprived, as would her restaurant. She encouraged us to keep warm at the Last Pronghorn Saloon, which never ran out of power. Juanita predicted the problem would be fixed within a couple hours. She advised to enjoy ourselves in the meantime. We had been through so much already.

A few minutes later, we were in my warm car, on our way to the bar.

IN THE DIMNESS of the Last Pronghorn Saloon, dozens of men and women, along with a few children, sought comfort in the winter night. Handsome cowboys bought drinks for an all-female punk band from Brooklyn. Off-duty border agents played pool with poets beneath a smoky light. A table of teenagers studied for college entrance exams near a jukebox that playing rollicking electric blues. A hermit with three fingers on his right hand showed an antique pistol to an unimpressed gallery-owner, a pale woman beneath designer sunglasses. Velvet portraits of country singers and neon signs for Texas beer lined the walls. Pronghorn antelope decorated everything else. With their actual numbers on the Narváez Plateau reduced to a few thousand, the pronghorn in the saloon—on wallpaper, on pitchers, in taxidermized mounts by the dart board—comprised the single largest herd in the area.

I held the door open for my brother as he ambled inside. Walking still hurt. We sat down on a pair of stools at the counter, where the bartender introduced himself as José Huang. He was a heavyset man dressed in a plaid navy-blue flannel jacket, dirty jeans, and russet boots. A ponytail ran down the back of his head from beneath his beige cowboy hat.

José poured my brother a glass of club soda and took a little more time with what I ordered. Setting down an imposing glass bottle—*Hecho En Oaxaca* written on the side—he reached under the bar and took out a vial labelled *Sal de Gusano*, unscrewing the metal cap and pouring the pink spice into his hand: rock salt, chili powder, ground up larvae. José ran his other hand beneath tap water, moistening the rim of the shot glass with his fingers before coating it with the worm salt. He

275

reached into a nearby icebox for a freshly cut lime wedge, setting it onto the seasoned rim.

Añejo, he said. Muy añejo. Enjoy.

I smiled. At my side, my brother was sitting with circles under his eyes. Every few seconds, he looked over his shoulder. His leg was jiggling against his stool. His hair's combination of dark brown and faded pink accentuated his strange mood.

I poked him on the shoulder. He jolted, then remembered himself.

Jesus, he said. Love you, sis.

Love you too, doofus.

We clinked our glasses. Jakob looked around the saloon.

Where are we? he asked.

At an antelope-themed honkytonk in Rosadero, Texas.

What is this place? I still don't know.

I don't know either.

I feel no connection here anymore, not even to the art.

We should come back in the summer. Give you some time and distance from everything.

In the summer? When it's a hundred degrees out?

It'll be nice. Sabana was telling me how the rain causes everything to bloom. The desert turns green. I'd love to see that.

José Huang looked over at us.

You hang around here in the summer, you best watch your ass, he said.

Excuse me? I said.

The bartender reached under the counter and brought out a glass jar. Inside the jar, the preserved body of an iridescent wasp menaced us, its amber wings extended several inches wide, its thick stinger aimed in strike. Jakob and I stared, unconvinced the jar had neutralized the threat.

This is a tarantula hawk, José Huang said. June, July, and August are the months when they come out of their nests. I got stung by one a few summers ago. Passed too close to a mesquite at the wrong time of day. Thought I'd been shot. You could have heard me in Mexico. Went into paralysis for five minutes. Felt like five centuries.

Somebody in the crowd yelled that the bartender showed that damned wasp to every tourist who came through. We ought to pay him no mind.

Jakob and I smiled, pretending we felt at home.

THE POWER CAME back on, just as Juanita Ochoa predicted. Along the borderlands, the night continued to unveil itself.

THREE O'CLOCK IN the morning came to El Paso. Farmworkers stirred and yawned on their sleeping mats in the Coatlalopeuh Church and Labor Center. Some lay in the pews of the chapel beneath stained-glass figures of Nahuatl and Catholic folklore. Others lay on the linoleum floor of the community center, where younger laborers were already gathering over instant coffee. For those who had work, chilis and pecans and cotton awaited them across New Mexico and Texas. The workers were all men with dark complexions and thick mustaches. They wore cowboy hats, shining belt buckles, cowboy boots, denim jeans, and denim jackets. Their hands were calloused, their skin weather-beaten. To pass the time before the arrival of the farm recruiters, some men read posters on the walls detailing their rights to fair wages and labor protections. Other men read posters for English classes and free medical check-ups provided by volunteer doctors.

Most mornings, Madre Lucia joined the earliest risers in the labor center before holding services in the chapel. She looked like Sabana, but in her sixties, dressed in a white pantsuit despite her religious position. She took the hands of the exhausted men, counseling them to turn to the spirits of the feathered serpent and the Virgen de Guadalupe for strength.

Four o'clock in the morning came to El Paso. Rafael Ybarra and Alejandro Bartolo Cenote Bautista walked out of their adobe house in El Segundo Barrio. A slim, kindly man in khakis, a button-down blue shirt, brown loafers, and gold-rimmed glasses, Rafael looked every part the businessowner. Alejandro, carrying a white apron and chef's hat, looked every part the apprentice.

On their route to the bakery, Rafael Ybarra waved at border agents in a nearby pickup truck. The agents returned the wave. Alejandro looked away.

Six o'clock in the morning came to El Paso. On the Paso del Norte Bridge, customs officers inspected and waved through the first commercial trucks of the morning from Mexico. The eighteen-wheelers rumbled into America, christening the new day one by one with the dividends of transcontinental commerce.

Across the bridge, Juárez lay aching.

HUES OF GOLDEN red blazed across the Mesilla Valley, bathing Mount Cristo Rey, casting deep shadows beneath the limestone statue of the Savior. From the American side of the border, Mia Jo thought she could see worshippers climbing the binational ridge from Juárez, young women who had disappeared outside the maquiladoras and reappeared on the streets as corpses. For a moment, hundreds of femicide victims had come back from the dead, treading up desiccated altitudes to beg the Christ King to forgive their murderers.

Though no amount of absolution could return these women to their lives.

Mia Jo Taylor parked Jace's pickup truck along the dirt road at the base of the mountain. As she stepped out, border agents on horseback directed their flashlights onto her. She pulled out her badge, yelling her rank. Before she could be questioned, Agent Taylor was sprinting across the road, one hand on the butt of her service weapon. She hopped the metal gate to the pilgrimage trail, running along its winding path, sprinting past turquoise crucifixes and three-dimensional dioramas depicting the Stations of the Cross.

As the pilgrimage trail rounded a bend, Mia Jo jumped onto the steep hillside below, tumbling across prickly-pears, sand-colored boulders, and dry bushes. On the other side of the mountain, the Anapra colonia came into view: houses constructed from cement blocks and tin, tire stacks and razor-wire. Dust was everywhere, insulating thin windows, engulfing the jagged streets, floating in the industrial haze. Plastic bags drifted in a faint breeze. Scraggly dogs trotted in packs, their eyes mean, their fur flea-bitten and coarse, their teeth sharp and stomachs hungry. The edge of the colonia vanished into the abruption of the desert. Apart from the peak of the Christ King, there were no apparent boundaries separating the city from the wilderness.

Mia Jo descended the hillside. From a nearby junkyard, teenage lookouts surveyed the agent through their binoculars. They sent text messages to their bosses, waiting for instructions. As Mia Jo raced into Juárez, she passed graffiti affirming the religious allegiance of those who had not yet fled.

¡Vivan Los Cristeros!

¡Viva Cristo Rey!

Mia Jo Taylor disappeared into the colonia. She would never reenter the United States.

WHEN THE MORNING rush at the bakery ended, Alejandro Bautista took a thirty-minute break. He hurried through El Segundo Barrio and Chihuahuita, stepping over potholed streets, passing elderly men with canes and straw hats, crossing intersections with murals devoted to civil rights organizers and Aztec warriors. He walked down South El Paso Street, negotiating a sidewalk teeming with shoppers and sellers. Bejeweled jeans, cellphones, piñatas, fresh fruit, cheap shoes, Quinceñera dresses, fast food, homemade meals, travel agencies, and pawnshops animated the corridor. This was where the working class of Juárez and El Paso did their commerce: the construction workers, nannies, cooks, landscapers, nurses, and bus drivers who kept the two cities running. Everything here was bought and sold in Spanish.

A few blocks away, the low brick buildings of Chihuahuita extended into the clean impersonality of downtown, boundaries of class and culture demarcated by the interstate. Combined with neighboring El Segundo Barrio, the two communities formed an island between the United States and Mexico, a bustling hybrid corralled by train tracks and the border fence.

Alejandro reached a bus station near the Paso del Norte crossing. Before approaching the ticket counter, he read the names of American destinations: San Antonio, Denver, Salt Lake City, Chicago, Los Angeles, Tucson, Phoenix. He purchased a ticket for Tucson, telling himself it would be easy to find a way from the Old Pueblo to Eloy.

Before returning to the panadería, Alejandro took a moment to stare at a massive painting dedicated to Teresa Urrea on a nearby warehouse. She was a handsome woman, with thick eyebrows and tightly braided hair, her body adorned by an elegant black dress. The daughter of a wealthy Mexican rancher and a Tehueco teenager, Santa Teresa's legend still echoed across the border: healer of the ill and disabled, an Indigenous rebel who organized against the dictator Porfirio Díaz, whose exile into the United States devolved into a traveling carnival show, her powers as a curandera diminished into circus tricks before her return home, when she vanished forever into the Sonoran Desert.

Though Alejandro did not know much about Santa Teresa, he could see Mariazul in the healer's eyes. Beginning his walk back to the bakery, his mind rehearsed the words of strength and comfort he hoped he could speak to her.

IN ROSADERO, MY brother and I slept until noon. Not even the morning bustle inside Adelitas Burrito could rouse us. I slept on a coach, my brother occupying the bed in his writing studio.

Stumbling out of his nook for coffee, he announced he wanted to do nothing at all. Aside from Javier's party tonight at the Naranjoven Gallery, Jakob had no reason to be anywhere.

We sat by the windows facing the high desert, our attention drifting from the grasslands to the photographs in the Justin Lehenwesen coffee table book. We sat there for hours.

By mid-afternoon, Juanita was done running her in-home restaurant. Kiki was done with school, and Sabana was done with her shift at Move Bricks Coffee—where I had already quit. All three women descended on the house, and, after some gentle persuasion, helped me re-dye my brother's hair to its full pink glory. With her grandmother's encouragement, Kiki Ochoa took over working my brother's scalp in the kitchen sink. Sabana and I hung back by the wall, where I expressed further chagrin about my abrupt resignation, and Sabana made tongue-in-cheek jokes about my performance as an employee. Juanita Ochoa joined us, watching Kiki from afar. She and Sabana spoke to one another in Spanish, their tone tinged with concern. I did not need to know the language to know their discussion. We watched the twelve-year-old from Nuevo Laredo tend to my brother's hair, both their expressions withdrawn, their body language so unlike ours, the same unhappiness in their eyes.

TWILIGHT GLIMMERED THROUGH the heart of El Paso. Cantinas and nightclubs burned with neon and Christmas lights; sizzling meat and spices wafted through the air. Stereos blasted Norteños and mariachi and cumbia and hip-hop, the rhythm booming through brick and iron. As shopkeepers shuttered their businesses on South El Paso, the last visitors from Mexico returned to the international bridge, hoping to reenter their country before too much daylight had escaped.

Alejandro strode past the storefronts in his oversized hoodie and jeans and sneakers, moving through the crowds with singular focus. He crossed the street to the bus station, where he submitted his one-way ticket for Tucson.

Within an hour, he was boarding for Arizona.

THE NARANJOVEN GALLERY swirled with artists and hipsters. Chillwave and neo-soul played out of speakers at a music booth in front of the Hall of Narcoliberals, curated by Javier's assistant, Alyssa. New installation pieces had taken residence along the wall by the reception desk: sculptures of mohair, panoramic collages of Pinto Canyon, television sets with melted glass screens.

Dressed in a leather jacket and bolo tie, Javier walked Jakob through the crowd as though they were still lovers. My brother, dressed in a black t-shirt and jeans and sneakers—just like me— nodded and shook hands. The room was filled with creatives, mostly young and white, clutching colorful drinks in their hands, providing critiques and networking. A few were staring at the floor, sullen and self-questioning.

I looked at Jakob across the crowd. He appeared almost emaciated. He caught my worried eye and gave me a brief thumbs up before returning his attention to the sculptor in front of him. Javier was holding onto his arm.

It was more than I could take.

I excused myself for a smoke break outside. As I made for the exit, I was followed.

ALONG THE SOUTHERNMOST stretches of Estevanico Avenue, Rosadero disappeared into blackness. On the outskirts of town, only the Veterans of Foreign Wars Hall provided any light, illuminating posters for a showing of a French New Wave film. In the distance, an invisible coyote yipped.

Then I noticed an SUV.

On a lightless side-street, the charcoal-colored vehicle crept up the block in silence, the engine calibrated to emit no sound. The windows were tinted. I could not see the driver, nor any of the other men I could sense were inside. A second SUV pulled up to the curb in front of the VFW Hall, rolling like a mobile tomb. A third SUV appeared in the shadows of an abandoned gas station.

Then, from the same door from which I had stepped out, sauntered a tall, broad-shouldered man in a white guayabera, bleached denim jeans, and snakeskin boots. He had spiky black hair and a smile like a lion's.

I could not move.

The man arrived at my side. Without a word, he took the lighter from my hand to ignite his cigar. As he returned my lighter, he looked up and down the street, scanning the rooftops of the casitas. Inside the gallery behind us, the party pulsed, revelers chatting and flirting, oblivious to the kingpin in their midst.

Enjoying the gala? the man asked.

I looked at him. I broke eye contact, then looked back, then broke eye contact again. He stared at me.

Do you know who I am? he asked.

I nodded.

Call me Dionisio, he said. I know who you are. Anna Rachel Tatevyan. Sister to Mr. Jakob Levon Tatevyan, the guest of honor. You and your brother are fortunate to be here. We all are. You can tell Rosadero is a safe place, where the artistic mind flourishes. In places of danger, you cannot devote yourself to anything but survival.

That's true, I said.

That is not to say violent crimes never happen in this part of Texas, he continued. I heard there was a shooting in Sierra Blanca, that a border agent got assassinated at a highway checkpoint. Did you hear about that?

I did.

Do you know why this man was killed?

Something about corruption. I'm not sure.

That was it. Corruption. A word that will always be attached to his name. Denton Pierce was as corrupt as they come.

The Prince of Nuevo Laredo puffed on his cigar.

Many years ago, I was stationed at Fort Benning, he said. I spent much time learning about—what do you call it? The Confederacy? Dixie? The Deep South?

You can call it any of those things, I said.

El Principe tapped his cigar, condemning a thick mass of ash to the ground.

Fort Benning is on the Alabama-Georgia state line. The people there have deep memories. They are still coping with the wounds inflicted by William Tecumseh Sherman. His name is still spoken like a curse. Do you know about the Savannah Campaign? The March to Sea?

I nodded.

Dionisio continued.

I learned about General Sherman in the very first course I took at Fort Benning. Our instructor emphasized the psychology the General used to paralyze the slave states. Aside from the strategic accomplishment of destroying the South's railroads and plantations, General Sherman's true legacy is that he was never forgotten by the enemies. Generation to generation, the memory of this Union hero's three-hundred-mile rampage passes on, as fresh as yesterday. Do you know why?

Why?

Because even now, over a hundred fifty years later, nobody can stop him.

Dionisio Ángel Verrado placed a large hand on my shoulder. He put his lips by my ear. He whispered.

There is a ranch in Brooks County, he said, a ranch with a gaping ditch where untold numbers of men, women, and children are rotting. Every day, more bodies come to fester. Many are disposed in garbage bags. The ditch will never close, Anna, because the corpses come by the hundreds. Every year. By the hundreds. You know about this now, this most heinous of open wounds. The wound will never close. Not even for a well-meaning woman like you. Now, you have one more secret you will carry with you and do nothing about.

He kissed me on the lips. Then he walked away, crossing the street towards the SUVs. As he stepped inside the middle vehicle, the other two rolled behind and in front, forming a caravan. Within seconds, they were speeding towards Ojinaga, a battering ram vanishing through an open door.

I slid down the outer wall of the Naranjoven Gallery. Nearby, the ash from the Prince of Nuevo Laredo's cigar remained, a thin stream of smoke trailing into the night.

ON THE INTERSTATE outside Lordsburg, the Border Patrol pulled over the bus bound for Tucson. Half a dozen agents stormed the coach, shining flashlights into the faces of passengers, demanding to see proofs of identification. They yanked immigration papers out of trembling hands, yelled in Spanish, seized luggage from overhead storage, dumped clothes into the aisle. As the agents made their way to the rear, Alejandro Bautista closed his eyes. He saw his sister, walking free and barefoot down the main road of their village. He saw the colorful tiendas of La Lancha and heard the birds of paradise singing in jungled mountainsides. He saw his parents laid to rest in an open-casket funeral, a priest eulogizing their passing with dignity. He saw himself with Mariazul, looking skyward as their mother and father soared over the Río Coatzacoalcos and above the glacial forehead of Citlaltépetl, their final rest completing the ecological cycle of home, peaceful and free from the prisons and landfills of the North.

Acknowledgements

On Thursday, August 17th, 2017, I visited Marfa, Texas.

Driving alone to the West Coast from the East Coast, I was returning to the Pacific Northwest after almost a year in Philadelphia, taking the long way in a car packed with most of my belongings. I was between lives, unsure of everything. Marfa was a place I came to on a whim, a place I knew almost nothing about, somewhere to spend the night between Austin and California. The afternoon when I arrived, heavy rains from a late-season monsoon had soaked the Chihuahuan Desert in hues of emerald and ocean-gray. High concept art galleries, clothing boutiques, old adobe casitas, and Border Patrol vans shared the same unlikely public space. In a gas station convenience store, Spanish was as common as English, and one could just as easily encounter an artist visiting from Mexico City or Europe. Outside, cowboy hats were worn by cowboys, mud caked on their pickup trucks from nearby ranches. The wide streets were almost empty, until a party broke out in front of the KRTS 93.5 studios, home to Marfa Public Radio. I checked into a motel on the eastern outskirts of town, where my eyes swept across an overwhelming horizon of prairie grass, yucca, prickly-pear, ocotillo, and agave. The night sky brought riches of stars and earthbound balls of luminosity, twirling and melting and flashing over the ground. In the distance, columns of lightning struck the countryside. Early the next morning, driving westbound on Highway 90 towards Van Horn, I listened to a radio interview with a long-time local resident, who appreciated the tourist dollars Marfa attracted, but was mystified by what these strange visitors saw in his hometown, and why they seemed to wear all-black and nothing else.

Looking down at my black t-shirt and black shorts, I knew I was in love. My first encounter with the town lasted less than eighteen hours, and I didn't do or see much of anything. But something in me sparked that would burn for over two years.

Light in Rosadero exists because of the awe stimulated by Marfa, Texas. This feeling would soon sweep me back across most of the borderlands, from Nogales to Tucson, Arizona, from Lordsburg, New Mexico to the city of El Paso and to the Rio Grande Valley, inspiring a manuscript I could never see coming.

Writing this novel would not have been possible without the love and generosity of my parents, who allowed me to take over a bedroom in the back of their forest home, working and reworking the manuscript for as long as I needed. My sister, too, deserves credit as my first reader.

This novel would also not be possible without the leadership and critical eye of S. Stewart, managing editor of Unsolicited Press, as well as the hard work of the rest of the Unsolicited team.

Thank you for reading.

About the Author

Jay Kristensen Jr. was born and raised in Seattle, Washington. He holds a Bachelor's in Social Work from The Evergreen State College in Olympia. Outside of the Pacific Northwest, he has also lived in Asheville, North Carolina, Philadelphia, Pennsylvania, and Tucson, Arizona. This is his debut novel.

About the Press

Unsolicited Press is a small publishing house in Portland, Oregon and is dedicated to producing works of fiction, poetry, and nonfiction from a range of voices, but especially the underserved. Our team has published books that aren't afraid to take on topics of race, gender, identity, feminism, patriarchy, mental health, and more. The team is comprised of hardworking volunteers that are passionate about literature.

Learn more at www.unsolicitedpress.com.